SCARS

A NOVEL

KEVIN DAUTREMONT, M.D.

ISBN: 978-1-4866-1926-9
eBook ISBN: 978-1-4866-1927-6

Word Alive Press
119 De Baets Street Winnipeg, MB R2J 3R9
www.wordalivepress.ca

WORD ALIVE
—PRESS—

Cataloguing in Publication information can be obtained from Library and Archives Canada.

"Drawing on his personal experience as a family doctor and a Christian, Kevin Dautremont has written a fast-paced, thought-provoking medical mystery filled with complex characters who struggle with unseen scars from the past, but find hope for the future."

—N.J. Lindquist
Author of *The Best of Friends and Manziuk & Ryan* series, editor of the *Hot Apple Cider* series

"An excellent suspense novel."

—DiAnn Mills
Author and three-time Christy Award winner

"Kevin Dautremont takes readers on a thrill ride against time in this story of loss, betrayal, and healing. Likeable characters, shocking twists, moments of humor, and hints of romance had me turning pages late into the night. Engaging and suspenseful, Scars cuts deep, compelling readers to ask: when faced with unspeakable tragedy, can anyone be trusted? Even God?"

—Sara Davison
Award-winning author of *The Watcher*, *The Seven Trilogy*, and *The Night Guardians Series*

To my wonderful wife, Lisa, without whose love and support this book would never have been written.

ACKNOWLEDGEMENTS

There are so many individuals who have taught me, mentored me, and helped me to reach this point. I wish to thank all the instructors and fellow writers at The Word Guild, Write! Canada, Write! Saskatoon, and at Jerry Jenkins' Christian Writers Guild. Thank you to the agents, friends, and editors that contributed to my growth as a writer. Special thanks to N.J. Lindquist, Janice L. Dick, and especially to DiAnn Mills. My deepest love and gratitude to my wife Lisa, my children and their spouses, and most of all, to my Lord and Saviour Jesus Christ.

"A bruised reed He will not break, and a smoldering wick He will not snuff out, till He has brought justice through to victory. In His name the nations will put their hope."
(Matthew 12:20-21)

PROLOGUE

"The evil that men do lives after them;
the good is often interred with their bones."
Julius Caesar, Act III, Scene 2

The storm surprised her.

Jennifer Sampson could have driven to the Baker farm, but she had been unwilling to risk anyone seeing her car. Safer to walk—only a couple of miles through the fields. The weather had been warm and dry for almost two months. The kind of early Montana spring she used to love. No rain and no worries.

It wasn't the same anymore. Was anything?

A fierce downpour started when she was halfway to her destination. Jennifer clutched the raincoat in her arms that she had wrapped tightly around a slim white envelope. By the time she reached the Bakers' road, her clothes were soaked, but hopefully the letter was still dry. Jennifer stood in the rain and studied the farmyard for several minutes. The sky had darkened into night before she crossed the ditch to the homestead. Mud clutched at her shoes and threatened to topple her. She fell. Once. Twice. At last she reached the gravel of the driveway.

As she edged into the yard, the wet clay sticking to her arms and legs began to trickle down onto her dress, into her shoes. It didn't matter. The letter was safe. Jennifer leaned against the edge of a building and caught her breath. A tremor ran through her. Light flickered inside the house, and she could see Amanda Baker moving about the kitchen.

Jennifer had inched halfway across the driveway when lightning flashed and changed the gloom to silver. Her neighbor stood staring out the window. No turning back now. She hurried to the porch, the floorboards creaking under her feet. Lightning flashed again.

Amanda threw open the door and pulled her into the house. Trembling, Jennifer contemplated the water pooling at her feet. Why had she come? Who would believe her? She took a step backward toward the night. "I can't stay."

The other woman's words echoed in the distance, but they made no sense. Jennifer struggled to focus, and gradually her confusion ebbed away. "I need you to hide this." Her hands shook as she unfolded the raincoat and held out the envelope. "Hide it. Don't open it. Keep it safe. Please do that for me?"

Jennifer's eyes locked on Amanda's as a shiver rippled through her.

"All right, dear. How long do you want me to keep it?"

Jennifer pressed the envelope into her grasp. "You'll know."

ONE

"I hold the world but as the world… A stage where every man
must play a part, and mine a sad one."
The Merchant of Venice, Act I, Scene 1

The ambulance doors snapped open.

Dr. Derek Kessler grabbed the end of the gurney and helped lift
it from the rear of the vehicle. The paramedic continued to pump
the ambu-bag while his partner dropped the wheels of the stretcher.
Overhead, the emergency room speakers chimed and repeated the
warning: Code Blue.

With practiced urgency, the code team moved through the ER
doors into the Stockton District Hospital while the paramedic repeated
his findings. Woman. Mid-twenties. Found on floor of farmhouse.
Respiratory arrest. No sign of trauma. Blood sugars normal. Previous
medical history negative. And no CPR prior to the ambulance's arrival.

"Who found her?" Derek felt her neck for a pulse. So young—too
young to die. He inhaled sharply and shook his head. *Focus.*

"Neighbor. Bringing her kid home. About 25 minutes ago. We were
on the scene ten, fifteen later."

"Got a name?"

"Yeah. It's Jennifer Sampson."

* * *

The incessant chirping of a psychotic bird eroded the last remnants of sleep. With a groan, Rebecca Andrychuk reached over to the night table. Maybe she could throttle the cursed beast. Not a bird. Instead, her hand closed over her pager. It had to be her secretary. No one else would be foolhardy enough to beep her. What time was it anyway? She peered at the clock. Eleven forty-seven, almost noon. Why had she stayed up so late? Blu-ray discs were scattered about the bedroom floor. The new Audrey Hepburn collection. She'd lost a lot more sleep for a lot worse reasons.

Rebecca silenced her tormentor and stared blankly at the message. Yes, it was from Paulina, texting to remind her of court in the early afternoon. Five minutes—just five minutes more sleep. But, as she rolled over, the empty space on the bed filled her vision. He had been gone for five, no, six months now. Wouldn't be coming back anytime soon. Probably never.

The pager went off again. Paulina would continue to beep her until she relented and phoned the office. Might as well get up.

* * *

"What's the rhythm?"

Team members slid Jennifer Sampson's body from the stretcher onto the casualty room bed while Derek moved to check her lungs. A nurse attached her to the cardiac monitor while another placed defibrillator pads on her chest.

"Still sinus tach," the paramedic said.

"Air entry's good. Both lungs filling. No spontaneous resps?" Derek pulled both lids open. "Pupils reactive but sluggish. Give it to me again. How long was she down?"

"Don't know for sure, Doc. The neighbor found her on the floor. She wasn't breathing, and there was no CPR till we arrived. Probably twenty minutes or more."

"Okay, get another IV going. Set up for a central line and a catheter. Maggie, can you do a femoral puncture? I need a full lab profile, the works. Call X-ray for a portable chest." He glanced at the ambulance attendant. "You find anything at the house? Pill bottles, pesticides, anything?"

"Nope. Nothing except a spilt glass of lemonade. Like maybe she fell out of her chair. No sign of any major trauma. No drugs or poisons around."

"Suicide note?"

"Didn't see one."

"All right, so why does a healthy woman suddenly collapse? Where are those labs?" Derek studied Jennifer's still form. There had to be clue somewhere. Her long blonde hair lay limp beneath her head. Her skin was pale and waxen, her lips and fingertips tinged a pale purple color and the front of her clothes tained with vomit. A wedding ring circled her finger. Something to live for. Someone.

A nurse called out. "I've lost her pulse. She's gone into ventricular fibrillation."

* * *

The facts are clear. Rebecca smoothed the front of her tailored suit jacket. *Be confident.* The case was sound, the evidence undeniable. Why then did she have to keep talking to herself? Her client was sure to win, if the case even made it to trial. All that should be required was the pretrial conference. Sitting back down at her office desk, she waited for her coffee to brew and reread the file. So, what was the problem?

The problem? Elma Sifton. Her husband had run up huge debts before he died. An undetected brain tumor had changed his personality and made him do a lot of strange things. The old woman had done everything she could, even selling off most of their land. Nothing was left except the original homestead, 160 acres. But she still owed a lot of money, most of it to Rebecca's client. He wanted the rest of the property, and the law was about to give it to him.

Rebecca shut the file. So why did that feel wrong?

* * *

"V fib? Charge to 200 joules." Derek grabbed the defibrillator paddles. A high-pitched whine filled the room. He shot a look at the code team. "All clear." The patient's body jerked in a sharp spasm and then lay still again. "Resume CPR. Where are those labs?" His vision stayed locked on the monitor while he checked her pulse and spoke to the nurse doing chest compressions. "Good. I can feel those."

"That's five cycles," the paramedic said.

"Okay, stop CPR. What's the rhythm?"

"Still V fib."

"Let's shock her again. All clear."

Jennifer Sampson's body arched and thudded back onto the stretcher.

"Do another set of cycles," He took the initial lab results from Maggie, the charge nurse, and studied the results. Blood sugar a bit low but not abnormal. White count and hemoglobin normal. He narrowed his eyes. *What's this?* Metabolic acidosis. Pretty severe. Why? That made no sense.

"We've done five more, doc."

"Stop CPR." Derek watched the monitor. The ugly, jagged scrawl of ventricular fibrillation vanished, and the blip of light danced evenly across the screen. Sinus rhythm. Derek blew the air out of his lungs and smiled. "Good job, team."

Time for a more extensive examination. He could detect no signs of head trauma. Her pupils reacted slowly but were equal. The fundi were normal with no sign of pressure on the brain. He checked her lungs again. Clear. No fluid. No sign of collapse. No rib trauma. The woman's abdomen was soft. Abrasions marred her left knee and left upper arm, probably from when she had fallen. When he carefully examined the wounds, he realized they weren't fresh. Maybe four to six hours old. If the fall had caused them, she'd been down on the floor for most of the morning before the neighbor found her. Derek studied her face. Pale, with dark ellipses below each eye, hair matted to her forehead, and a cold sheen on each cheek. Her chest rose and fell as the respiratory technician continued to pump in oxygen. The only sign of life.

He touched her forehead. *What happened to you, Jennifer Sampson? What caused this?*

"Do you want her on a ventilator, Doc?" the tech said. "There's no respiratory effort."

"Yeah, we'd better. Go ahead and do it."

The rest of the lab tests arrived. Derek watched the charge nurse push a vial of sodium bicarbonate into the IV and then scanned the pages. Liver normal. Pregnancy test negative. Even the toxicity screen was clear. He grimaced. No answers there. "Repeat the blood gases. We need to correct that acidosis. How's her urine output?"

"There isn't much." Maggie tilted her head, her dark ponytail brushing her shoulder.. "What do you think happened?"

"Not sure. Poisoning of some sort. An organic acid maybe. I have no idea what we're dealing with. We can't test for it, and even if we could, we don't have the meds to treat her." He spoke to the ward clerk. "Call for the air ambulance. We've got to get her out of here. She needs dialysis." Derek hovered over the prone body of his patient. "I don't know what, and I don't know why. Could be accidental. Could be suicide. Do you know her, Maggie?"

"I know of her. It's a small town, Doctor. Isabel Vermette's the neighbor who found her. She's still here in the quiet room with the patient's daughter. She might know something."

"Any next of kin?"

"We've been trying to reach Mrs. Sampson's husband, but no success yet."

"Okay, I'll talk to the neighbor. Watch the patient and be careful with the fluids. We don't want to overload her." He touched the unconscious woman's wrist. Her pulse remained steady but weak. Derek frowned and headed for the doors.

* * *

Isabel Vermette lifted her head when Derek entered. "Is she…?"

"She's stable. For now. But I don't have enough information. Is there any chance she might have done… something to herself?"

The woman's eyes widened and she shook her head. "No. Absolutely not."

"You're sure?"

"I was bringing Olivia home from a sleepover. Jenn's a good mom. She wouldn't do anything stupid."

The little girl lifted her head from Isabel's lap and peered at him. Derek froze. His mouth fell open, and he reached toward her. She looked just like Sarah. The eyes. The hair.

Jennifer's daughter sat up. "Where's my mommy?" she whispered.

Derek lowered his hand and took a step backward. "We're taking care of her. She's very sick."

"I wanna see her."

"Not right now. Maybe soon." The child started to cry. He knelt in front of her and gently grasped her shoulder. "I promise I'll do my best to make her better."

"Dr. Kessler?" A nurse rushed into the room. "We need you STAT."

Derek scrambled to his feet and hurried after her to the casualty room. Maggie had resumed compressions. She called out as he raced in, "She's flat lining."

TWO

Sound travels at night.

That was why they'd always told her to keep her window shut. But she liked to have it open a little bit. It made her feel safer.

Gravel crunched beneath tires on the driveway, and a car door opened and closed. The little girl reached over to pull the window shut.

Daddy was home.

THREE

"Perdition catch my soul, but I do love thee!
And when I love thee not, chaos is come again."
Othello, Act III, Scene III

The heart monitor mocked him.

Derek watched the glowing green line waver and curve across the screen. No heartbeat. Nothing. He laced his hands together behind his head and squinted at the ceiling. His frown deepened into a glare. *Are you going to do it again? Let her die too?*

"That's five cycles of CPR, Doctor."

"Okay, Maggie, push another atropine, and then repeat the epinephrine." The monitor remained unchanged.

"Do you want more bicarb?"

"How many has she had? Three? No, the blood gases should be here right away." He moved to her side to shine a light into Jennifer's pupils. Wide black pools of fading hope.

I'm losing her.

* * *

Rebecca paused at the foot of the stairs of the Stockton County courthouse and peered up and down the street. To the west, the Lewis Range of the Rocky Mountains preened high above a brief cushion of foothills. Eastward the land stretched away, an undulating olive and brown patchwork dotted with farmhouses and ranches. Visitors and tourists always looked westward, while locals turned the other way. The mountains were beautiful and scenic and majestic, but those who lived in Stockton knew their livelihood lay out on the plains. Grain, cattle, and oil—those were the tickets.

She dropped her head. Neither direction held any appeal for her. The mountains made her feel surrounded and confined, while the openness of the prairie left her exposed and vulnerable. She didn't fit into one or the other. When Rebecca glanced upward, her client waited at the top of the courthouse steps. Forcing the tightness to ease from her neck and arms, she smiled and hurried up the stairs.

The man rubbed his beefy hands together. "I'm sure glad we're finally getting this done. I've got plans for that land."

"We have to win the case first."

"You said it was a sure thing."

"Yes, but you never can tell for sure." Rebecca pulled open the heavy wooden door of the courthouse and held it for him.

"Shoot, I'm not worried. The place might as well be mine already."

Rebecca's eyes narrowed as he strode through the courthouse doors. Shouldn't he be twirling the end of a big, raven-colored mustache? Suppressing a sigh, she followed him in.

* * *

The team sensed it. Derek could tell by the sag of their shoulders, the flatness in their gazes. They wanted him to do something.

"Here are the blood gases, Doctor."

"Give her another bicarb." Derek glared at the monitor. "Repeat the atropine and epi." Nothing. No heart activity. "Charge the defibrillator."

"She's not fibrillating."

"Charge to 200."

"But there's no cardiac activity."

"I have to try." Still nothing. "Charge to 300."

"It's not working."

"Again."

"Doctor…"

Derek stared at the defibrillator paddles and then at the monitor. The green line remained flat. He blinked and set the paddles down slowly. When he spoke, his voice was barely a whisper. "Time of death?"

* * *

Rebecca wiped her forehead with a tissue and snatched a glimpse of her client. How could he look so cool? It had to be ninety degrees in here. She had just chanced a peek at her wristwatch when Judge Farr called a recess. Had he noticed? Her head hurt too much to care.

It had to be a migraine, but why now after all these years? A wave of nausea hit her. Covering her mouth, she hurried into the washroom and splashed cold water on her face.

"Are you all right, honey?"

Rebecca lifted her head and tried to focus on the woman. The nausea overtook her and forced her head down. Her skull throbbed. The woman's palm pressed against her back, her voice soft, mumbling something. What? The hot needles behind her forehead faded and the nausea lessened. Easing herself upright, she rotated to stare at the elderly woman. Her lids were closed and one hand swayed in the air. *What is she doing?*

The woman opened her eyes, lowered her arm, and smiled. "Are you feeling better now, sweetie?"

"Uh, yeah," Rebecca said. Her vision cleared. She recognized the woman. Mrs. Sifton. "It's only a headache. I should go."

"Maybe you should see a doctor."

"I'm okay." She cocked her head. "What were you doing just now?"

"I was praying for you."

"Prayer?" What was the use of that? "Listen…" *Now, be polite.* "Thanks for wanting to help, but I don't believe in God."

"That's okay, honey. He still cares."

Rebecca shifted away from the women's warm face to stare at her reflection in the mirror. *Yeah, right.*

* * *

Derek lowered his head and shuffled forward, pausing outside the quiet room. They had been close. Had almost saved her. Almost. He swallowed to ease the parched dryness of his mouth. *What can I say?* Cardiac arrest. Car accident. No matter what, who had the right words? He stood at the entrance to the room and caught Isabel's eyes. Fear. Doubt. Olivia's were different. Trust. Only trust. That made things worse. He tried to turn away but couldn't. "I'm sorry."

Isabel sobbed, reaching for Olivia and holding her tight. The child continued to stare at Derek. Her lip quivered slightly, and the cobalt-blue of her irises glistened.

He couldn't breathe.

* * *

"Do you really think this is the best I can do?" Her client scanned the notes she had given him. "Old Man Sifton owed me a lot of money."

"I know that," she said, "but you get the outbuildings, the surface and mineral rights. Mrs. Sifton keeps her house and the ten acres it sits on. It's fair. She'll accept it. Besides, I know Judge Farr. He's not too happy with our case."

"We could lose?"

"There's a chance."

"Shoot. Okay, make the deal."

Rebecca nodded, sharply. Now she was lying to a client? To protect some old lady? What would her father say? He was real lawyer. To him winning was everything, the only thing. No concern for collateral damage, including his own family. She clenched her teeth. Once she'd dreamed of being just like him, but only before, way before what he did to them, to her. A bitter coldness invaded her body. *Breathe. Don't give in.* Her jaw spasmed and relaxed, the tension oozing from her. Glancing down, her head jerked. She had crushed the files she'd been holding. *He won't win. Not this time.*

Carefully she smoothed out the papers. Her father would never make this offer. He wasn't some hick small-town lawyer. No, not him. Powerful, rich, feared even. The kind of lawyer people want. She let the air out of her lungs as if collapsing a balloon. There had to be something more to life than this.

* * *

Derek pulled himself from the quiet room. Leaning against the wall, he massaged his brow with the heels of his palms. The regular hum of the emergency ward had returned. He peered into the casualty room. Through a gap in the curtains he could see a lone nurse hovering over the stretcher, waiting to move the body to the morgue, waiting to hide his failure.

Shaking his head, he trudged toward the front desk. Jennifer's chart waited for him, the blank page accusing. What could he write? Why had she died? He had to know. He spoke to the ward clerk. "I need to speak to the police."

* * *

Sheriff Eugene Paschek hated bulletproof vests. They were hot and they chafed. Made him look fat. Okay, fatter. But, since they were standard operating procedure, he would have to accept them. He hated other stuff too, but especially hot shots and Bible-thumpers. He'd heard this new doc was both. His vision shifted to the passenger seat of his patrol car and he snorted. It appeared the same could be said for his new partner.

Deputy Joseph Standingready of the Stockton County Sheriff's Department. Should have been more help than he was. The rednecks saw him as another Indian, and the natives saw him as another cop. It didn't help that he was Cree whereas the locals were Blackfoot. They hadn't ever gotten along. Paschek tolerated him so far, but he didn't have confidence in him. He preferred having a partner with a mean streak, one who wouldn't hesitate to use his nightstick if necessary, and who would have his back. This guy Standingready might be a little too nice. That worried the sheriff.

He turned the patrol car off the highway and onto the gravel lane that led past the Sampson house. Didn't know much about Jennifer Sampson, but he'd been told she was high maintenance. Now the husband Shooter, him he knew all too well. Tyler Sampson got his nickname from the drinks he downed at whatever bar was handy, and he wasn't always careful about driving afterward. With his last DUI, the judge had told him detox or jail. Paschek hadn't seen him since.

The sheriff stepped from the patrol car and studied the house. Small and neat—virtually a cottage—with a neatly manicured lawn and flower garden. Pleasant, nice even. He turned and caught the rookie staring off at the distant mountains. Paschek grunted to catch his attention.

"Sorry, sir." The rookie hurried to stand by the sheriff. "It's quite the view."

Paschek shook his head and pointed northward. "That way's better."

"What's there?"

"Nothing. Few trees by the Flatiron Creek. Otherwise, nothing at all. No place to hide, all the way to Canada. That's the view I like." He started to walk along the path, but a spasm of pain shot through his left thigh. Shot was the right word. He grabbed his leg while instinct forced him to reach for his nine-millimeter. His lips twisted in a harsh grimace as he straightened and eased the grip on his pistol. *It still hurts. Six years, and the stupid thing still hurts.*

"Are you all right, sir?"

"Shut up and follow me." Paschek climbed the stairs to the front door and tried the knob. It turned easily. He let the door swing open and stood silently before inching over the threshold. The sunlit kitchen glistened. Everything clean and in its place. Almost everything. A cut glass tumbler lay broken in the middle of the floor, glass shards and a small amount of yellow liquid spread out beneath it. A matching pitcher half-filled with lemonade sat on the table.

"There's the lemonade," Standingready said. "Do you want me to collect some of it?"

"No, Deputy. I don't. Not yet." The sheriff motioned for his partner to be still and strolled into the kitchen. He pulled a pencil from his breast pocket and used it to open the cupboard doors and drawers. All the contents were stacked with care in groups of twelve. Dishes, bowls, cups, even the cutlery in the drawer. Neat and tidy, obsessively so. Something registered as not quite right in his brain and he scanned the stacks again. Only ten cut glass tumblers. One lay on the floor in pieces. Had the little girl broken one? That would have driven Jennifer crazy, given the order she clearly demanded in her home. Paschek surveyed the table and the kitchen floor and frowned. *Or did someone take one? The perp, maybe?* He reopened one of the cupboards and peered inside.

"Deputy, go get the police tape. We need to make sure the house is secure. And then you can collect those samples."

"Yes, sir. You think there's been a crime?"

"Maybe. Just maybe."

* * *

Rebecca's migraine had returned. And it had brought company. Her court case had barely concluded when her brain was assaulted by relentless pounding against her skull. The hot needles were gone. They'd been replaced by an ice pick that jabbed from one temple to the other, then twisted. It took all her effort to keep a blank stare plastered on during Judge Farr's closing remarks, and she even managed to smile at her client. He seemed satisfied. She felt nauseated.

Mrs. Sifton wasn't right about everything. That prayer mumbo jumbo hadn't helped much, but maybe her advice would. Maybe Rebecca should see a doctor.

* * *

The waiting room stretched to overflowing. Derek peeked at the growing stack of charts and grimaced. *Time to get to work.* He made a vain attempt to settle the unruly curl in his chestnut hair before grabbing the first file. He needed to get a haircut soon or it would be completely unmanageable. As he started to read, Maggie approached.

"Don't worry about those, Doctor. I called in an extra physician to help clear the backlog. Dr. Naidu said she had a quiet afternoon booked. She'll be right over."

"Thanks, Maggie. Chandra's a big help, and I know the staff love working with her." He tossed the file back onto the pile and headed to the exam room. Isabel Vermette stood in the doorway. Derek stopped in front of her. "Are you okay?"

"Olivia wants to see her mom. I didn't know what to do."

The little girl had shrunk into the corner of the quiet room, her knees pulled up to her chest, arms wrapped tightly around her legs. Kneeling beside her, he studied her with gentle scrutiny. "Do you understand what's happened, Olivia?"

"Yes." Her lips trembled. "Mommy's dead." Derek struggled to hold her gaze. He cupped her palm in his, and she squeezed tighter than he thought possible. "Is Mommy in heaven?"

"I hope so."

"Can I see Mommy? Please?"

He rose and led her toward the doorway. A disturbance in the emergency ward entrance caught his attention, and after motioning for Isabel to take the child, he peered out of the room.

"Where is Jennifer? Where is my daughter?" A tall, white-haired man strode down the hospital corridor, pushing through a knot of staff members. A woman, slight and frail, followed at his heels. The color of her skin matched the gray of her hair. The man thrust himself into the exam room. "I said, where is she?"

Olivia Sampson raised her head and stared at her grandparents. Then she screamed.

FOUR

The voices were louder now.

Mama was shouting. She was angry. She was always angry. Daddy never got angry, even when his breath smelt bad and he had trouble walking. Once, she ran into the table and knocked it over. His bottle fell off and broke. Even then, he didn't get angry.

Because Daddy loved her.

FIVE

"When in the why and the wherefore
is neither rhyme nor reason."
The Comedy of Errors, Act II, Scene II

Sheriff Paschek stood in the middle of the Sampson home and rubbed his chin. Knowing there'd been a crime wasn't enough. He needed proof. The Crime Scene Unit from the Department of Criminal Investigation was a couple of hours away. He had to give them more, or they wouldn't even think about making the drive. Slipping on a pair of latex gloves, he moved carefully through the room. No sign of a struggle and no suicide note. Nothing that could be ingested accidentally. He opened the garbage can and peered inside. Coffee grounds, egg shells, a frozen orange juice container, nothing else.

The rest of the house was clean and neat, spotless even, with feminine touches everywhere. Other than a few items in the bathroom and the clothes in the closet, there wasn't much to indicate that a man had ever lived here. Paschek pulled open a cabinet in the living room. A bottle of wine and a partial bottle of bourbon. The level of the whiskey bottle had been discreetly marked with a thin pencil mark. He twisted his lips in a tight smirk. *Interesting.*

He peered at the front door. Standingready remained on the threshold, shifting his weight from foot to foot. Good. Staying alert, watching and learning. Exactly what Paschek wanted him to do. "You have those samples I told you to get?"

"Yes, sir." His partner held out two vials of lemonade, one from the jug and one from the spill on the floor. Only a few drops could be salvaged from the half-dried puddle, along with some of the dried residue. The sheriff hoped it would be enough.

"Okay. Take them to the car. I'm going to check out the garage, and then I'll join you." Paschek headed out the door from the kitchen. The garage was a marked contrast to the house. A car sat parked in the center of the concrete floor, its hood open. Greasy auto parts and oily rags lay in piles around the vehicle. Tools were scattered across the work table and on the floor.

He moved to the center of the garage and slowly turned in a circle. He spotted something under the work bench and bent for a closer look. Clean and new and out of place. Five black plastic bottles in a package that had held six. Paschek squinted as he read the label.

Gas line antifreeze. Ethylene glycol.

The sheriff bagged the bottles and headed to the patrol car. Time to get this investigation underway for real. First, he'd call to see if the hot shot doc could confirm his suspicions. After that? Wait and see.

* * *

Derek's mouth dropped open. Olivia continued to scream. Her grandfather marched forward and pointed at the little girl.

"Olivia! Stop that." Silence fell over the room. The man scowled at Derek and glared at the woman with him. "Tabitha, keep the child quiet." He stepped closer to the physician. "I'm Samuel McKenny, and Jennifer Sampson is my daughter. Where is she?"

"Mr. McKenny, I am very sorry. Your daughter was found not breathing, and then her heart stopped. We were able to get it started again, but it wasn't enough. We lost her."

The old man gritted his teeth. A shadow passed across his visage. "What are you saying?"

"I'm sorry. She didn't make it. Jennifer is dead."

He staggered as if he'd been punched then surged forward and raised a clenched fist. "You did it. With your science and your lies. You let her die."

Derek recoiled and lifted his hands. "We did everything we could."

"Everything?"

He flinched at McKenny's accusation. No, not really. He hadn't prayed.

"Where is she? Where is my daughter's body?"

"In the casualty suite. I'll take you to her."

"I know the way." He pushed past Derek. Tabitha followed but staggered to a stop when her husband snapped a command. "Stay with the child. I'll take care of Jennifer."

She shrank back to the chair and collapsed into it. "Yes, Father."

Derek blinked. She called her husband Father? He didn't think anyone did that anymore except maybe someone in a weird religious cult. Who *were* these people?

Olivia trudged over to stand beside her grandmother, taking hold of the woman's arm but keeping her gaze fastened on Derek. *Just like Sarah.* He shook himself, pushing the thought away. *Don't go there.*

Swallowing hard, he hurried to follow her grandfather.

The old man marched through the ER to the casualty room and tore open the curtains. With a cry of protest, the nurse moved to block him, but she stepped aside when Derek waved her off. McKenny reached out and touched his daughter's forehead. He lifted his other hand and closed his eyes. The young doctor watched his lips moving silently and hesitated. Should he pray as well? *Isn't it too late?* He moved toward Jennifer's body and reached for her other hand.

"What do you think you're doing?"

He snatched back his hand and lifted his head. McKenny was glaring at him. Derek blinked. "I thought I should pray with you."

"You? Pray?" He jabbed a finger into Derek's chest. "You let her die, and now you pray?"

"I thought…"

McKenny shook his head vehemently. "It's no good here. There's too much evil. Too much unbelief."

Derek's stomach tightened. Maybe they *were* part of some cult. "What are you talking about?"

"It's vital that I take her away from here. To holy ground. There I will raise her up." He bent to lift Jennifer's corpse from the stretcher.

Derek reached across the bed to grasp his arm. "You can't do that."

McKenny tried to shake him off, but Derek pushed his arm down, away from Jennifer, before letting go. "We can't release the body. It's a coroner's case now. There will have to be an autopsy."

"Absolutely not. I forbid it." The elderly man attempted to raise his fist again, only to have the motion stopped when Derek seized his wrist.

The color drained from McKenny's face, leaving him even grayer than before. His vision drifted to Jennifer's body. Derek reached out to touch his arm, but he swatted it away. "No. There will be no autopsy. I will not consent to it."

"As I said, this is the coroner's case. Even if you were next of kin, the coroner wouldn't require your consent."

"She's my daughter."

"And her next of kin would be her husband."

A red flush spread over the old man's face. "Her husband? That man is worthless. He took her away from the faith and away from her family. He probably caused this. He's not even here. He—"

"Doesn't matter. He's still next of kin. We're trying to reach him, but if we don't, the autopsy will still go ahead."

"You can't—"

Derek raised his hand. "I know this is a sad time for you. I'm sure you want to take care of your wife and your grandchild. They need you now."

Air hissed between McKenny's gritted teeth as he spun around and stomped out of the casualty room. Derek shot a look at the nurse. She shook her head and ducked away.

* * *

Rebecca lifted her head from the desk and moaned. Two more ibuprofens hadn't helped. The past few clients must have wondered what was going on. She'd been able to make it through, but it hadn't been fun. At least it had all been simple stuff, and when she punched in the day planner on her computer, it listed only one more case.

She eased open her office door and leaned against the jam. Paulina looked up from her keyboard and waited. Sunlight filtering in through the blinds reflected off the woman's polished brass name plate, forcing Rebecca to shield her eyes. Secretary. Should read Babysitter and Big Sister.

"Is the next case here?"

"'Fraid not. Seems she's a no-show."

"All right. Listen, this headache is getting the best of me. I'm heading to the hospital. I know what you're going to say, and the answer is no. I can drive." She grabbed her handbag and nodded at Paulina. "Who was the appointment for, anyway?"

"New client. Young mom from north of town. Sounded really down when she called. She said she wanted to talk about something but wouldn't say what." Paulina punched a button to change the screen on her monitor. "Name's Sampson. Jennifer Sampson."

* * *

Paschek grimaced and snapped off the police car's radio. The ward clerk argued but finally put him through. Everyone was too busy. The sheriff had to remind her who he was. He finally got hold of the ER doc, Kessler or something, and told him what they'd found. Okay, the doc had some smarts. He said right away that ethylene glycol could have caused the victim's death.

Kessler asked if it was suicide or an accident. Paschek started to tell him it was none of his business but relented and gave him his opinion. Suicide—possible but not probable. Accident—didn't fit the scene. That left one possibility. The doc could read between the lines. With that

Paschek cut off the call. He'd had enough of having to explain things to civilians.

He pulled a small bag of M&M candies out of his pants pocket and peered inside the bag. Only a couple left. Green ones. With a grimace, he shoved the bag into his pocket and glared at his partner. "You get through to Helena?"

"Yes, sir, the Crime Scene Unit is on the way, and the rest of the DCI homicide unit will probably come out later."

"Probably?"

"The duty officer wasn't totally convinced. Kept asking why we hadn't called the Kalispell office."

"'Cause I wanted the guys from Helena. I know how it works. We'll get those lazy bastards off their butts soon enough." Paschek surveyed the Sampson home. Quiet, serene. But, there was something else, something angry and brutal. He could sense it. "You stay here and keep an eye out. I'm going to check on things at the hospital. Someone from base will come and get you."

"Okay, sir."

"Oh, and Deputy?"

"Yes, sir?"

"Don't touch anything."

* * *

He was beginning to clear the backlog. Derek finished writing the prescription and handed it to the patient's mother. "We'll put Susie on an antibiotic, and her ear infection should be better soon. Best keep her home from daycare for a day or two."

"How did you know she was in daycare?" The woman swung the child onto her hip and grabbed her purse.

"She's the third one today, so I figured it was a good guess." Following the mother and child out past the main desk, Derek caught a glimpse of Chandra Naidu entering an exam room and nodded at Maggie. "I owe Dr. Naidu big time."

"I'm sure she doesn't mind."

That might be true. Chandra was a good friend. She and her husband John invited Derek for dinner every few weeks and he always enjoyed their time together. It was almost like being home. "What's next?"

"Bert Cavanaugh's in Casualty Two. He fell and sliced his arm. He is going to need sutures."

Derek hurried down the corridor toward the room Maggie had indicated. He'd seen Bert Cavanaugh on numerous occasions. Today, though, the man's tremor was worse than usual. His head bobbed and jerked in a series of bird-like twitches. He tried to sit up as Derek entered the room, but a spasm shook his whole body. His condition was deteriorating.

"Hi, Bert. What happened?"

"I … I fell." The patient lifted his left arm. "Into a glass table." The gash on his forearm was long and deep. "Guess I'm getting clumsy."

The physician shook his head. Bert wasn't clumsy. He had Huntington's chorea, and gradually but with certainty it was killing him. The physician tried to wash the wound, but the irregular flicking of Bert's arms made it impossible. He snapped the call button to summon help. With his left arm held still by a nurse, the patient's other abnormal movements became more pronounced. His right arm flopped about on the bed, a salmon stranded on the shore, while his tongue darted in and out like a snake's. While Derek finished stitching the wound, Bert stared down at his injured arm. "'This was the most unkindest cut of all.'"

"Huh?"

"It's from Shakespeare's *Julius Caesar*."

"Sorry, Bert, I didn't have much time for English lit in med school."

"Ha, that's okay. Hey, nice job, Doc. I owe you a coffee."

"I'll hold you to that." With the nurse's help, Derek finished dressing the wound. "Now, I want you to ride in a wheelchair out to the taxi stand and take a cab home. Rhonda will get a chair for you, okay?" He moved to leave, but his patient reached out to stop him.

"Before you go, Doc," Bert said, "could you pray for me?"

Derek looked at his friend and sucked in his bottom lip. Taking a slow deep breath, he dipped his head. His words felt cold and stilted at first, but Bert's twitching fingers on his gave him strength. Together, they ended with an "Amen".

Moments later, as the nurse wheeled the patient toward the exit, Derek hurried out of the room and almost ran into another physician. "Dr. Cudworth. Sorry, I didn't see you."

Dr. Simon Cudworth, Stockton District Hospital's head of surgery and Chief of Staff, scowled, his features hard and stiff. Without a word, he stomped out of the ER.

Derek scratched his head. What was that about? He continued to the desk where Dr. Naidu stood writing in a chart. "Hey, Chandra, thanks for helping out."

"No problem. I'm finishing off the last case." She turned to a slim, graceful woman and held out a prescription. Stylishly dressed in a powder-blue skirt and blazer, the patient was an attractive woman with shoulder-length red hair framing a heart-shaped face. A spray of freckles across her nose enhanced her polished appearance with a touch of playfulness. When she looked at Derek and smiled, the mysterious green of her eyes captured him.

"This is Rebecca Andrychuk. She came in with one of her rare migraines but responded to sumatriptan, so I'm giving her a script for more. This is Dr. Derek Kessler."

The woman stepped forward. "Good afternoon, Dr. Kessler. I heard there was a new ER physician in town."

"Uh, yeah." He hesitated before taking the offered hand. "I've only been here a few months." Hadn't her eyes been emerald? Now they were more hazel. A wave of heat rose from his collar, and he dropped his gaze. He was still holding her hand and released his grip.

"Rebecca's a lawyer here in town," Chandra said. "She took care of the paperwork when John and I bought our house."

"I was glad to be able to help." Rebecca's shifted her gaze from one physician to the other. "Chandra's pretty popular around here."

Heat stretched past Derek's ears. He started to speak but hesitated when she glanced at the ring on his left hand and stiffened.

"Thanks for your help, Chandra." Her voice was formal. "I'll be on my way. Pleased to meet you, Dr. Kessler."

"Uh, yeah. Good to meet you, too," he said. *Uh, yeah? Did I just say that? Twice?* Great, he sounded like an idiot. He tried not to, but couldn't help watching her walk away. When she reached the ER entrance, she glanced back. Their eyes locked for a second until he blushed again and turned away.

"Derek. Hey, earth to Derek."

He blinked. "Sorry, what were you saying? I missed it."

"I'm sure you did. I could see you were a bit… distracted." Chandra grinned. "Anyway, since everything's caught up now, I'm heading out. You'll be okay?"

"Yeah, no problem. Thanks again." He surveyed the Emergency Department. The exam rooms were empty and the waiting room deserted. Not the quiet room. "Maggie, are the McKennys still here?"

"Uh huh. They sent Olivia home with the neighbor, but they stayed, even after their daughter's body was taken to the morgue."

"Maybe I should talk to them."

"I'm not sure that's a good idea."

"You're probably right, but I should try." He trudged down the hallway. Samuel McKenny appeared in the doorway of the quiet room. He grimaced and then retreated out of sight. When Derek reached the threshold, the older man stood in the middle of the room like a statue, staring at a spot on the wall. Tabitha McKenny shook her head. Derek noted how her pale flesh trembled in sagging folds from her jaw line, as if she had lost a lot of weight. *I guess there's really nothing to say.* He shrugged and started back down the corridor.

A man's voice reached him from the main desk. "Please, can you help me? They told me the ambulance brought my wife in. Can you tell me what happened? Where is she?"

Derek hurried to the desk and inclined his head in Maggie's direction. "It's okay, I'll handle this. Excuse me, sir, are you Mr. Sampson?" The man wore a dark jacket with the hood up, and his jeans were covered with streaks of oil. When he shoved back the hood, Derek sucked in a quick breath. "Tyler?"

"Derek? What's happening? Where's Jennifer?"

"She's your wife?" How did he not know that? He and Tyler had been friends for months.

Tyler grabbed the physician's arm, his voice shrill and wavering. "That's what I said. Where is she?"

"Oh man, I am so sorry."

The young man staggered back a step. The color drained from his face. "No."

"We did everything we could, but we couldn't save her." Derek squeezed the man's elbow. "Come. I'll take you to her."

Tyler yanked his arm from Derek's grasp. "This isn't funny. She's not dead." He stood frozen, mouth open, staring into nothing. A tear etched a path down his cheek. He shivered when Derek placed a hand on his shoulder.

"I understand," he said. "I do." He squeezed his friend's shoulder. "Come on. Let me take you to her so you can say good-bye."

Tyler nodded and trudged after him down the corridor.

When they reached the basement room, Derek shoved his hands in his pockets and tried not to shiver. It was cold. Morgues always were. Tyler Sampson hovered beside his wife's body. He smoothed the limp blonde hair from the waxen forehead and hesitated before touching her lips with his fingertips. "She's not here anymore. She's really gone."

Derek inched closer and reached out but hesitated. With a slight shudder, he lowered his arm.

Tyler dropped his head. "I don't know what to do."

"That's okay."

"Don't even know what to feel."

"That makes sense." Derek focused on a distant spot. "I didn't know you were married."

"I am, or was. I guess we never talked. About that, I mean. We'd see each other at church and all but…" He drifted away from the morgue table and wiped his face with both hands. "What's next?"

"The coroner will be involved. There needs to be an autopsy."

The young man lowered his hands. "Why?"

"Her death. We can't explain it."

"Oh."

"And the police have to decide what to do next."

"The police?"

"Afraid so." The two men walked from the room, past the security guard posted at the doorway. "It's their job to find out what happened, why Jennifer died. It's mine, too."

Tyler shuffled down the hallway. When they entered the ER, he shook himself. "I need to take care of Livy now. Where is she? Where's my daughter?"

"She's not here, Isabel Vermette took her—"

"There's the one you should be talking to." Samuel McKenny's shout cut him off. "Not me. He's the one who killed her." He shoved past a man in uniform and shook his fist at Tyler.

The policeman surged forward between the two men and pushed them apart. "Mr. McKenny, I suggest you go back in that room and sit down. Deputy Blackburn will finish speaking to you." He twisted around and motioned to Tyler. "Hi, Shooter, I haven't seen you for a while. This is different from our usual… circumstances."

"I need to go. I have to get my daughter."

The policeman shook his head. "She's okay for now. I'm sorry, but I'm required to ask you a few questions."

"Can this wait, Officer?" Derek stepped to Tyler's side. "Mr. Sampson's had quite a shock."

"It's Sheriff. And no, it can't wait." He jerked a thumb toward the empty staff room. "In there, Shooter." As the sheriff moved to follow, he glanced over his shoulder at Derek. "This won't take long. I'll talk to you later."

"Me?"

"Yes, Doctor. That's what we do in a murder investigation."

SIX

The front door slammed.

Mama was crying. The little girl could hear her on the driveway. She used bad words. The child didn't know what they meant, but she knew they were bad. The words frightened her.

Her mother shouted again and then a car engine revved.

Mama was driving away. She'd be back later. She always came back. But for now they were alone.

Just her and Daddy.

SEVEN

"Thou errest: I say there is no darkness but ignorance."
Twelfth Night, Act IV, Scene II

Medicine was a wonderful thing. The drugs Dr. Naidu had given her had cured Rebecca's headache completely. No hocus pocus, no magic formula, just good old pharmaceuticals.

She had driven to the office to grab a few files and was about to leave when the phone rang. She hesitated. *Let it ring. Probably nothing. Maybe they'll just quit trying.* When it rang again, her shoulders slumped. *Oh, all right.*

"Andrychuk Law Office."

"Rebecca? Is that you?"

She grimaced at the man's voice. Not him. Not now.

"Hello?"

"Hello, Philip."

"Hey, it's great to hear your voice, babe."

"Why? Did Sylvia kick you out? You remember Sylvia—your wife?"

"No, she didn't kick me out. She's off on a shopping trip to San Francisco or New York or someplace."

Rebecca leaned a hip against the corner of the desk. "Philip, why are you calling? It's been what, five, six months? And you didn't exactly leave on the best of terms."

"I know that, but I missed you."

"You missed me?"

"Yes."

Rebecca glared at the phone. She should hang up, but instead she held the receiver to her ear. "Why should I believe you?"

"Because I mean it. Really. I've got next weekend free. I'd love to see you again."

She massaged her temple with her free hand. "You think you can call me out of the blue after all this time, and that will make everything all right?"

"Listen, babe, I'm sorry. I know I was wrong. But I need to see you. I booked a suite at the Chateau in Glacier. You remember the room, don't you? The view was special."

She lowered her hand and swallowed. Hard. "That's not a good idea."

"Come on. I already made reservations at Le Triumph for dinner. Say you'll come."

"I'll… I'll think about it."

"Great, I'll see you there. I have to run, but I can hardly wait. See you, babe."

Rebecca dropped the phone onto the base with a clatter. What had she done? The thought of seeing Philip again, after what he had put her through over the last few months, made her ill. She cradled her head in her hands. What in heaven's name had she done?

* * *

Derek leaned back in the white plastic chair as Tyler hobbled into the staff room, his limbs stiff and mechanical.

"I do understand." He whispered after his friend. Derek wished he couldn't comprehend what his friend was going through, but he could, all too well. He touched the plain gold band on his finger. The memories still hurt. He gritted his teeth and squeezed his lids shut. The counselors kept saying it would get better, that it would hurt less. They were wrong.

* * *

Sheriff Paschek shut the door to the hospital staff room and motioned for Tyler to take a seat. He stood over the young man and stroked his chin. The smile on the sheriff's face did not reach his eyes. "Okay, Shooter, I know you want to get to your daughter, so I'll be brief."

"Please don't call me that." Tyler stared at the floor, his voice barely audible.

A tremor rolled along the young man's fingers. *Good.* "Call you what?"

"Shooter. My name is Tyler."

"Okay, you want Tyler now, fine. I thought you were proud of your nickname. Big guy in the bar scene. The oil stud drinking everyone else under the table."

"Not anymore. I've changed."

"Is that so?"

"I haven't had a drink in almost five months. One hundred and forty-two days."

"So you're in AA now."

"Yeah, and some other stuff."

"Wait, don't tell me. You got religion."

Tyler's lips paled.

"No comment, eh?" Paschek smirked. "If you're on the wagon, how come you've got half a bottle of bourbon in your house?"

"That was Jennifer's. First Sunday of each month, she would have a whiskey sour." Tyler lifted his shoulders. "Said she was toasting her father. I never understood it."

"That's your story? Fine, whatever you say." The sheriff dropped onto the chair opposite. "Let's get on with it. I know it's been a rough day. I'll try to make this quick." He stretched out his legs. Pulling a notepad and a pen from his shirt pocket, he wrote the time and date at the top. "How long were you and Jennifer married?"

"Almost five years."

"And how were things between the two of you?"

"Okay."

"Just okay, huh? You only had the one child?"

"Yeah, Olivia."

"A nice kid. You like her?"

"Of course."

"Good. Do you love her?"

"What are you getting at?"

"Nothing—nothing at all. Except that I remember your Uncle Billie. He loved little girls, too. Of course, they weren't his, and he went to jail over it."

"He wasn't my uncle," Tyler said through gritted teeth. "He was my Dad's cousin. That stuff doesn't run in families. Not in mine." He lurched up from his chair. "We done now?"

"Easy there, Shooter," Paschek sneered. "I've got a couple more questions. Why don't you sit down and relax?"

When Tyler continued to glare at him, the sheriff tossed the notepad and pen on the table and stood. He slipped his thumbs under his gun belt and waited. Finally, Tyler exhaled loudly and sank back down. Paschek grinned and settled on the hard chair again. "Okay. So how come you only had one kid?"

"'Cause Jenn didn't want any more."

"But you did, eh? Was that a problem between the two of you?"

The young man narrowed his eyes. "That's personal."

Paschek held up his hands. "I'm just asking. It's not an interrogation." He peered at his notepad as if he'd lost his place. "Was Jennifer depressed?"

"No."

"Did she ever talk about... suicide?"

"No, of course not." Tyler's clenched his fists on the table until his knuckles turned white. "She wasn't depressed. She wouldn't hurt herself."

Paschek's frigid grin did not change.

"Is that what you think? That she killed herself? She wouldn't."

"You're probably right. It was likely an accident. An accident involving gas line antifreeze."

Tyler's head jerked. "What are you talking about?"

"We think that might be what killed Jennifer. And we found a package of the stuff with one bottle missing in your garage. Know anything about that?"

Tyler's eyes bulged. "I bought a package recently. Ran out of it last winter, so when I saw it at the hardware store I thought I'd stock up, even though it's early. I haven't even taken any bottles out of the package yet."

"I see." Paschek folded the notebook and slipped it into his pocket. "The hospital had a hard time reaching you earlier. Where were you?"

"Out on the rigs. We were working halfway to Havre."

"They contacted the company. You weren't on the rig."

"I was on a long change."

"Long change?"

Tyler shifted in his chair. When he spoke, his voice was even, his words slow and steady. "It's a shift change. We'd been doing the graveyard—the midnight shift—and it was our turn to change. You get off at eight in the morning and don't go back until four the next day."

"So, you were off for over thirty hours?"

"Yes."

"That's a fair bit of time." Paschek rose and swaggered across the room to lean against the door. "Where were you?"

"At the motel, the one up on Highway 2, the Derrick. I had breakfast with the rest of the crew and then got some sleep."

"All of you?"

"Yeah, all of us. For about six or eight hours, anyway."

"Then what?"

"I guess the other guys headed to the pool hall or the bar."

"But not you? You stayed at the motel?"

"That's what I said. I stayed at the motel."

"The whole day? What did you do?"

"I slept some more. When I woke up, I watched TV and read for a while."

"You? Reading? A book?"

"The Bible."

"Oh, that's just perfect." Paschek snorted. "Anything else? Or did you work on your sermon all day?"

Tyler blew air slowly out through his teeth. "I went for a walk. I watched a couple of movies. Got a pizza from the motel and went back to bed. Took the phone off the hook 'cause I needed to sleep. I was still there when my foreman came and told me about Jennifer."

"You seem to have done a lot of sleeping."

"It's the only way I can handle shift change."

"During all this time did anyone see you?"

"No." Tyler's voice was hoarse. "I was alone." He massaged his forehead. "No one else was there."

"No roommate?" Paschek tilted his head, studying the man in front of him. He'd seen a nature show once featuring snakes and mice. The mice had the same appearance that Shooter did—right before they were eaten.

Tyler frowned. "Uh, yeah, we all had roommates. The company won't pay for single rooms. Mine was Chuck Newton. But he wasn't there, probably at the bar the whole day."

Paschek nodded. "Sounds like Newton. You got a vehicle out there by the rigs?"

"Yeah, my truck."

"What kind?"

"A 2012 Ford 150, black. It's paid for. Anything else?"

"One last question. You had more than thirty hours off work. Why did you stay at the motel? Why didn't you go home?"

Tyler's shoulders slumped. For a moment, he didn't answer. When at last he spoke, his voice was barely above a whisper. "Because she didn't want me. She didn't want me at home."

* * *

The ER was quiet. Derek glanced at his watch. As he had a few free minutes, he hurried to the hospital pharmacy. "Hi, Charlie, got a minute?"

Charlie Watson, the hospital's main pharmacist, looked up from his computer. "Sure, Doc. I was just reconciling the narcotic prescriptions. What can I do for you?"

"I've been reading about a new IV antibiotic, a fourth-generation cephalosporin. I'd like to get a stock of it for the ER."

"No worries." The pharmacist grabbed his notepad and moved to the counter. "Give me the particulars, and I'll get someone to look into it next week."

"That'll be fine. I'll check back in with you in a few days."

"Nope, not me." The pharmacist laughed and tapped the top of the notepad. The date August 27th had been written, underlined, and circled. "I've got tomorrow off and I'm leaving for my vacation in"—he twisted to look at the clock on the wall behind him—"about twenty minutes."

"That's nice."

The door to the pharmacy opened and a nurse rushed in. "Charlie, I need some meds." She skidded to a stop at the counter. "Oh, sorry, Doctor."

"That's okay." Derek waved a hand through the air. "You go ahead. We're just chatting."

The pharmacist frowned. "What is it now?"

"Dr. Stadler admitted a patient and he wants her on diclofenac cream for her arthritis."

"Why didn't he just order an anti-inflammatory?"

"She has ulcers and can't take any by mouth, and she's also got bad hemorrhoids so suppositories are out of the question."

"Oh, all right, I'll have to compound it, though. I'll send it up when it's ready." He inclined his head toward his desk. "I'll leave reconciling the log for the next guy. No problem."

Derek's pager vibrated, and he slipped it off his belt. It was the ER. "Time for me to go, or I'll be the one with the problem."

* * *

"Dr. Kessler, good of you to join us." Paschek was waiting when Derek entered the emergency department. "I could say I'm sorry for making the ward clerk page you, but I'm not."

The police officer motioned toward the staff room as Tyler Sampson shuffled through the open door. He'd been pale earlier. Now he was ashen.

Derek hurried to his side and took his elbow. "Are you all right?"

"Huh?" Tyler blinked, as if struggling to focus. "I'll be okay. I've gotta get Livy. Where is she?"

"Isabel took her home. Said she'd take care of her until you came."

Sheriff Paschek cleared his throat loudly. "Dr. Kessler, would you please step in here? Now."

The physician leaned in and whispered to his friend, "I'll be praying for you. Let me know if there's anything I can do."

Paschek slid between them and waited for Derek to walk into the staff room before following him and closing the door. With a deep frown, he sat and made a show of leafing through the pages of his notepad. Derek eased onto the other chair and studied the sheriff. When Paschek was finally ready, his scowl had not changed. "Okay, Doc, tell me all about Jennifer Sampson."

The ER physician pulled out his notes from the pocket of his white coat. "Jennifer Sampson was a twenty-six-year-old woman who was brought in by ambulance in respiratory arrest. She arrived in the ER at 11:42 and subsequently went into full cardiac arrest. We were able get her heart beating and were arranging a transfer to Billings. Unfortunately, she arrested again and couldn't be revived. Time of death was 13:54."

"Why the transfer?"

"Her condition and her blood work made me suspect poisoning, possibly with an organic acid or solvent."

"Could it be gas line antifreeze?"

"I suppose. We're not equipped here to detect that, let alone treat it. The only thing that would help is dialysis."

"You notice anything else?"

"Not much. She had several minor abrasions on her arm and knee. No sign of any significant trauma."

"Past history?"

"Not much in the chart. Normal childbirth. Otherwise nothing."

"Any marks on her? Burns? Needle tracks? Anything?"

Derek shook his head. "No, nothing that I saw, but I'm not a pathologist."

"So the next step is an autopsy."

"Yes, and we're in luck there, Sheriff."

Paschek's grimace deepened. He set his pencil down and squeezed his right fist till the knuckles cracked. "What makes you say that?"

"The district is part of a new visiting specialist program. For the next few days, we'll have a pathologist on site, Dr. Warren Chiu from the University of Montana."

"Dr. Chiu?"

"Yeah. He's one of the top forensic pathologists in the Northwest. He'll be arriving in a few hours."

The sheriff nodded. "All right. When he gets here, I'll speak to him." He spun around and strode from the room.

Derek sagged against the back of the chair. *Guess I've been dismissed.*

* * *

Rebecca locked the office and walked to her car. *Forget the phone call, and forget about Philip.* She glanced back at the squat red-brick office building. The stack of unfinished files she'd left on her desk mocked her and she hesitated. "Never leave things undone," her father would always say. In spite of his words, or maybe because of them, leaving things undone had become the story of her life. Pulling open the car door, she slumped onto the leather seat.

Her movements almost automatic, she reached out and ran her fingers along the car's dashboard. A smile touched her lips as she lifted her keychain and gazed at the small photo of her mother. The reverse of the key fob had an engraving of a red bow, similar to the one her mother had placed on top of the car when Rebecca had been accepted into law school. When he found out about the gift, her father disapproved. A Mustang convertible was hardly practical for Montana winters. "Trade it in for an SUV," he had demanded. Typical. Any party could be ruined by a good argument.

She'd give anything to talk to her mother again. Just once. Her father had taken that away. Rebecca started the Mustang. He'd taken it all away.

An irrational urge to disappear from her own life seized her. *Hit the highway and drive—head south and keep going. There's enough money in the bank.* She wheeled out of her parking space and headed for the exit. *Pull it out and enjoy life. For a long moment she sat at the edge of the lot. Which way to turn?* Right led to her house. Left to freedom. Her finger twitched on the turn signal, aching to push it down. *For how long? Six months, maybe a year. Then what?* She snorted, shoved the lever up, and turned toward home.

Her thoughts churning, Rebecca stared at a street sign and exhaled with a small grunt. She had missed her exit and would have to turn around at the next set of lights. Her eyes narrowed. Something was going on at the new hospital. Two police cars were parked next to an ambulance outside the emergency department. *What's that about?* Maybe Dr. Kessler was still working. She could pull into the hospital and ask him what was going on. Maybe say her migraine had returned. An image of the doctor, his eyes locking with hers, an adorable blush creeping up his neck, flashed through her mind.

Rebecca straightened and gripped the steering wheel. *Stop it.* Philip was enough trouble for her. She couldn't get involved with another man, especially not another married one. She drove on, not stopping until she had parked in her building's lot.

When she stepped into her main floor condo, she sighed in relief. The monochrome palate of ivory and stainless steel was broken only by a large bouquet of blood-red roses in the middle of the dining table. After shrugging off her jacket, she collapsed onto the sofa. Tilting back her head, she allowed the stillness of the room to wash over her.

A moment later, chills swept across her skin. Her eyes snapped open and she swung her legs over the edge of the coach. Surging to her feet, her heels clattered on the marble floor. She stopped before a small table holding three silver picture frames. A retriever, an Australian sheep dog, a beagle. Rescue dogs she had pulled out from pounds or puppy mills. She had spent hundreds, maybe thousands, on vet bills, trying to heal them. Ultimately, each time she had realized she couldn't. She had given each away, unable to give enough care, enough companionship, enough love.

Another shiver rippled through her. *Stop it. You like being alone. You're used to it.* She grabbed her phone. Who should she call? Paulina? Her neighbor, Judge Farr? Was there anyone she could reach out to? The device slipped from her fingers.

Rebecca staggered into the bedroom and crumpled to the floor, her back to the wall. She couldn't hold it in any longer. Her sobs echoed through the empty condo.

EIGHT

The little girl shivered in the silent darkness. She pulled the blankets up to her neck and stared at the ceiling. *Just be still.* She clutched the blankets with both hands. *Keep quiet.*

The bottom stair creaked. A soft whimper escaped from her lips.

Daddy was coming.

NINE

"Though justice be thy plea, consider this, that, in the course
of justice, none of us should see salvation."
The Merchant of Venice, Act IV, Scene I

Sheriff Paschek smacked his desk. His coffee mug jumped and splashed
some of its muddy contents onto the papers he'd been studying. He
swore under his breath. "Marsh, get your butt in here."

"Yes, sir?" The senior deputy stuck his head into the room.

"That post-mortem report here yet?"

"No, sir. The hospital promised we'd have it by nine this morning.
It's only a little past eight."

"I know how to tell time." Paschek narrowed his eyes. "The new guy
here?"

"Yes, sir. Deputy Standin' Reedy is here."

The sheriff crossed his arms. "Deputy, you look like you swallowed a
whole lemon. Send in Deputy Standingready." He grabbed his mug and
tipped it toward him, examining its contents. "Then run down to the
diner and get me some decent coffee."

"Yes, sir."

The sheriff pulled open a desk drawer. Empty. He slammed it shut.
"And get me some M&M's."

"Yes, sir. You want me to pick out the green ones?"
"Don't get smart with me, Marsh. Just do what I say."

* * *

The morning was going well. Absolutely no sign of a headache, and Rebecca had phoned in when Paulina beeped her the first time. She didn't have any court cases today, only appointments at the office with lots of people to see and talk to and no time to feel sorry for herself. No need to feel lonely. Only happy thoughts.

The sun sparkled through the windshield of the car as she arrived at her office. Was it time to finish yesterday's case? Paulina should be typing the papers for Mrs. Sifton to sign, but they might not be ready yet. That old woman was different somehow. She really seemed to care. Not many people were that way anymore, at least not many that Rebecca knew. She smiled as she strode through the office door. The only ones she truly knew cared about her were Paulina and Judge Farr. At least she could be grateful for them.

* * *

Derek didn't enjoy running. He hated getting up early, did not relish the burning in his muscles when he pushed through the last half-mile, and wasn't thrilled about getting hot and sweaty before he'd even had a cup of coffee. He did it anyway.

Stepping from the shower beside the doctors' lounge, he tossed his towel aside and pulled on a set of scrubs. He studied his reflection as he ran his fingers through his damp hair. He looked tired. His diet had been poor of late, and sleep, well, sleep hadn't come easy for a long time. Maybe he should try harder to forget. He touched the gold band on his finger. But that was why he ran. It helped him to remember.

* * *

Paschek sipped his coffee and lifted an eyebrow. Hazelnut. Marsh must be angling for a raise or a day off. Or maybe something else. The sheriff shifted his gaze to the new deputy across the room. Standingready stiffened under his gaze. Which made Paschek strangely pleased. "You know how to make decent coffee?"

"No, sir." The deputy snapped to attention.

Shaking his head, Paschek pointed to a chair. "Relax already. All you gotta do is ask Marsh where to get some."

"Yes, sir. If you say so, sir."

"You got a problem with Marsh, Deputy?"

"Not me, sir."

"All right. Don't let there be one." He grabbed one of the bags of M&M's and tore it open. "Tell me about the Sampson place."

"What do you mean, sir?"

The sheriff poured the candy out on his desk blotter. "Don't tell me you stood there and did nothing?"

"Not exactly."

"All right. What did you see?"

Standingready shifted on his seat. "You uh, you told me not to touch anything in the house. Sir."

"Uh huh." Paschek picked candies out of the pile and popped them into his mouth. Red. Blue. Orange.

"You didn't say anything about outside the house."

The yellow ones were next. "Get to the point, Deputy."

"I noted that the yard was carefully maintained. The lawn had recently been mowed. There were fresh clippings on the walk."

"So?"

"I searched around. Checked the garden shed. There wasn't a lawnmower anywhere."

Paschek munched on the last of the brown M&M's. "So someone else cut the lawn. Maybe saw something." He pushed a scattering of green candies into a pile. "Good work. Get on the phone and check with the neighbors. Find out who it was."

"Yes, sir. Thank you, sir."

The sheriff scooped up the remaining M&M's and yanked open the bottom drawer of his desk. "What are you waiting for? Get going." He leaned over and dropped the candies into a Mason jar. When he straightened, he was alone.

* * *

His shift hadn't started yet, so Derek headed to the cafeteria for a quick breakfast. He picked up his tray and turned away from the cashier, surprised see Simon Cudworth waving at him. His forehead wrinkled. Something must be up. The hospital's top surgeon and chief of staff had barely acknowledged his existence until now. "Dr. Cudworth."

"Dr. Kessler, take a seat." The surgeon observed him through narrow slits. "You in the ER today?"

"Yeah. Just starting."

"I see." The surgeon wiped his face with a napkin. "Nice call on that dissecting aneurysm last week." He pulled his chair closer. "You showed excellent instincts."

"Uh, thanks."

"So far, that is."

Derek looked up from his tray. "I don't follow."

"I passed through the ER yesterday. Saw you with that Huntington's patient." He knit his hands together. "I didn't like what I saw. Or, rather, what I heard."

"Excuse me?"

Cudworth's smile was cold. "You want to get all religious on your own time, that's fine. But not in my hospital." His left hand slowly clenched into a fist on the table. "Dr. Kessler, you're a physician. We deal in science, not sorcery."

"Let me get this straight." Derek crossed his arms. "You are actually objecting to me praying for a patient?"

"Of course not." Cudworth crumpled the napkin into a tight ball and tossed it onto Derek's plate. "I just want you to keep it out of the ER. Keep it to yourself." The surgeon drained the last of his coffee and stood. "You like it here, don't you? It could be really good for you." He rounded the table and bent to whisper in the younger doctor's ear. "Go with the flow. Don't rock the boat. I promise you, it'll be safer that way."

When he had gone, Derek shoved his tray away. He had lost his appetite.

* * *

Rebecca accepted a stack of files and a mug of coffee from Paulina as she strode through the office door. "How's the morning?"

"Not bad. Three appointments and those real estate forms."

"Nice." She settled into the black leather chair behind her desk. Paulina still stood in the doorway. Rebecca tilted her head. "Anything else?"

"There is, yes. Judge Farr called."

"Oh."

"He sounded serious. Said he wanted to see you about something." Paulina shifted her weight from one foot to the other. "He'd like you to come to his office."

Rebecca bit her bottom lip. "Did he say when?"

"Yes. This morning."

The air conditioner blew a cold blast of air against the back of her neck. So much for happy thoughts.

* * *

His coffee was getting cold. Should he send Marsh out for more? Paschek swirled the murky liquid around in his cup before setting it down. No, he had something more important for the man to do.

"Deputy," he said when Marsh entered his office, "I want you to follow these leads from Jenn Sampson's appointment book."

Marsh took the sheet of paper the sheriff held out and glanced at it. "What about this one in Helena? You want me to run down there?"

"Nah, get one of the locals. Henke owes me. Call him." Paschek sipped his coffee and scowled. "You'll require a court order, though. That one's some sort of counselor and likely won't talk without one."

"No problem." The deputy studied the list. "I can do the rest. This one's next to the court house. I'll go see her first."

"Who's that?"

"The lady lawyer—Rebecca Andrychuk."

* * *

Despite Derek's ruined breakfast, it should have been a decent day. Fridays could be crazy in the ER, but for a change he had help. Arthur Stadler was a semi-retired family physician who filled in occasionally. He wasn't fast, but he knew his stuff, and the two of them should have been able to handle whatever came their way with ease. In theory, anyway.

The morning rush had been cleared out easily enough. Flus, colds, and sprains mostly. Derek had been worried at first about an elderly obese woman with chest pain, but then she belched, and the pain disappeared. The lab tests were normal and he sent her home. The next case didn't go as well.

He had barely finished suturing a laceration when Maggie LaPerriere appeared in the doorway. "Doctor, the ambulance is bringing in a young girl, Lucy Friesen. She's in rough shape."

Derek grimaced and hurried to the ER desk. The radio crackled when he took the microphone. "Kessler here."

"Unit Two here," the radio hissed through the static. "We're transporting a seven-year-old leukemia patient. High fever. Tachycardia. Shallow breathing. Pressure low. Mom found her unresponsive this morning. We couldn't get an IV started. ETA ten minutes."

"Okay, we'll be ready." Derek turned to Maggie. "Where's Dr. Stadler?"

"He went for an early lunch."

"Get him here STAT. I'll put in a bone needle to get fluids into her."

The charge nurse shook her head. "I'm afraid all our intraosseous needles were recalled and haven't been replaced."

"That's just wonderful. I'll have to insert a central line."

"Is that a problem?"

"Yeah, I've always struggled getting a line on kids. Is one of the anesthetists available?"

The ward clerk checked the OR's computer listing. "No, but I think Dr. Cudworth just finished his case."

"That's excellent news, Doctor," Maggie said. "Dr. Cudworth regularly teaches placing central lines. He's an expert."

"All right, see if he's available. Do you know what stage of treatment Lucy is in?"

"I talked to her mom a couple of weeks ago. At that point they had just initiated her third round of chemo."

"That would put her more than halfway through, meaning that her white cell count will be in her boots. We need an IV line. If not, there may not be much we can do to help her."

* * *

The coffee was bitter in her stomach, and Rebecca pushed the cup away. This was not good, not good at all. She straightened the stack of files on her desk and grabbed the top folder. After only a brief glance at the first page, she dropped it and peered at her watch. "What time did the judge want to see me?"

Paulina picked up the document and handed it back. "He didn't say. I'm sure he meant when your work was done."

"Right." Rebecca opened the file and closed it. *Concentrate.* Her gaze shifted to the window. It really was a beautiful day. "Say, Paulina, what do you know about the new emergency doctor in town?"

"Dr. Kessler? Seems nice. George saw him last week for his gout. He liked him."

"Hmm." Rebecca twirled a pen around in her fingers.

"He's renting one of those apartments over on Ninth. Been there for four or five months."

"On Ninth? Aren't those pretty small? I thought they were all bachelor suites."

"They are. What's wrong with that?"

She shrugged. "Nothing. I'm a little surprised that a married couple would stay there, that's all."

"I don't think he's married. At least there's no Mrs. Kessler in town. No, I'm sure he lives alone."

Oh. Rebecca reached for the file she'd dropped. Better be careful. Alone could still mean married. She was relieved to hear the front door to her office open to announce the arrival of her first appointment.

* * *

"What have you got?"

Derek jerked his head as Simon Cudworth marched into the ER. "Seven-year-old leukemia patient, unresponsive, with fever and dehydration," he said as the paramedics pushed the gurney into the casualty room. He placed his palm on the little girl's forehead. Her skin was hot and dry to the touch, her respirations rapid and shallow.

The surgeon pursed his lips. "What did you want me for?"

"The paramedics couldn't get an IV started, and there's no bone needles. I was hoping you could place a central line."

"Fine," Cudworth grunted. "Get me a tray." The surgeon moved the child's head to expose her neck. Wiping the skin with disinfectant, he pressed his fingers to her neck, clearly feeling for landmarks to identify her jugular vein. "Give me the needle."

While the senior surgeon worked, Derek continued his examination. He peered intently into Lucy's pupils. No sign of pressure on the brain. He pulled up her T-shirt and reached for his stethoscope but froze at the sight of the child's skin. She was covered in dozens of small, reddish-purple spots—tiny points of bleeding under her skin. Petechiae. He sucked air into his lungs. Meningococcal meningitis. He touched the girl's head and whispered, "Oh, Lord."

A snort from Cudworth seized his attention. The surgeon was glaring at him, nostrils flared in an angry challenge. "Don't tell me you're planning to pray."

Seconds thudded by. Without warning, a sudden spasm shook Lucy's body. Her jaws clenched tight, her body arched upward, and her limbs jerked from side to side. Derek grabbed her head with both hands. "She's having a seizure."

* * *

Rebecca usually appreciated the fact that her office was only half a block from the courthouse. Not today. All too quickly, she arrived at Judge Farr's office.

Marilyn, the judge's secretary, greeted her. "The judge has been expecting you. He said to send you in."

Judge Farr's inner chamber smelled of leather and old books, with a faint hint of cigar smoke. The odor evoked memories of her childhood, and Rebecca shuddered. She hesitated at the doorway, a little girl once more, alone and lost.

"Rebecca, welcome." Judge Farr waved her in. "Have a seat." He was a short, slightly plump man, with a halo of frosted hair that hovered atop a face lined and tanned from years of serious thought and serious fly fishing. "Would you like a coffee?"

"No, thank you, sir. I'm fine." She sat rigid, a trickle of sweat curling down between her shoulder blades.

"All right."

He eased the door shut and settled onto his plush, chocolate-brown chair. He knit his fingers together and paused. *Here it comes.* It was sure to be a reprimand about the Sifton case, which she likely deserved.

"My dear, I need to tell you… I spoke with your father yesterday."

Rebecca blinked. "You did?"

"Yes. He asked about you."

"Did you tell him where he could go?"

"Rebecca. He does care. I think he's lonely."

"Lonely? I remember how he handles loneliness. Whatever he's feeling right now, he deserves it. After what he did to us, to me." She stood. "Was there anything else, Judge? Or am I dismissed?"

"Please, sit. I'm your friend. I've known you all your life." He sighed. "Fine. Nothing more about your father." He held up a file. "Mrs. Sifton. Want to talk about her?"

Not particularly. Rebecca sank back down and slowly nodded.

* * *

The child writhed and shook on the stretcher. Cudworth lurched back a step and swore. "Hold her still."

Derek protected the little girl's head while Maggie and another nurse draped themselves on top of her to stop the jerking movements of the seizure. He shot a heated look at the surgeon. "We need that IV line."

"What do you think I'm doing?"

His gaze dropped to the little girl's flushed cheeks. *I can't lose her.* He squeezed his eyes shut. Not another one.

TEN

The little girl shivered.

Daddy had told her not to be scared. He said he loved her, that he would never hurt her.

She couldn't stop shaking.

ELEVEN

"You would play upon me; you would know my stops; you
would pluck out the heart of my mystery."
Hamlet, Act III, Scene III

"Autopsy report's here," Marsh said from the doorway.

Sheriff Paschek glanced at the clock and scowled. It was after eleven. So much for medical efficiency. "I thought you were going to interview that lawyer?"

"I was, but I thought you'd want this first."

Paschek held out his hand, and Marsh handed him the file. Paschek flipped it open and scanned the first page. Typical medical mumbo jumbo. He skipped to the summary and began to read out loud. "Cause of death: cardiac arrest secondary to severe metabolic acidosis." More crap medical jargon. "Acute respiratory and renal failure due to..." *Ah, here we are.* "... organic acid poisoning." Paschek turned the page. "Chemical analysis of stomach contents and blood toxicology samples couriered to the University of Montana confirm the presence of ethylene glycol." He looked up at Marsh. "You know what that is?"

"Nope. 'Fraid not."

"It's what we've got locked in the evidence locker. What I found in Shooter Sampson's garage. Gas line antifreeze." He dropped the post-mortem report on his desk. "Our murder weapon."

* * *

Rebecca stamped from the office. How dare Judge Farr betray her like that? He knew her father, knew what he was like. The man had never cared for anyone but himself. If he was trying to get hold of her now, he must want something. She stalked in the direction of the exit then stopped and spun toward the judge's secretary.

"Marilyn, was yesterday the first time my father called?"

A pink flush crept across the secretary's face. "Well, I don't know…"

"Please." Rebecca stepped closer.

Marilyn's shoulders slumped. "All right. No, it wasn't. He's been calling the judge about twice a month for awhile now."

Rebecca jerked back. The warmth drained from her face, and she gritted her teeth. Her thoughts raced. *No, I won't let him back in.* On trembling legs, she backed out of the office. *Not now, not ever.*

* * *

"I got it." Cudworth stepped away from the gurney and raised his hands in triumph. The little girl continued to convulse.

Derek's eyes were fixed on Lucy's face. She was turning blue. "Keep her still. Don't lose that IV." Cudworth crossed his arms and leaned against the wall. Keeping one hand on her forehead, Derek reached down to grasp Lucy's leg. "Maggie, push lorazepam two milligrams IV. Then get respiratory and the lab. She's going to be okay."

* * *

The case was starting to come together. Paschek liked what he had so far. Still, it wasn't enough, not yet. He stuck his head out his office door. "Standingready, any luck finding out who cuts the victim's lawn?"

"No, sir. The McKennys didn't know anything about it. I was able to figure out who the nearest neighbors are, but that's all. There was no answer at the Baker place, and the Hendrys' phone has been busy all morning."

"So, what are you going to do about it?"

"Sir?"

Paschek shook his head. Rookies. "Grab a set of keys. We'll head over there. You know, do some real police work." He held out his hand. "I'll drive."

* * *

Derek stepped from the treatment room and leaned against the wall. He dropped his chin to his chest and rubbed his forehead. That was too close. If they hadn't got that central line in...

"They're taking the little girl to the ICU now, Doctor."

"Thanks, Maggie. I'll talk to her parents and then check on her. Ask the ICU nurses to set up for a lumbar puncture."

Dr. Cudworth finished the note he had been writing and handed Lucy Friesen's chart to a nurse. He slid down the counter, closer to Derek. "You had me worried there for a moment, Kessler."

"Yeah, I thought we might lose her."

"Not that. I knew I was going to get the line."

Derek stiffened. "What, then?"

"I thought you were going to forget what you are. A doctor, not a preacher." Cudworth inspected his fingernails. "That little girl was saved because of good medicine, not because of any supernatural delusions." He reached out and tapped Derek on the chest. "I'm glad you remembered that."

Derek rubbed his forehead with the side of his hand. Was it true that God had absolutely no place in a place where people were sick and suffering? He dropped his hand. *Who knows?* Maybe his boss was right.

* * *

Rebecca's lunch was cold.

"Do you want me to heat that up?"

Rebecca glanced over. Paulina stood in the doorway. "Heat it up?"

"Your soup." Her secretary took the bowl from Rebecca's desk. "You haven't touched it."

"I'm not very hungry."

"I could tell. You've been sitting there staring into space for fifteen minutes. Should I put this in the fridge so you can have it later?"

"I guess so." Rebecca leaned back in her chair and rubbed her eyes as Paulina left the room. The meeting with Judge Farr still stung. What was her father up to?

A knock on the door frame brought her upright. Paulina was back.

"Sorry, Ms. Andrychuk." *Why so formal?* "There's someone to see you."

"Who?" Something in her secretary's tone tightened up Rebecca's stomach, and she pressed a hand to her abdomen.

"A police officer."

* * *

Paschek always drove. He liked it that way, and so that's the way it was. He glanced over when Standingready cleared his throat. "You got something to say, Deputy?"

"Uh, yes, sir. It's just—well, how can you be so sure this was murder?"

Paschek exhaled. "I haven't been a hick Montana sheriff all my life. I put in my time on the beat. Denver. Narcotics mostly, but a couple years on homicide."

"Wow."

"No, there was nothing 'wow' about it. Just hard, dirty work." Paschek stared at the horizon. "Not much fun."

"That why you quit it?"

"I quit so I could put in a few years without night shifts, and rapists, and motorcycle gangs. Nice and quiet. Stockton was going to be my swan song until I retired." He gripped the steering wheel a bit tighter. "Didn't count on stuff following me here."

The hum of the air conditioner was drowned out when the car turned off the pavement onto a gravel road. Standingready raised his voice. "This case, why do you think it was murder?"

"Not think—know. Jennifer Sampson was poisoned. The labs and autopsy confirm it. Ethylene glycol, gas line antifreeze. Causes loss of consciousness and then heart and kidney failure. Just two or three ounces can be fatal. It was in the victim's stomach and in the broken glass but not in the jug of lemonade. The stuff is supposed to taste really sweet, but the lemonade would mask that."

"Maybe suicide?"

"No evidence. No note. No depression. Everyone interviewed denied it. And then, there's her appointment book. She had an appointment with a lawyer on the morning she died and another with a psychologist in Helena on Monday. All signs point to murder, not suicide."

"Did you see anything at the house that made it look that way?"

"Definitely. Jennifer Sampson was obsessed with the place. Everything was clean and orderly. Everything matched. All the kitchen stuff was in sets of twelve. Everything except those cut-glass tumblers. Counting the broken one, there were only eleven." Paschek grunted. "That wasn't perfect. Jennifer Sampson wouldn't go for that. But she couldn't do anything about it if she was already down on the floor when the twelfth glass went missing. At first I thought maybe it had broken earlier and been thrown away, but the more I consider the case, the more I think the murderer took it."

They were passing the Sampson house, and both men turned their heads to look as they drove by. Vans from the Crime Scene Unit were parked in the yard. They would be collecting evidence for the rest of the day, at least. Once they were done, the doors would be sealed until the DCI decided whether or not to get involved. The yellow police tape fluttering in the breeze might be the end of it, unless Paschek could prove that he was right.

He drummed his fingers on the steering wheel. "There was opportunity. Jennifer was alone in the house Thursday night and Friday morning. Isabel Vermette said she had the little girl at her place for sleepovers a lot. The grandmother sometimes babysits but not this week. No one else was around. Then, there's the means. A pack of gas line antifreeze. One bottle missing. That was stupid. Maybe the killer meant to dispose of it and forgot or didn't have a chance. Or he thought no one would figure out that she'd been poisoned. Who knows?" Paschek's face twisted into a grimace. "We need more."

"More evidence?"

"Yeah, but mostly motive. I've got an idea, but I want to be sure."

"You said 'he'."

"That's right, I did." Paschek smiled grimly as he turned off the road into a farm yard. "I've got a suspect, and I'm going to nail his hide to the wall."

* * *

Derek slumped onto a chair at the nursing desk and lowered his chin to his chest. From the back room, he could hear Maggie's muffled tones. She was tearing into Art Stadler over a pager with dead batteries and a cell phone that had been turned off. Dr. Stadler slunk from the room and grabbed a chart. A pair of sturdy white shoes appeared on the floor at his feet. Maggie. Was it his turn?

"Dr. Kessler, may I speak with you?"

Derek rubbed his eyes and nodded as Maggie settled on the chair next to him. "What did you want to say?"

"You did a good job. You saved that little girl's life."

"But Cudworth…"

"Is a fine surgeon, a very good technician. You, however, are an excellent doctor."

"Thanks, Maggie."

"I'm not telling you this to stroke your ego. My primary concern is the patients." Derek raised an eyebrow. "I've watched you these past few months. You do a better job when you trust in yourself. Don't let Dr. Cudworth or others like him shake you. Have a little faith." Maggie stood and, one hand on her hip, wagged a finger in Derek's face. "Listen to me. I'm Métis. Descendant of French fur traders and Native Americans. My people came to Montana from Canada in 1885, after the Northwest Rebellion. I know what it's like to be fired upon." She leaned closer. "Don't quit. Don't give up. Keep fighting."

Derek grinned and stood. "Thanks, Maggie. I appreciate it."

"I'm not done yet." She took Derek by the shoulders and turned him toward the exit. "You need a break. Get out of the hospital for a while. Go have some lunch."

"But the patients..."

"Will be fine. Dr. Stadler can look after things." She gave him a push. "Go."

Derek shuffled to the exit. When he glanced over his shoulder, Maggie was still standing and watching. He shrugged and pushed open the door.

* * *

"Good afternoon, ma'am," the police officer said as stepped into the office. "You're Rebecca Andrychuk?"

"I am." Rebecca glanced at Paulina, who stood in the doorway, arms crossed and a wary look on her face. "It's okay, Paulina."

The officer waited until Paulina had closed the door before turning back to Rebecca. "I need to ask you a few questions."

"Certainly, Deputy..."

"Marsh."

"Well, Deputy Marsh, would you like a cup of coffee?"

"Thanks, but not just now. Maybe later." He crossed the office to lean against the side of her desk.

"Okay." Rebecca leaned back in her chair, increasing the distance between herself and the officer. "You said you had some questions?"

"That's right, I did." His smile was oily. "How long have you been here in Stockton?"

"Three years now."

"And you're single?"

"What does that have to do with anything?"

"I'm checking background facts. Did Jennifer Sampson have an appointment to see you yesterday morning?"

"Sampson?" Rebecca leaned forward and ran a finger down the page from the day before. "Oh yes, she did have an appointment, but she didn't show."

"Do you know why she made the appointment?"

"No idea. She didn't tell my secretary anything when she booked it."

"That'd be the lady who showed me in?"

Rebecca pointed through the glass in the office door. Paulina remained standing just outside. The look on her face had not changed. "Yes. Paulina Zales."

"Okay." Marsh glanced at the notebook he'd pulled from his pocket. "Had you ever seen Jennifer Sampson before?"

"No, she's a new client. I've never met her."

"So you don't know why she wanted to see a lawyer?"

"I'm afraid not."

"I guess those are all the questions I have, then. Thank you for your time." He closed his notebook and pushed away from the desk.

"What's this all about?" Rebecca stood. "Is this lady in trouble?"

"You could call it that. She's dead. We're investigating the case right now."

"Dead?" Rebecca jerked, her eyes wide. "You mean she was murdered?"

"I'd better not say anymore. The sheriff wouldn't like it." Marsh held out his hand. "Thanks for your assistance, Miss Andrychuk. If I have any more questions, I'll call you. Maybe take you up on that offer of a coffee."

Rebecca disengaged her hand. "Certainly, Deputy. You may call my office and speak to my secretary anytime."

Marsh grinned and touched the brim of his hat with the tip of his index finger. After he'd sauntered out of the office, Paulina closed the door firmly behind him. "What did that man want?"

"You don't like him?"

Her secretary shuddered. "Gives me the creeps. He chases after anyone in a skirt and doesn't like taking no for an answer."

"I'll remember that. He was here about that new client who missed her appointment yesterday. She won't be rescheduling. Sounds as though she was murdered."

Paulina's hand flew up to her face. "A murder? In Stockton?"

"Apparently." Rebecca trudged back to her desk. Who would have thought?

* * *

Derek sat alone in the restaurant booth, a slice of strawberry rhubarb pie untouched beside him. He ran a thumb through the condensation on the glass of ginger ale on the table before him. Rows of silver bubbles rose through the amber liquid to burst at the top of the glass like so many unfulfilled promises.

"Doc. Hey, Doc. Are you okay?"

A hand fell on his shoulder. Derek looked up. Bert Cavanaugh stood beside him, leaning heavily on a cane. "Hi, Bert. Sorry. I didn't hear you."

"No problem, Doc. Can I sit down, or are you waiting for me to fall over?"

Derek held out his hand. "Have a seat, please."

Bert struggled to get his body moving in the right direction and then flopped onto the bench opposite Derek. His head twitched in a staccato rhythm, and his arm jerked into the air. "Nancy, bring me an iced tea, please." He slid a little deeper into the booth and fixed his eyes on Derek. "What's happening? You look awful."

"It's been a rough couple days."

"Want to tell me about it?"

Where to even start? Derek sighed. "There was a little girl in the ER today. If it hadn't been for Simon Cudworth, she likely would have died." Derek clenched his hands into fists. "Yesterday was worse. There was a code—a young woman stopped breathing. I lost her, couldn't save her. I even prayed. No help." He paused. "No point."

Nancy set a glass of iced tea in front of Bert, and he smiled at her. "You know what, Doc? I think you're wrong there. I understand you're hurting. Disappointed, maybe even mad at God. That's okay. He's got big shoulders. But it's always worth praying. God is listening, and He does answer. It's just that sometimes, well, sometimes He says no." A sharp tremor worked its way up Bert's spine to pulsate down both arms and he spilled some of his iced tea.

Bert squeezed his eyes tightly and gritted his teeth. The tremor passed. "Let me tell you something. I'm a living, breathing miracle. I shouldn't be alive. I've had this Huntington's for almost thirty years. Most patients with it are dead in half that time. Why do you think I'm still here?"

Derek shrugged.

"I'll tell you. Prayer. Prayer, and maybe God's not done with me yet." Bert took a long drink from his iced tea. His hand held steady, the tremor almost gone. He studied Derek's face. "It was so hard for Marie when I was diagnosed. She cried herself to sleep most nights. Said she'd make a terrible widow. We never expected the Lord to take her first. We didn't count on the cancer."

Both men were quiet. Bert sipped his ice tea, struggling not to spill any. "I don't understand why it happened this way," he said. "I still don't like it. Losing Marie, this lousy disease, any of it. But I've learned that God's in charge. I can accept that."

"Aren't you afraid to die?" Derek played with the paper from his straw, twisting it around his fingers.

"Shakespeare wrote, 'The valiant never taste of death but once. Of all the wonders that I yet have heard, it seems to me most strange that men should fear; seeing that death, a necessary end, will come when it will come.' But you need a better answer." The jerking movement had returned to his right hand, but Bert ignored it. "The Apostle Paul was a lot wiser than the Bard. He said, 'To live is Christ, and to die is gain.' I'm ready, Derek. I'm ready either way." He reached out slowly, his hand fluttering like a moth. He tapped a finger against the physician's hand, touching the gold band on his finger. "I can see it hurts. Do you want to tell me about it?"

Derek pulled off the ring and read the inside inscription. *All my love, Cassie.* He slipped the ring back on his finger. "I was married. I had a wife and a daughter." He glanced around and then leaned back in the booth. The sounds of the restaurant seemed to fade to silence. "They died," he said, "almost two years ago now. A long story."

Bert clasped his hands together. "Derek, my friend, I have all day."

TWELVE

The door opened.

The little girl wanted to cry, but she knew Daddy wouldn't like that. He had told her to be strong. Be brave. And remember that he loved her most of all.

She closed her eyes.

THIRTEEN

"Demand me nothing. What you know, you know.
From this time forth I never will speak word."
Othello, Act V, Scene II

As the police cruiser turned into the Hendry yard, a boy on a riding lawnmower crossed the lane in front of them. Paschek smashed his foot down on the brakes, and the car skidded on the gravel. Swearing harshly, he exploded from the patrol car and stomped over to the youngster. The boy jumped off the lawnmower and bolted into the house. Paschek gestured impatiently for Standingready to get out of the car. "Let's go."

A woman appeared in the doorway as the two officers approached the house. "Can I help you, Sheriff?" she said.

Paschek touched the brim of his cap. "Yes, ma'am. That your boy on the lawnmower just now?"

The woman frowned and glanced over her shoulder. "Kyle, get out here." She waited a moment then shouted again, "I said out here. Now."

The boy shuffled into view. He pushed the screen door open with his foot and stepped onto the porch. "I didn't do nothin'."

"Then why's the sheriff here? Were you driving on the road again? You know your father said…"

"I ain't hurting nobody."

The woman clamped a hand on the muscle between the boy's neck and shoulder. Kyle winced and tried to twist away. She squeezed harder. "No more back talk." She let go of him and shifted her attention to Paschek. "It won't happen again, Sheriff."

"Thank you, Mrs. Hendry, but that's not what we're here about. This here's Deputy Standingready. He wants to ask Kyle a few questions."

Standingready stepped forward. "Do you know the Sampson place, Kyle?"

"Well, duh." He sidestepped quickly when his mother raised her hand. "I mean, yes, sir. It's only a mile away."

"Do you cut the grass for them?"

"Yeah, but I always drive over in the ditch." He glanced at his mother. "Almost always."

"How often are you there?"

"Every week. Even if it don't need it."

"Were you there this week?"

"Yeah."

Standingready straightened and placed his hand on his gun belt. "What day would that have been?"

The boy's eyes widened. "Yesterday. It was yesterday. Sir."

"Did you see Mrs. Sampson?"

"Nope."

"Didn't she pay you?"

"Nah, she pays me ahead of time. That way I don't gotta bug her for it."

"So you didn't see anyone."

"Didn't say that."

Mrs. Hendry started to lift her hand again, but Sheriff Paschek stepped forward. "Now, Kyle, you don't want to be an uncooperative witness, do you? You know what we do with uncooperative witnesses?" The boy shook his head. Paschek leaned forward and whispered in his ear, "You don't want to find out." He moved back a pace, his eyes locked on Kyle. "Now, answer the deputy's questions."

Standingready cleared his throat. "What did you see, Kyle?"

"I seen, I mean, I saw someone else. It wasn't Mrs. Sampson. Her car was parked like always. I saw a pickup truck leaving right before I got there."

"Who was driving it?"

"Don't know. I couldn't see."

"All right, what kind of truck was it?"

"Ain't sure. But it was black."

Paschek's eyes narrowed as he moved to stand over the boy. "Was it Tyler Sampson's truck?"

"Don't know."

Paschek leaned forward, his face inches from Kyle's. "Think, boy. Whose truck was it?"

The boy edged closer to his mother. "I don't know."

"Sheriff, please," Mrs. Hendry said. "The boy's barely twelve. Tyler's not around much in the summer. I don't think Kyle's even met him."

"I see." Paschek stepped back and touched the brim of his cap once more. "Thank you for your cooperation. We may need to talk to Kyle again later."

He strode back to his vehicle and climbed in. He nodded to his deputy as he started the car. "That's one more piece of the puzzle. Places Shooter at the scene."

"Could have been someone else," Standingready said.

"No way. It was Shooter, all right. Like I said, one more piece."

* * *

She should have eaten lunch. Not that Rebecca was hungry, but food might have helped settle the churning in her stomach. She was starting to feel nauseated, and when she stood the room swirled in front of her. Clamping a hand over her mouth, Rebecca brushed past her next clients and rushed to the washroom.

Moments later, she straightened, steadying herself with a hand against the side of the stall. A stray shaft of sunlight sliced through the window to stab at her eyes. Rebecca clenched her eyes tight and groped for the bottle of headache pills Dr. Naidu had prescribed. She'd managed to get the lid off when another spasm of pain rocked her. The splash that followed forced her eyes open. She peered into the toilet bowl and groaned. "Oh no."

* * *

The telephone receiver bounced twice before settling in its cradle. Paschek glared at the offending instrument and fumed. He jabbed a finger at the intercom. "Standingready, get in here."

"Yes, sir?" the deputy said as he entered the room.

"Is Marsh back yet?"

"No sir. He dropped off his report on the interview with the lady lawyer but then went out on a call. Drunk and disorderly."

"How come you didn't go with him?"

"Uh, Deputy Marsh felt it was best if he went alone."

"He did, did he?" Paschek shook his head. "Well, when he does get back, tell him he's in charge." He reached up and pinched the bridge of his nose.

"Something wrong, sir?"

"Yeah, there is. Those idiots at the Department of Criminal Investigation." He slammed a fist down on the desk. "'Not enough evidence.' Bunch of jerks. Too lazy to get off their butts and do some work."

"So they're not coming?"

"Aren't you listening? That's what I said. They're not convinced that there was a crime in the Sampson case. It'll be different when Melansen gets back."

"Melansen?"

"Detective Oliver Melansen. Old friend of mine. Out of state right now, but he'll be back tomorrow, then we'll get some action." Paschek bent over and opened the bottom drawer of his desk. He pulled out the Mason jar of green M&M's and gave it a shake. Over half full. *That's enough.* He shot a look at his deputy. "You still here?"

"Yes, sir," Standingready said. "You wanted me to tell Deputy Marsh he's in charge?"

"Why do I have to keep repeating myself? I'm going out of town for a few hours, so Marsh will run things until I get back." He tucked the Mason jar under his arm and strode to the door. "Don't you dare call me unless it's... Actually, don't call me at all."

* * *

"This report came for you," Dr. Stadler held out a stack of papers as Derek reentered the emergency department.

"Thanks." Derek scanned the top page. Jennifer Sampson's autopsy report. When Art Stadler spoke again, he set the papers down.

"The ER has been pretty steady, although I've managed to keep things under control." Stadler leaned in and lowered his voice. "Maggie cracked the whip a couple of times, but I guess I deserved it." He signed off the chart he was holding and tapped it with his finger. "This was quite the case."

"What about it?"

"Migraine sufferer comes in because she dropped her meds in the toilet and her regular doctor's office was closed."

"Not another drug seeker."

"That's the thing. She wasn't after narcotics. She actually did drop her sumatriptan in the toilet. She brought the pill bottle with her to show me. Who would have guessed it?" Stadler grinned and straightened his tie. "So I gave her some intranasal stuff, and she started feeling better right away." He dropped his voice to a whisper. "Course, she wasn't hoping to see me. Asked for you right off."

Derek stiffened slightly. "Who did you say she was?"

"I didn't, but here she comes." Stadler jerked his head, and Derek turned to see Rebecca appear in the doorway of Exam Room Two. The lawyer smiled and walked over to the desk.

"Good afternoon, Dr. Kessler," she said with a nod. "I wasn't expecting to be back here so soon."

"Uh, yeah. Dr. Stadler was telling me. I'm glad you're feeling better."

"Arthur took good care of me." Rebecca patted the older physician's arm. Stadler gave a mock bow and, after handing her a prescription, disappeared down the hallway. Rebecca held up the paper. "Next time I'll be more careful with my meds." Her smile faded when she saw the post-mortem report on the counter top. "Jennifer Sampson. Oh." She pressed a hand to her chest. "Was she really murdered?"

Derek snatched up the file. "I shouldn't say... I mean..."

"No, I'm sorry. I shouldn't have asked. I understand. Confidentiality and all that."

"Did you know her?"

"No, not at all. But I, well, I guess I sort of heard about it." Rebecca bit her bottom lip. "A deputy came to my office earlier. Mrs. Sampson had booked an appointment to meet with me yesterday, which of course she missed. He asked a few questions, but there wasn't much I could tell him." She opened her purse and dropped the prescription inside. "I'd never met her. I guess now I never will." She closed the purse and slung it over her shoulder. "Anyway, I'd better be going. Nice to see you again, Doctor." She touched his hand briefly, and then she was gone.

Derek stood in silence, the last remnants of her perfume settling into the recesses of his brain. He glanced down at his palm. Her hand had been soft and cool in his, so much like Cassie's. He shook himself and reached for a chart. Time to get to work.

* * *

The squad car's radio hissed and crackled before falling silent. Paschek watched the mile markers race by to merge with the horizon. Another twenty miles and he would be out of range and off the clock. The jar of M&M's rattled on the seat beside him in rhythm with the hum of the tires. The sound mocked him with its unending drone. *Just like the job. No time off. No time away.*

The radio crackled again. "COM to Sheriff Paschek. Come in."

Paschek cursed and rolled to a stop on the side of the road. "Paschek here. I told you I didn't want any calls, Standingready." The voice on the radio faded out. The sheriff cranked up the amplification and spoke again. "I said no calls."

"Marsh here. Something's come up."

"It better be important."

"It is. What's your 10-20?"

"I'm almost out of the county. What is so important?"

"The Sampson case. New evidence came in. Just what you were waiting for." The radio buzzed with static. "Enough to close the case."

The squad car's tires squealed as Paschek spun the vehicle around and headed down the highway. "I'm on my way."

Fifteen miles down the road, he glanced over at the jar of green candies. "You'll just have to wait. You always have to wait."

FOURTEEN

She did cry.

It wasn't until later, after he left. But she did cry.

She tried hard not to. She tried hard to do all that he had told her. Not to be afraid. Not to cry.

And especially to always do one thing.

FIFTEEN

"There is a tide in the affairs of men, which, taken at the flood,
leads on to fortune; omitted, all the voyage of their life is
bound in shallows and in miseries."
Julius Caesar, Act IV, Scene III

His shift was over. Derek lingered at the main desk, finishing up his charts, reviewing lab tests, and sipping a cup of truly awful coffee. He pulled out Jennifer Sampson's post-mortem report and read it again. She was only twenty-four. Way too young. He glanced at the listing for next of kin. Too young to leave a husband and a child alone. He pursed his lips. How old was the little girl? Four, maybe five. The same age Sarah had been.

Derek tossed the report onto the desk. He closed his eyes tightly and dropped his head into his hands. How could this girl look so much like his daughter? The same blonde hair, the same brown eyes. The way her bottom lip trembled when she was trying not to cry. The way she asked for her mommy. Derek surged to his feet. Too many deaths. Too many failures. He had to do… something.

He snatched up the report. There, beside Tyler's name, home phone and cell phone numbers. Clutching the papers, he hurried from the department. He had to try.

* * *

Dr. Stadler's treatment had worked. Her headache was completely gone, and she had even caught up on the last of her cases. Rebecca dropped the final stack of letters and case files on Paulina's desk and settled in her office chair. She straightened the desk blotter and moved the pens into a tidy row before reaching to turn off her computer. She paused with her finger on the mouse and cocked her head to the side. Why not? No harm in simply checking things out.

Rebecca selected a search engine and typed in Philip's name. She scrolled down the list of entries, looking for anything of note. She clicked on a magazine article about some charity fund-raising gala. Philip would never miss such an event. Sure enough, he was listed as a major donor, and there he was in couple of photos. His wife Sylvia was with him, looking elegant in a chic gown. Rebecca grimaced as she surveyed the picture. Sylvia had posed with her hand draped over Philip's arm—not to be possessive, Rebecca was certain, but to flash the huge diamond on her finger. No wonder she hadn't kicked him out.

Philip wasn't watching Sylvia or the camera in the picture. Rebecca followed his sight line and shook her head. He was looking down the blouse of the pretty blonde standing beside him. Typical. She clicked on the second photo, a close up. Philip was handsome in his Armani tuxedo, and he had a smile that could melt a witch's heart. Or a lawyer's. Rebecca touched the screen with her finger and smiled. Maybe he was worth another try.

She leaned back and chewed on a fingernail. With a sharp nod of her head, she clicked back into the search engine. Her typing was slow and methodical. Andrychuk, Maxwell.

* * *

The door to the station house slammed behind him as Paschek strode to his office. Marsh had risen from the reception desk, but the sheriff silenced him with a glance. First things first. He pulled the Mason jar of M&M's from under his coat and slipped it into the bottom drawer of his desk before returning to the front office. He stood, hands on hips and surveyed the room. The three deputies' desks were unoccupied while Marsh stood by the entrance. The coffee maker gurgled in the background, drowning out the steady hiss of the air conditioner. One of the waiting area chairs held a middle-aged woman. "Okay, Deputy. This better be good."

"It is, sir." Marsh gestured to the woman. "This is Amanda Baker. She phoned and said she had evidence about the Sampson case. I had her bring it down right away."

Paschek frowned. "You should have gone out. We'll talk about that later." He shifted his attention to the woman. "All right then, Mrs. Baker. You said you had evidence. Did you see something? Hear something?"

"I have something. A letter."

"Okay. Go on."

"Jenn came to see me a few months ago. She gave me the letter for safe-keeping and told me not to open it until… well, she said I would know. We've been away, so I just heard about what happened. Such an awful thing. That poor child. I wish I had done something sooner."

"Where's the letter now?"

"I took care of it," Marsh said. "Photographed it and sealed it in an evidence bag." When Paschek frowned again, he continued, "I used gloves. Didn't touch it."

Paschek looked back at the woman. "We have to check everything for prints. Did anyone else handle it?"

"No, just me and Jennifer. As far as I know, anyway."

"Did you read it?"

"Yes. I should have right away, but she was so insistent. I knew something was wrong, but I never guessed." Amanda's eyes were wet with tears. "She was scared, scared for her life. The letter made it clear. Jenn thought she was in danger. That he might kill her."

"Who was she scared of?"

"Her husband, Tyler. She thought he was planning murder."

Paschek's grin was wide and wolf like. *I think he might have done just that.*

* * *

There was no answer at the Sampson home. Derek should have guessed. Why would you want to stay where your wife had just died? When he finally reached Tyler on his cell, the younger man informed him that the police had the house sealed. Still investigating things, they had said, still looking for answers. The Vermettes were putting them up for a few days. Tyler wasn't thrilled with the arrangement, but it was better for Olivia than staying at a hotel. At least it approached normal. As if anything could.

Tyler jumped at the chance to get out of the house. Coffee? Anywhere would be great. A half hour later they settled at a corner table in a downtown snack bar. Derek sipped from his cup. The coffee was surprisingly good, the donut not so much. He set it down on the napkin. "Where's the nearest Dunkin's?"

Tyler shook his head. "Would you believe Seattle?"

"You're kidding, right?"

"Afraid not. This is Stockton. You're lucky to get anything around here." Tyler stared into his cup.

Derek held his breath for a moment before reaching over to squeeze Tyler's shoulder. "It hurts. I know about that."

"How could you?" Tyler pushed the mug away. "How could anyone? Unless you lost your wife, you couldn't possibly understand."

Derek's voice was barely a whisper. "I do understand. I lost them both. My wife and my child." The air had gone out of the room. Would either of them ever breathe again?

Tyler raised his head. "Does it ever stop hurting?"

"No. But it changes. Less like a knife. More like… an ache, an emptiness." He took another sip and grimaced. The coffee was getting cold.

Tyler cleared his throat and spoke softly. "I'm sorry, man. About your family. I didn't know."

"How could you? I never told you. I guess we never talked about anything too deep."

"Looks that way, don't it? If it hadn't been for Bert, we'd have never gotten past first names." He cleared his throat again. "Guess guys are like that."

"Maybe. This was real bad, though. I mean, I didn't even know you were married." Derek slowly broke his stale donut into little pieces. "How long... how long were you...?"

"Married? It'll be six years this December—I mean, it would have been if..." Tyler buried his face in his hands and made a hoarse choking sound. Derek started to reach out again but stopped when the young man looked up. Tyler's eyes were red but dry. And there was something in them. A hint of something hard? Must be the fatigue. What else could it be?

"I saw the report," Derek said. "The autopsy report."

"Yeah?" Tyler turned to stare out the window. "What did it say?"

"Jennifer died from poisoning. Gas line antifreeze."

Tyler's hand jerked, knocking the cup of coffee. The lukewarm liquid sloshed over the edge, splattering across the table. Derek grabbed a handful of napkins from the middle of the table and held them out. Tyler didn't move to take them. "Paschek said something about antifreeze, but that doesn't make any sense."

"Could Jennifer have—I mean, do you think there's any chance she..."

"No. No way. Jenn would not have killed herself." The young man gripped the edge of the table, his face red and his knuckles white. "She wouldn't."

"Okay, I believe you." Derek dabbed at the puddle of coffee. "You're right. It doesn't make sense."

"I shouldn't have bought them."

"Bought what?"

"The antifreeze. I bought them a month ago. Stupid." He chewed on his thumbnail. "I had trouble with the truck last winter. Kept freezing up on me. Thought I'd be smart and stock up early. Dumb, just dumb. Like Jenn always said." He traced a line through the last drops of coffee.

The hands of the clock on the wall shuffled forward as time drained slowly away into oblivion. Without meeting Derek's eyes, Tyler muttered, "I have to go." He tapped the table beside the wreckage of Derek's donut. "You could go north. Get a Tim's."

"A what?"

"A Tim Horton's donut. From Canada. You could go get one." He stood and turned to the door. "That's what I'd do if I could." He seemed to shrink further into himself. "I'd just go."

* * *

There were even more entries this time. Rebecca shouldn't have been surprised. Her father always went for the high-profile cases, those with the double bonus of lots of attention from the media and a hefty paycheck. Rebecca was scanning the list when a recent posting caught her attention, something she had never expected to see: Maxwell Andrychuk's name and the phrase *pro bono* in the same sentence. Had to be a mistake. Maybe it was referring to his opponent. She clicked on the link.

It was him. An immigration case he had taken all the way to the state court of appeals. Rebecca read and reread the details, pausing repeatedly to shake her head. Everything about the case was surprising. Not only had her father taken a case with no chance of payment, but it was one that could prove unpopular with his usual country club set. Homeland security had ordered the deportation of an East Indian woman and her child, and Maxwell Andrychuk, of all people, had fought to keep her in America.

It looked like he'd won. That was at least expected. Rebecca couldn't remember her father ever losing. Then again, maybe he only talked about the cases he'd won—or rather, lectured her about them. Never a real conversation. Still, a lecture was better than the other possibilities. Especially after he'd been drinking. Rebecca bit her lip. Things got much worse after he'd been drinking.

She finished the article. It sounded like a good case, and she had to admit that it looked as though her father had done a good job. He'd proven that it was a case of mistaken identity, with the result that the woman and her child were allowed to stay. At the end of the text was a link to a photo. Rebecca hesitated before clicking on it. Max Andrychuk stood grinning at the camera with his arm around his client's shoulders. She cringed. The woman was young and very pretty. The little girl was gorgeous. A fierce wave of bile rose in Rebecca's throat. The images explained everything.

* * *

Paschek closed his office door and marched back and forth. Amanda Baker was in the outer office waiting for a deputy to finish typing her statement. Marsh and Standingready were rigid statues against the wall of the office, careful to stay out of the sheriff's way. Paschek's smile was vicious as he smacked his fist into an open palm. "We've got him now."

Marsh glanced sideways at his fellow deputy and muttered, "I knew it was Shooter."

Paschek paused to glare at his men. "Like I told you, we have a suspect. He had the means and the opportunity. The letter gives us the motive." Marsh started to grin but sobered quickly when Paschek stopped in front of him. The sheriff grabbed a copy of the letter and ran a finger along the lines. "The handwriting's the same as in Jennifer Sampson's appointment book. Neat and precise. An expert will check it later, but I'm sure she wrote this." He narrowed his eyes and handed the copy to Marsh. "Read it again. Out loud."

The deputy cleared his throat. "I'm Jennifer Sampson, and I live in Stockton, Montana. If you're reading this, then something has happened. Maybe I'm dead. If I am, I know who did it. My marriage is over. I don't love Tyler anymore, and I want out, but he won't let me. If I try to leave, he'll kill me. He's an alcoholic with a terrible temper. I am afraid of him." The paper crinkled in Marsh's hands as he moved it up. "He thinks he's smart, that no one will know it was him. But I'm not stupid. I know a lot more about computers than he does, and I found what he's been looking at. I thought he was talking to girls or looking at porn, but I found out the truth. He's researching how to kill someone, how to use poison. I know he's planning something. I can't tell anyone.

No one will believe me. But if something happens, they'll know. Take this letter to the police. Please, do it for me. Jennifer."

"Keep an eye on Tyler Sampson." Paschek's voice was soft, his eyes hard. "Don't pick him up, but don't let him out of your sight. Marsh, send a man up to the motel to check on his alibi." He glanced at his watch. "Melansen should be on his way back to Helena right about now. I'll call him first thing in the morning, and then we'll get things moving." His voice dropped to a whisper as he stared out the window. "I've got you, Shooter. This time I've really got you."

SIXTEEN

Some things she tried to remember. Others, to forget.

But one thing she knew for certain. The one command she must always obey.

Never tell anyone.

SEVENTEEN

"The course of true love never did run smooth."
A Midsummer Night's Dream, Act I, Scene I

The sun was halfway to its zenith by the time Rebecca stirred from her bedroom. She frowned at the coffee machine when it gurgled at her cheerfully. *Just make the coffee and shut up.* After filling her mug, she trudged to the window. A small bird, hanging upside-down from a branch while it pecked away at a pinecone, peered at her from the spruce tree in the yard. The nuthatch seemed to stare in amused wonderment, its small striped head tipping from side to side while its black eyes flashed.

"Oh, you think you're funny, do you?" Rebecca tossed her auburn hair back over one shoulder and snorted at the bird. "Wait until winter, and then we'll see how happy you are." The nuthatch righted itself and chirped before flitting to the feeder hanging from a branch and tapping its beak against the empty container. "Go next door. Judge Farr always has stuff out." The bird tapped the container again. "Okay, okay. I'll put out some birdseed later. You're no different than anyone else, you know." Rebecca smiled in spite of herself and sipped her coffee. "Everybody wants something."

She shuffled to the kitchen table and sank onto a chair. The problem with Saturdays was there wasn't enough to do. The morning plodded on, inching toward the noon hour. The clock was a tyrant, scolding her to get busy and do something. No more lazy conversations with songbirds. It was time to get moving. Rebecca sighed and rested her head on one hand. *I don't want to. What's the point?*

The memory of Philip's phone call jabbed at her like a splinter. Every thought was disrupted by its presence. She needed to make a decision. But why? To be fair to Philip? Hah, that had nothing to do with it. Why had he called? Why couldn't he stay out of her life? But he had called. Somebody wanted her. On some level, that felt good. He didn't love her, she knew that. He probably wasn't capable of love. But he could be kind and considerate. He was always fun to be with. Didn't she deserve a little fun? She gulped down more of the coffee. The first mouthful was rich and full, but the aftertaste was bitter.

Rebecca stared into the mug as other memories assaulted her. The stifled sobs coming from her mother's bedroom when her father was once again working late. The look in her mother's eyes on that final morning. That last betrayal had killed something in her. It was only time until death consumed her fully. Rebecca would never forgive her father for that. He had killed her mother as surely as if he had forced that bottle of sleeping pills down her throat. Rebecca had lost both parents that day. She had lost her whole world.

The last harsh dregs of coffee settled into the pit of her stomach. Bitterness stirred within her. Hadn't she turned out exactly like him? Wasn't she the "other woman"? Did she even care? There had to be something else, something that gave life meaning, purpose even. She suddenly thought about Mrs. Sifton. The strange little woman had lost everything, yet somehow seemed happy, joyful even. She'd actually prayed for Rebecca. She really seemed to believe in something—something bigger than herself.

Rebecca lifted the silver coffee pot, and peered at her reflection. Her hair was disheveled and the lack of makeup made her look tired, old even. She had always liked her freckles, but now their joyful spray could not offset the sadness in her eyes. She needed more, more to believe in, to strive for. Like what Mrs. Sifton had. Rebecca shook her head and poured herself another cup of coffee. Whatever it was, she didn't have it.

* * *

He could have slept in. Derek wasn't scheduled to be in the ER that day, and no one would care if he spent it resting. But he couldn't do it. He lay and watched as the ceiling slipped from the first claret blush of dawn to the fierce glow of morning. He used to love mornings, waking up next to Cassie, hearing Sarah starting to move around in her bedroom. Now, he woke up alone.

He groaned and buried his head in the pillow. Some mornings Cassie had woken first. When she did, she would lean over and kiss his ear until he couldn't fight it anymore and had to open his eyes. He closed them now and pictured her in his mind—long blonde hair, eyes a miraculous blue. And her lips…

Derek jerked upward, his eyes wide, his mouth gaping. The vision had blurred and then cleared. Hair now red, eyes a playful green, yet somehow poised and professional. He rubbed his eyes and shook his head. Where had that come from?

* * *

The kitchen clock assaulted her senses as it chimed the hour. Rebecca jerked her head up and looked around in bewilderment. It was after three. How? She rubbed her eyes and opened her day planner. Was she supposed to be doing something? The page was empty. Nothing. No appointments, no plans. It was too late to drive to Billings. She could go into Great Falls. Whoopee. The only good thing about that place was that it wasn't Stockton.

The decent stores here were all closed for the day. Everyone would be busy with their families or at a ball tournament or something. Maybe she could work? Rebecca rifled through the small stack of papers on the table—not enough to fill the rest of the day, only an hour or two.

Moving to the living room, she ran a finger along the row of Blu-rays. *Boring. Didn't like it. Seen it five times.*

Rebecca stood in the center of the room, hearing nothing but the sound of her breathing. She stared at the telephone. Her address book beckoned her, but she didn't really need it. She still knew Philip's cell number by heart. At least it would get her away from this town, if only for a weekend. Maybe it was worth it.

* * *

His apartment was too small. The couch, bookshelves, and table meant that three or four strides were all Derek could manage before having to turn around. You couldn't pace in such a small space. Derek always paced when he was upset, trying to figure something out, or feeling guilty. Only Cassie could make him stop. He shook the memory out of his head and looked around. The apartment was a dump. The furniture was old and worn, the fixtures dated. He really should find himself a new place. Maybe a house. No, too permanent. Permanence implied that things had settled, healed even. They hadn't.

A heavy cloak of guilt draped itself over his shoulders. It dragged him down and sheltered him at the same time. Things were bad enough already, and now he had allowed thoughts of another woman to creep in. Another setback. Once more he had failed to live up to God's expectations. Which made sense. He failed because he was a failure. *Give up. Leave.* But then what? He'd done that already. That's what moving to Stockton had been about—leaving the pain and the memories in Ohio and going far away, starting over. Unfortunately, the memories had come with him. They never left.

He stared out the window of his apartment, eyes focused on some distant point well beyond the horizon. A new thought came like a light breaking through a dense blanket of cloud: *What would Cassie do?* Derek sighed. That was the problem. He knew what Cassie would do. Search for God's direction and then obey it. For him, it was different. Knowing what to do was hard, but obeying was harder. The Bible lying on the couch caught his eye, and once again he felt a gentle nudging. *Let it go.*

Let go of the pain. Forgive. He grabbed his sneakers and bolted for the door.

It was too hot to run, but Derek went anyway. Physical pain was easier to manage. Helped to block the voices in his head, push aside the torment. This time it didn't help. The third time around the block, his gait slowed. He tried to concentrate on his breathing as he passed beneath a large mountain ash, but a raucous squabble captured his attention. A mountain jay was arguing with a squirrel over the tree's bright red berries. The squirrel scolded the jay fiercely as it hopped from branch to branch. The jay flapped its wings defiantly, but at last relented and flew to the uppermost branches. There were enough berries for both.

Derek walked on, his thoughts returning again to Cassie. He knew what she would say at this moment. *See? God takes care of the animals. Even the jays and the squirrels are in His hands. He provides for them.* Derek closed his eyes. He could imagine her cupping his face in her hands, almost feel her skin against his. *And you're much more valuable to God than they are. God will care for you too.*

He grimaced and shook his head. If that was true, He had a funny way of showing it. The squirrel chattered again, continuing to berate the jay. It stood on its branch, looking up at the bird, so indignant Derek could almost picture it shaking its tiny fist at the sky. He wanted to do the same. He wanted to scream and shout and curse at God. But even that felt futile.

The chirping of his cell phone broke into his thoughts—a merciful interruption. He glanced at the screen. Bert. He tried to keep his voice steady and even. It didn't work.

"Hello."

Bert's request was simple. With his regular driver ill, and his Huntington's in full flare-up, he needed a ride to the Saturday-evening church service. Maybe they could invite Tyler along. "He's staying at the Vermettes' while the police continue their investigation at his home. He could probably use an outing."

Derek swiped at a bead of sweat sliding down his temple. "I usually attend the Sunday-morning service, but I could go tonight if you prefer."

Bert laughed. "Actually, I'll need a ride tomorrow morning as well."

Why not? "All right, Bert. Whatever you need."

"Thanks, man." Bert disconnected the call.

Derek glanced back up at the mountain ash. The jay and the squirrel had stopped bickering and were both watching him. Derek shook his head. That was weird.

The phone was ringing when he stepped into his apartment. It was the hospital.

"Sorry to bother you, Dr. Kessler. I know you're not on duty, but we have a… well, we have a situation."

"What kind of a situation?"

"Mr. McKenny is here. He's raising a big stink about his daughter and says he won't leave until he talks to you."

"McKenny?" Derek pinched the bridge of his nose. *You have got to be kidding me.* "Okay. I'll be there in half an hour. Have him wait."

"Thank you so much, Doctor. I'll tell him."

Derek disconnected the call. What on earth did McKenny want with him? Whatever it was, it couldn't be good.

* * *

His hair was still wet from the quick shower when Derek strode into the ER. The duty nurse at the desk leapt up before he was fully through the door.

"Thank goodness you're here," she said. "That man has been out here every two minutes looking for you. I was getting ready to call the police."

"Where is he now?"

She jabbed her finger toward the department's quiet room and sank back onto her chair, closing her eyes, clearly relieved that McKenny was someone else's problem now.

Derek paused at the doorway and peered into the room. McKenny sat with his arms folded across his chest, glaring at a blank wall. Derek took a deep breath and forced his fists to unclench. Fight or flight reaction. He glanced over his shoulder. The duty nurse and the rest of the ER staff were watching him. No chance for the flight option.

He stepped into the room.

EIGHTEEN

"Canst thou not minister to a mind diseas'd, pluck from the memory a rooted sorrow, raze out the written troubles of the brain and with some sweet oblivious antidote cleanse the stuff'd bosom of that perilous stuff which weighs upon the heart?"
Macbeth, Act V, Scene III

Rebecca bit her bottom lip. Her hand hovered over the phone, frozen in place. Life was supposed to be fun, wasn't it? *You're born, you live, and you die. That's all and nothing more. Might as well pack in as much fun as you can on the way. Oh yeah, are you having fun yet?*

"No, I'm not." She glanced around the empty room. *Great, now I'm talking to myself.* She pulled her hand away from the phone and dropped onto the couch. Rebecca wrapped her arms around herself and shivered. *Is this all there is?* Her chin plummeted to her chest as tears surged over her cheeks.

A sharp rapping sound pulled her head up. The nuthatch was back, reminding her of the pledge to put out more feed. Another broken promise. The bird sat on the windowsill and watched her intently. It tapped the window again. "Okay, okay. I give up. I'll get you your birdseed." The little bird flitted to the top of the spruce tree and watched as Rebecca trudged out to the deck. She stood on her tiptoes to reach the bird feeder and managed to spill half the bag of birdseed onto the ground. The nuthatch chirped and flapped its wings to scold her. Rebecca shook her finger at the creature. "I meant to do that. It gives the rest of the birds a chance to get some. Now, eat your lunch."

She stood in the condo and watched as the nuthatch picked through the birdseed for the choicest bits. After a few minutes, it flew back to the windowsill and looked up at Rebecca. The bird cocked its head from side to side, its eyes fixed on hers. Then, in a sudden flurry, it was gone.

"You're welcome." Rebecca reached up and touched her cheek. Her tears had dried.

* * *

"Mr. McKenny?" Derek took a single step into the room. "You wanted to speak with me?"

The old man grunted and rose to his feet. "You're here. About time."

Derek's eyes narrowed for a brief moment before he marched into the room. Taking a chair, he motioned for McKenny to be seated. When the man remained standing, Derek said, "What can I do for you, Mr. McKenny?"

The old man hesitated and then wilted back onto the chair, dropping his face into his hands. When he looked up, his eyes were red. "They won't let me have her."

"Excuse me?"

"The hospital. You let her die. Then they took her and cut her up. Now, they won't let me have her body." McKenny's lip trembled. "I… we… her mother and I need to… we need to bury her, to finish this."

"They haven't released Jennifer's body to the mortuary yet?"

"No."

"Won't they be releasing her to Tyler?"

"He knows. He agreed to let us do this. He owes us a lot more than that. Will you help or not?"

Derek stared into McKenny's face. Their eyes locked for a full moment before McKenny tore his gaze away. Derek nodded. "Give me five minutes, and I'll see what I can do."

It took more than five minutes. The weekend charge nurse didn't know what the holdup was, and the chief lab tech could only tell him that the post-mortem report was complete except for the specimens sent out to the university. Dr. Chiu had finished everything else that morning and was at a trout stream somewhere. Derek had to keep searching for direction, and he was getting frustrated. The problem was it was difficult to find many administration types in a hospital late afternoon on a brilliant summer Saturday. *Not happening.*

He finally reached someone on the phone. Derek wasn`t sure what the man actually did, but he sure had a nice title: Senior Vice President and Chief Administrative Officer of the Prairie View Health District. At least he knew what was causing all the difficulty.

"I don't know why someone else couldn't handle this."

Derek flinched. Whining was never pleasant. When it was used by someone who sounded as if his already nasal voice had been distorted by sucking on sour pickles, it was awful. "No one on duty knows what to do. Dr. Chiu has signed off on the autopsy, and the funeral home has been notified. I don't understand why the body has not been released."

"Dr. Chiu? He's the medical examiner?"

"Yes, he's our visiting pathologist. Isn't his signature enough?"

"Not when it's a forensic post-mortem. The coroner is the only one who can release the body."

"Okay, I'll call the coroner. Who would that be?"

"Well, the coroner is an elected position, and it doesn't pay much." The administrator wasn't whining anymore. His voice was still irritating. "Last county election, only one person ran. He was elected without opposition."

"Who was it?"

"Sheriff Paschek."

Derek pushed the heel of his hand against his forehead. "You have got to be kidding me."

This day kept getting better and better. Derek glanced at his watch. He was supposed to pick up Bert and Tyler for church in three quarters of an hour. Maybe he could slip out the staff entrance. Having to deal with Old Man McKenny was bad enough, having another conversation with Sheriff Paschek was simply too much. Derek peered around the door into the quiet room. McKenny continued to sit staring at the wall. He looked smaller than Derek remembered. The physician shook his head and reached for the phone. How bad could it be?

* * *

The game was going into extra innings. Paschek refilled his bowl of chips and grabbed another cold one from the fridge before throwing himself back in his easy chair. He wasn't really a Mariners or a Rockies fan like most of the county, but inter-league games were always interesting. Todd Helton fouled off three straight pitches to keep the count full, and the Seattle manager responded by making the call for a pitching change. Paschek leaned forward in his chair. "This could be it."

Helton had just stepped into the batter's box when the phone rang. Paschek cursed and pushed the pause button on his digital video recorder before snatching the device off the table beside him. "What?" he snarled.

"Sheriff Paschek?"

"Yeah, what is it?"

"I'm sorry to bother you, Sheriff. This is Dr. Kessler."

"Okay, Doctor. Get to the point, will you?"

"I'm at the hospital, and we have a bit of a problem."

Paschek grunted. "By 'we', I take it you mean 'you.' I don't have any problems there."

"Sorry. You're right, it is my problem, but you're the only one who can solve it."

Waving his hand in a circle, Paschek pushed off his chair and stood. "Speed it up, will you? The ball game is waiting."

"Mr. McKenny is here at the hospital. He wants to take his daughter's body to the funeral home for burial, but it hasn't been released yet."

"So?"

"As the county coroner, you're the only one who can sign the release form."

"Let me get this straight. You're calling me to help out Old Man McKenny? From what I hear, you two didn't exactly hit it off earlier. Didn't he try to punch you?"

"Well…"

"And now he's going around telling anyone who will listen that you let his daughter die. Course, no one actually listens to McKenny. The guy's a nutcase. Still, makes no sense, you wanting to help him."

"I feel that I should."

"Why? You a masochist? Or just stupid?"

"I'm asking you to sign the release form for the body. That's all."

"Don't raise your voice to me, Doctor. You want to get along in my town, you'd better get along with me." The phone line crackled with static. Paschek dropped back into his chair and shook his head. "Fax me the form. Hospital's got my number. I'll fax it back."

"Thank you, Sheriff, I really—"

Paschek snapped his phone shut and punched at the remote control to restart the game. After all that, Helton proceeded to strike out.

* * *

The rear hatch of the hearse opened with a hiss. Derek handed the signed release forms to the mortuary attendant. The young man glanced over the papers, initialed a couple places, and then scrawled a signature across the bottom. He tore out one of the copies and returned the top page to Derek before turning to his partner. "Load it up."

Derek put a hand on the attendant's shoulder and jerked his head toward the rear door of the hospital. "Try to watch how you speak, okay? That's the dead woman's father."

The driver peered around Derek and grimaced. "Old Man McKenny? Oh yeah, I heard about this one. No worries. I don't want that guy on my case." He raised his voice as he gestured to the attendant. "Bring the deceased, please. We need to transport her to the funeral home."

McKenny shuffled closer, his face grim and his jaw clenched tight. He stood in silence, watching every move the men from the funeral home made as they slid the shrouded remains into the hearse. McKenny nodded sharply and looked away as they pulled the hatch closed.

Derek watched the old man. When he had first met him, he'd seemed tall and erect, his shoulders square and stiff; now he seemed to have shrunk somehow. There was an air about him that Derek couldn't quite identify. Remorse? Regret? The physician took a step toward him.

McKenny whirled and glared at him. "Don't think this lets you off the hook. Just because you did the right thing now and got them to release Jennifer doesn't excuse what you did earlier. You still let her die. You still failed her." He spun away and marched to his car.

As McKenny followed the hearse away from the hospital, Derek stood with his hands dropped to his sides. The sense of something wrong was clearer now. Beneath the anger and bitterness was something deeper, something Derek recognized: guilt.

He shook his head and glanced at his watch. He had another commitment to keep, and if he didn't hurry, he would be late picking up Bert for church.

* * *

Derek, Bert, and Tyler arrived at the church on time and hid out in the back row. Their talk was light and superficial, all about sports and the weather while the possibility of friendship developed. Bert kept trying to steer things deeper, but the younger men had resisted. After several weeks, however, their resistance was crumbling.

"In the fallen world we live in," the pastor was saying, "pain is inevitable. Christ Himself was described as 'a man of sorrows, acquainted with grief.' There is no promise that the joy of the Lord will replace the suffering and pain of this world, only that it will support us *through* the pain and disappointment."

Derek glanced over at Bert. It was amazing. Each week Bert would stumble to the last bench in the church, barely able to stand or walk. But as soon as the pastor started to preach, his tremors and shakes would stop. Somehow, each week he was given a brief remission of his Huntington's. Derek couldn't explain it. One more thing he didn't understand.

"To summarize," the pastor continued, "first we need to let the emotions hit us fully. Acknowledge the pain and take the time to reflect on it. Secondly, we must bring that pain to God and express it fully to Him. Lastly, subordinate the emotions and the pain to the purposes of God." He paused and gazed out over the congregation. "If we fully grasp the truth that our deepest needs—to be loved, to be secure, and to be significant—are totally and completely met in Christ, we can offer up our pain and allow God to use it to minister to others. We can fulfill our deepest calling. We can glorify Christ."

Before the choir could return to the platform for the closing number, Tyler was on his feet, heading for the door. Derek started to follow but hesitated.

Bert's hand fell on his shoulder. "It's all right," the older man said. "I can get a ride with someone. Go with him."

Derek hurried after Tyler, glancing over his shoulder as he did. Bert's head jerked to the side while his hand spasmed into the air. The Huntington's was back.

* * *

At the snack bar, Derek and Tyler found a corner table and sat. Tyler was silent. He cradled the steaming mug of coffee, fixated on the dark liquid. Derek sipped his own cup and waited. He shifted his weight from side to side and rubbed his hands. Tyler was still quiet. Derek chewed on his bottom lip and finally broke the silence.

"How's Olivia doing?"

"She's okay. She likes Isabel and Anton. Good people. They're letting us crash in their basement until the cops let us go home. Crime scene, they say." He seemed to run out of energy then, and returned his gaze to his coffee. "Was that planned? The sermon?" Tyler said at last. "Did he know about Jennifer?"

"Pastor Josh may have heard about it. I mean, it is a pretty small town, but I think he had already prepared his sermon. Most of the time, preachers prepare what they're going to say a few days ahead of time."

"I guess. I don't know if I could do it—what he said about pain, I mean."

"Yeah, I understand."

Tyler nodded. "You mentioned your family. How... how did it happen?"

Derek slumped against the back of the chair, a heavy weight descending onto his chest. When he spoke, his voice was low and hoarse. "Her name was Cassie. We were married shortly before I started my residency. We had a little girl. Her name was Sarah." He turned and looked out the window. "She would have been six now." The glare from the sun made his eyes water. "They were both killed. Car accident. Two years ago." He shifted his attention to Tyler. "It feels like yesterday."

"Oh man, I'm so sorry. I didn't know."

"How could you? I never talk about it. It still hurts."

"Yeah, it does."

Both men were quiet. Derek sipped his coffee without tasting it. Tyler fixed his eyes on Derek's face. "Did you love her?"

"Yes, I did. More than anything."

"I felt like that about Jenn once."

"Once?"

"Yeah, at the start. It seemed great. We had so much fun together—at first. Things started to change after Livy was born."

"How come?"

"I dunno. Jenn liked to keep everything neat and perfect around the house. Babies aren't very neat. Livy is a really good kid, but even the best kid makes messes. Jenn hated that." Tyler drained the last of his coffee. He contemplated the dregs for a moment before continuing. "We started to drift apart. Jenn made it clear that she didn't want any more kids. We... we hadn't slept together in a couple of years. I don't think she loved me anymore. Maybe she never did."

"I'm sorry, Tyler."

"I treated her good. I really did. Never hit her or anything. Felt like it once or twice. Maybe even threatened to. But I wouldn't. Really. Even when she threw divorce in my face. Me busting my butt on the rigs to keep her in style, and then she says that. I... I might have said something. I didn't mean it, but I did say the only way our marriage was ending was if one of us was dead. I meant as in 'till death do us part', but I guess I can see how she might have taken it another way." He looked out the window, eyes fixed on the distant horizon.

"I was always a partier. They called me Shooter. I could throw it back with the best of them. When me and Jennifer started coming apart, I began drinking heavier. Then I got a couple DUI's—"

Derek's head snapped up. His skin went cold, his eyes wide. A memory tinged in red flashed across his mind. He lurched to his feet, knocking over his chair.

Tyler blinked. "You okay, man?"

"I have to go. I have to go now." Derek stumbled to the door and away from the open-mouthed look on Tyler's face. He barely heard the young man's last words.

"Derek? What did I do?"

NINETEEN

"This above all: to thine ownself be true, and it must follow,
as the night the day, thou canst not then be false to any man."
Hamlet, Act I, Scene III

Derek had recognized what McKenny was feeling because he was all too familiar with it himself. Guilt. And now he had piled on more by the way he had treated Tyler. Derek sat in his darkened apartment and cradled his head in his hands. When would he ever learn? When would he start listening? He pulled out his cell phone and stared at the screen. His mouth went dry, and his throat tightened. His thoughts tumbled through his mind in random waves of fear and doubt. *Let it be. You're a good guy. Everyone makes mistakes. Cut yourself some slack.*

Derek clamped his eyes shut and clenched his fists. No, no more coward's way out. He needed to deal with this. He punched out a text message to Tyler.

Sorry about that. My bad. See U in the morning & explain? U going 2 church?

No. 2 tired.

See U after? Pick U up 4 lunch?

All right. C U then.

Derek closed his eyes and stretched out on the sofa. Maybe he could do at least one thing right.

* * *

The only thing worse than a Saturday in a small town was a Sunday. Rebecca punched her pillow and buried her head under the blankets. No use. That stupid clock was too noisy. She lifted her head and scrunched her eyebrows together. That was no clock. She groaned and closed her eyes. It had to be the bird again.

Rebecca followed the tapping to her front window. There he was, pecking away at the glass. She shook her finger at him. "There's no feeder out there. If you want food, it's at the back." The nuthatch disappeared in a flash of gray and cinnamon feathers. A black SUV parked across the street caught Rebecca's eye. "That's new to the neighborhood. Wonder whose it is?"

She made her way to the back of the condo and peered through the rear window. No sign of the nuthatch at the bird feeder yet. "Get going or you'll miss breakfast." She noted the time on the oven clock. "Better make that lunch. Actually, might be a good idea for me, too." Hurrying back to her bedroom, Rebecca glanced into the mirror hanging in the hallway. "And as for you, stop talking to yourself."

* * *

Pastor Bucknell's message was worth hearing a second time. Derek considered inviting Bert along for lunch, but the Huntington's seemed worse than usual. When that happened, Bert typically went straight to bed to rest. Derek dropped him off at his house and pulled onto the highway out of town, following the instructions from the GPS on his phone. A few miles later, a large black sign proclaimed that he had reached his destination. Derek grinned at the cast-iron cowboy throwing his rope over the head of steer frozen in midstride. *Welcome to the country.* He turned into the lane and came to a sudden stop. The way was blocked by two police cars.

* * *

Rebecca finished buttoning her blouse and followed the inviting aroma of fresh coffee into the kitchen. Her hair was still damp from the shower, but she could style it later. Right now she wanted food and caffeine, not necessarily in that order. The doorbell rang as she finished pouring herself a mug.

Deputy Marsh stood on her front step and smiled broadly when she opened the door. He touched the brim of his hat and nodded. "Good afternoon, Ms. Andrychuk. I was hoping to catch you at home."

Rebecca blinked. "I wasn't expecting another visit from the police." She looked at him and hid a grimace. His shirt was open at the collar more than regulation allowed and was stretched tight across his chest. The deputy had rolled his short sleeves up to expose his biceps and flexed his muscles while lifting the cap from his head. *He's posing for me.*

"I have a few more questions, Rebecca. May I call you Rebecca?"

"I prefer Ms. Andrychuk. Is this an official visit? Where's your police car?"

"That's my SUV across the street." He stepped closer. "I guess you could say this is more of a social call. Can I come in?"

"I don't think that's a good idea." She placed a hand on Marsh's chest and tried to push him away. Her effort was futile.

"Come on, Becky. Is that coffee I smell? Why don't you be polite and offer me a cup?"

"No. I think you should leave."

"Aw, come on. It's just a cup of coffee." Marsh pressed forward.

"Please, just go." She pushed harder.

Marsh grabbed her wrist. His smile twisted into a leer. "I like what you've done with your hair. It's quite sexy."

"Afternoon, Rebecca." A man's voice broke in from the front walk. "Is there a problem?"

Rebecca peered around the deputy and smiled. "Oh, hi, Judge. No, no problem. Deputy, you know Judge Farr, don't you? He's my neighbor. Judge, this is Deputy Marsh. He was just leaving. Weren't you, Deputy?"

Marsh shuffled backward and slapped his cap on his head. "Yeah, I guess I was."

"I see," the Judge said. "I'm glad you are taking you duties as an officer of the law so... seriously. I'll be sure to mention it to Sherriff Paschek."

"No need for that, sir. I'll be on my way." Marsh scuttled across the street and tore off in his vehicle.

The judge stepped around the shrubbery separating their doorways and took Rebecca's arm. "Really, my dear, are you all right?"

"I am now, Judge." She gave him a peck on the cheek. "Thanks for being my knight in shining armor."

"Do you want to do anything about this? A word in the right ear, and I could have that deputy patrolling the Marias Pass in Glacier—up to and including January."

"No, it's okay. I can handle it." She hugged him. "Don't worry. I'm a big girl. Look, I was about to make lunch. Why don't you join me?"

"Best offer I've had all day."

"Wonderful," Rebecca held the door open for him so he could go inside. "Tell me, what do you know about birds? Nuthatches in particular."

* * *

Derek pulled up to the police cars as two deputies exited the house, each holding on to one of Tyler's arms. Paschek and an older officer followed them out. Derek hurried from the car.

"Tyler," he called, "what's happening? What's going on?" Tyler could only shake his head as the two deputies brushed past.

"Dr. Kessler," Sergeant Paschek said, stabbing Derek's chest with his index finger, "what are you doing here?"

Derek took a step backwards. "I... I came to talk to Tyler. What's happening?"

"Mr. Sampson will be unavailable for a while, maybe a long while."

"What do you mean?"

"You'll find out soon enough."

The older officer held out his hand. "Sheriff Paschek, would you be so kind as to introduce me?"

Paschek rocked back on his heels and jerked a thumb at Derek. "This is Doc Kessler, the one I mentioned earlier. Kessler, this is Detective Melansen from the Montana Department of Criminal Investigations. He's in charge now, and together we're going to see that Shooter Sampson gets what he deserves."

"Thank you, Sheriff." The detective shook Derek's hand. "Good to meet you, Doctor. I will want to speak to you later, but that can wait. Right now, we're taking Mr. Sampson in for questioning."

Derek watched as Tyler was placed in the rear of one of the patrol cars. "Will he be all right?" He looked back at the detective. "He's a friend of mine."

Paschek pushed past Derek. "You've got poor taste in friends, Doc. I hope your medical skills are better than your people ones." He glanced at Melansen before stomping to the second police vehicle. "I'll be waiting in the car."

Melansen lifted his shoulders. "I'm not sure what you did to tick him off so much, but I'd suggest you stay out of Eugene's way for a while."

"What about Tyler? What's going to happen?"

"If you want to help him, Doctor, I have one suggestion. Get him a lawyer."

TWENTY

"If you prick us, do we not bleed? if you tickle us, do we not
laugh? if you poison us, do we not die?
And if you wrong us, shall we not revenge?"
The Merchant of Venice, Act III, Scene I

A *lawyer?*
Derek stood frozen as the two police cars drove out of the yard.
Should he get involved? If they were only taking Tyler for questioning,
it would be easier to stay out of it. And, considering Paschek's attitude,
maybe safer as well. He glanced over his shoulder at the house. Tyler's
little girl Livy stood on the porch with Isabel. Her eyes met Derek's, and
he squirmed under her gaze. He had let her mother die. Couldn't he at
least help her father?

Derek sighed. He knew only one lawyer in all of Stockton, and he'd
only recently met her. He didn't know if she took criminal cases, or if
she would be willing to help. Derek studied Olivia Sampson. It felt as
if Sarah and Cassie were watching him over her shoulder. He nodded
toward the little girl. He would try.

* * *

Judge Farr didn't stay long. He had things to do, a life to live, but at least he cared. At least someone did. After he'd gone, Rebecca stood in the middle of the room, hugging herself as a quiet emptiness settled over the condominium. Not even a bird broke the brittle sense of cold that fell like a shroud over the room. The telephone caught her eye. She still had not made a decision about Philip. He could never fill the gap in her soul, but maybe, just maybe, he could cover it up for a while. Was it worth it? Wouldn't it hurt just as much afterwards? She blew out a breath. Grabbing a Blu-ray at random, she threw it into the machine and slumped onto the sofa as it whirred to life.

She couldn't concentrate. Finally, she gave up and turned off the TV. Her thoughts raced as she sagged against the cushions. Philip and her father. Her father and Philip. They both wanted back into her life. She didn't want the one and was unsure about the other. In the silence of the condo, she spread her hands in an imploring gesture.

"Your honor, I plead the court's indulgence and ask for a recess until I can get some common sense." The rattling ring of the telephone made her jump, and she lowered her arms and reached for the device. "Hello?"

"Is this Miss Andrychuk?" a man's voice asked.

"Yes. Who is this?" She shifted to get more comfortable against the arm of the couch.

"I'm sorry to bother you. This is Derek Kessler, the new emergency room doctor."

Oh. Her eyes widened. *Oh, my.* "Can I help you with something?"

"I got your phone number from Chandra Naidu," Derek continued. "I'm calling because I need help with a legal matter. A friend of mine was picked up by the police an hour ago. I'm afraid he might be in a lot of trouble."

Rebecca rubbed the side of her hand across her forehead. "Who are we talking about?"

"Tyler Sampson."

"Sampson? As in Jennifer Sampson? The girl who was killed?"

"Yeah, Tyler is her husband. The police think he did it."

"Did he?"

"I… I really don't think so." He was silent for an instant. "Look, Miss Andrychuk, he needs help. You're the only lawyer I know in town. I was hoping you could do something for him. Please."

Rebecca chewed her bottom lip. She hadn't handled any criminal cases for a couple of years, and most of those had been legal-aid types she had taken to spite her father. Still, she had enjoyed the courtroom battles. She was even good at them.

"Miss Andrychuk?"

"I'll see what I can do, but no promises. Where is he now? The sheriff's station?"

"Yes, I think so."

"Okay, I'll head over and see what's going on."

"Thank you, Miss Andrychuk. I appreciate it."

"One more thing."

"Yeah?"

"The name's Rebecca."

"Okay, Rebecca, as long as you call me Derek."

"All right then. Derek."

* * *

The interrogation room was sparsely furnished. A heavy table in the center of the floor was flanked by a pair of chairs. Tyler Sampson slumped in one of them. Paschek stood leaning against the wall, watching the time click away on the industrial-style wall clock. Tyler kept his head down. He didn't look up when Detective Melansen entered the room. The senior officer took the other chair and settled onto it. He adjusted the microphone on the table and placed a Styrofoam cup in front of Tyler.

"Just water," he said. "I'd offer you some of the sheriff's coffee, but I'm afraid you might complain about police brutality."

Tyler's face remained grim. "No, thanks. I don't need nothing."

Melansen sipped from his own cup and then carefully set it down. He propped his elbows on the table and steepled his fingers. "Okay, Mr. Sampson, we have a few questions for you. You understand that you have not yet been charged with a crime?" He waited till Tyler nodded before continuing. "You have the right to remain silent. Anything you say can be used against you in court. You have the right to speak to a lawyer and have one present. If you cannot afford a lawyer, one can be provided for you. Understand?"

"Yeah, I understand."

"Do you want a lawyer?"

"Do I need one?" Tyler looked up, his eyes red and weary.

"That's not for me to say." Melansen sighed. "Look, Tyler, it's up to you. You can answer our questions or not. You can have a lawyer present or not."

"Don't make no difference. Ask away."

Melansen took another sip from his cup and settled back in the chair. He nodded to Paschek. The sheriff's smile was hard and tight as he stepped forward. He had known the detective for a long time, and they had worked together before. That fact meant Melansen would keep him involved in the case. Paschek wasn't about to pass up the opportunity. He crossed his arms and towered over the young man. "This is official this time, Shooter, so I'm going to start with the same questions from the hospital, for the record. You understand? Good." Paschek ran through his questions, watching Tyler as he answered. After several minutes, the sheriff eased himself down on the edge of the desk. "Okay, Shooter, we know you and Jennifer were having problems. Want to tell us about that?"

"Yeah, we were having trouble. Jenn didn't seem happy anymore. I don't know why."

"Was it your drinking?"

"No, I told you I quit. If anything, things got worse between us when I sobered up, but we were going to work things out."

"Oh, were you getting counseling or something?"

"Jenn was. Some guy in Helena. She didn't want me to go. Just pay the bills."

Paschek cocked his head. "You resent that?"

Tyler shrugged. "I was used to it. I learned real early that Jenn liked nice things, and that when she wanted something, she wanted it right away. And she usually got it."

"So what was the problem? One of you having an affair?"

"Ha, no chance. I wasn't and, well, Jenn didn't really like anything… physical."

Melansen set his tea down. His voice was soft when he spoke. "So you'd grown apart."

Tyler studied the detective. "Things were good at first, great even, but I think Jenn started to believe her father."

Melansen raised one eyebrow.

"Samuel McKenny," Paschek said. "Religious fanatic—runs his own church and thinks everyone else is going to hell. He doesn't like you much, eh, Shooter?"

"No, not much."

"Why is that, Tyler?" Melansen asked.

"He never approved of me. I think Jenn started dating me just to defy him. Part of the reason she married me was to get away from him."

Paschek moved to stand behind Tyler and bent forward to hiss in his ear. "He thinks you killed her." When the young man didn't react, he added, "And he's not the only one." He picked up the file folder from the table and withdrew a piece of paper that he set in front of Tyler. It was a copy of the letter Amanda Baker had brought to the station. "Read it."

Tyler recoiled from the page as if it were something deadly. After a moment, he lifted the letter from the table. As he read it, the color washed from his face, and his hand shook. "Where did you get this?" His voice cracked.

"Maybe you should start telling us the truth," Melansen said. A knock sounded on the door. Melansen jerked his head at Paschek and the sheriff walked over and opened the door. It was Deputy Standingready.

"What do you want?" Paschek snapped.

"I'm sorry, sir, but there's a woman here who says she is Tyler Sampson's lawyer. She insists on being present at the interrogation."

"Who the blazes is it?"

"She said her name's Rebecca Andrychuk." Standingready was forced to step aside as Rebecca pushed her way past him.

"You know who I am, Sheriff." She smiled and strode into the room. "I have been retained to represent Mr. Sampson."

Paschek tried to block her way. "You can't do that. The victim was your client. She listed an appointment with you in her day timer."

"An appointment she never kept. I have never met Jennifer Sampson. There is no conflict, so I will be representing Mr. Sampson."

"Oh, yeah? Who retained you?"

"His friend, Dr. Kessler. Now, I don't believe you want to interfere with my client's rights, do you?"

"He waived his right to have a lawyer present."

"I'm sure he's changed his mind by now." Rebecca maneuvered around the police officer. "Haven't you, Tyler?"

Tyler tore his gaze from the letter he still held in his hands to look up at her. "Yeah, yeah, I have."

* * *

Paschek stormed over to the waiting area where Detective Melansen sat nursing his second cup of tea. Melansen twisted his mouth into a grim smile and lifted one hand. Tyler Sampson was entitled to speak with his lawyer as long as he needed, no matter how that lawyer had been retained. Rebecca and Tyler had been behind closed doors for almost an hour. Melansen tapped his watch and held up one hand with fingers spread wide. Five more minutes, and then Paschek could interrupt.

"Detective?"

Paschek and Melansen both swung their gazes toward the interrogation room. Rebecca Andrychuk stood in the doorway. The detective took a slow sip of his tea before rising from his chair. "We still want to ask your client a few questions."

"Are you planning to charge him with anything?"

"No. Not yet."

"You do realize that he was nowhere near Stockton on the morning Jennifer Sampson died."

"Oh, of course. He was at the motel with his oil field crew."

"Yes, he was."

"Sheriff, would you tell Ms. Andrychuk what we learned?"

Paschek's voice was harsh. "We learned that no one saw him. His roommate cannot vouch for him and neither can the motel staff. He ordered a pizza all right, but he ordered it at noon Thursday. He had them deliver it Thursday evening and specifically told them to leave it by the door. No witnesses." The sheriff paused. "No alibi."

Melansen held up a file folder. "And then there's the matter of the letter Jennifer Sampson wrote."

"I saw it," Rebecca said. "It'll never stand up in court. No judge will allow it to be admitted. It's hearsay."

"Perhaps." Melansen stroked his chin. "But I spoke to the DA. He thought he might be able to get it admitted. Something about state of mind."

"You know I'd fight that."

"Yes, Ms. Andrychuk, I expect you would."

"I don't think my client should answer any more questions right now. He has nothing to hide, but this has been a very stressful time. Unless you plan to charge him, I would like to take him back to his daughter."

Paschek opened his mouth to speak, but Melansen waved him to silence. "Very well. We'll be in touch. I'm sure you know what to tell your client."

"Yes, I do. Don't leave town."

* * *

Waiting sucked. Derek ground his teeth and stared at the cell phone on the counter. His apartment wasn't getting any bigger, and he still couldn't walk around in the place. Cassie had been the patient one. She would smile, pat his arm, and remind him that God was in charge. He had hated it and loved it. She had simultaneously been his foil and his balance. It sounded corny, but she had completed him.

He turned to the cluster of photographs on the little end table. Sarah at the beach. The three of them together. And lastly, one of Cassie alone. He picked that one up and traced the image with his finger. How had someone so beautiful ever fallen for him? It was all the more amazing since they were so different. Cassie was a natural athlete, he was a wannabe. He was intellectual and analytical, she relied on her feelings. She could be over-sensitive and emotional, he could be as dense as a brick. She always trusted in God completely, Derek had constant doubts and questions.

Still did. Like why was he here and Cassie and Sarah were gone? Why had they paid the price for his neglect? For his selfishness? For his sin?

The phone rang harshly and he jumped and dropped the frame. It struck hard on the scarred linoleum, the glass cracking with a sharp snap. Derek snatched it up. "Oh, no."

The phone rang again and he grabbed it and stabbed it on. "Yes?"

"Hello, Dr. Kessler? It's Rebecca Andrychuk. I was able to see your friend. The sheriff hasn't charged him with anything yet, so I got him out of there and dropped him at the Vermette place."

"Good. I mean, I'm glad. You said 'yet.' Do you think there will be charges?"

"There might be. The DCI is still gathering evidence, but it's clear that Tyler is their main suspect."

"DCI?"

"The Montana Department of Criminal Investigations. They help out the county sheriffs with any major criminal investiagions. Usually, they take over the whole thing, but this time it looks as though they're letting Sheriff Paschek keep his hand in the mix. Enough to muddy the water, anyway."

"I don't understand."

"Our Sheriff Paschek is a bit of a bulldog. He seems sure Tyler's guilty, and he's not apt to let go of that idea easily."

"Do you think Tyler will be okay?"

"I'll do what I can."

"Thank you, Ms. Andrychuk. I appreciate this." Derek paused and smiled. "It sounds like you're going to take the case." At least that was working out.

"I guess it does, doesn't it? I promise I'll do my best. At least, I will if you stick to our deal and stop calling me Ms. Andrychuk. It's Rebecca, remember?"

"Right. Then thank you, Rebecca."

"Everything else okay? You sounded upset when you answered the phone."

"It's nothing. I mean, I dropped something, that's all." Derek set the cracked frame on the end table. "It's okay."

"All right. Look, I don't want to bother you, but I need a lot more information. It would help if I knew more about Jennifer Sampson's death. Can we get together to go over a few things?"

Derek glanced at his watch. "Sure, my shift doesn't start until eleven. Do you want to meet somewhere?"

"I'm in my car right now, so I could drop by your place. You're in the apartments up on Ninth, right?"

"Um, yeah." Derek ran his fingers through his hair. He didn't have many people over and couldn't remember ever having had an attractive young woman to his apartment. He wasn't sure he should start now. "I'm in 3B."

"Okay, I'll see you in a few minutes. Bye."

Derek stared at the phone lying silent in his hand. He trembled slightly. What was happening? He shot a look at the ceiling, imagining God high above watching him. *What are You doing now? What is going on?*

TWENTY-ONE

*"Love is not love which alters when it alteration finds, or
bends with the remover to remove."*
Sonnet CXVI

R ebecca drove up to the apartments and pulled into a parking spot
near the entrance to Derek's building. She started to check her
hair and makeup in the mirror then caught herself. *This is strictly
business. Nothing personal.* Rebecca picked up her briefcase and
climbed out of the Mustang to examine the apartment complex. The
concrete buildings were arranged around a central courtyard. The grass
was half dead from neglect and surrounded by asphalt cracked and
split by too many scorching summers and frigid winters. No views
of the mountains here. Nothing but flat prairie broken only by fuel
depots and storage facilities. It was not the type of place she would
have expected a doctor to live in.

Derek had told her that he lived in the third building, and she
soon found his door. He had said B, hadn't he? She reached for the
doorbell but hesitated. Why was she nervous? Rebecca squared her
shoulders and rapped on the door, perhaps a bit louder and more
sharply than necessary.

"Miss Andrychuk... Rebecca. Come in, please." Derek held the door open for her. Rebecca stepped over the threshold and followed him up the short flight of stairs leading to the apartment. She kept her face calm and professional while she glanced around the room. It was definitely cleaner than she had expected but was quite sparse. It barely looked lived in.

"Would you like coffee?"

"Yes, please." She set her briefcase on the coffee table in front of the couch and trailed after him as he crossed the small space to the kitchen area. When he glanced back, a smile touched her lips.

Derek scooped grounds into the basket of his coffee machine and added water. "Do you take anything in it?"

"Just cream. Milk will do."

"There might be a carton in the fridge. Would you mind looking?"

"No problem." Rebecca pulled open the door and peered in. It was pretty bare—mustard, ketchup, a couple of containers of leftover takeout that had seen better days. She found a quart container of milk, but when she picked it up and shook it, it was obvious that the contents were no longer in their original liquid state. "Um, on second thought, I'll take it black." When she handed the milk carton to Derek, he started to lift it to his nose as if to smell it, then appeared to think better of it and dropped it into the garbage.

"Sorry about that."

"It's okay. I take it you don't cook much."

"Not lately, although I have been known to make a mean Eggs Benedict."

"Oh, well, that's something I'd like to see some time."

"Uh, yeah. I guess... ah, well, uh..." Derek glanced away quickly and finished making the coffee. Was he actually blushing again? It had been a long time since Rebecca had made any man blush once, but twice? *Better change the subject.*

"So, Dr. Kessler, Derek, what I need from you is more information on Jennifer Sampson's death. Can you fill me in on what happened? Any detail might help."

"Sure, I'll try." He handed Rebecca her coffee and they made their way back to the living room. "Take the armchair, please. It's the most comfortable." When she complied, he sat opposite her on the couch. He opened his mouth as if to speak, then closed it again.

Rebecca set her coffee on the table. "I can assure you this is all legal. Tyler is still the next of kin and has given me permission to discuss all aspects of his wife's case with you."

"It's not that." Derek's voice rasped, and he cleared his throat. "It's that I still think I failed somehow, that I could have saved her."

Rebecca leaned back and crossed her legs. "Tell me all about it."

* * *

Derek sat immobile on the couch, his eyes fixed on the floor. What was happening here? This was Tyler's lawyer. He needed to meet with her to try and help his friend, but he was beginning to feel things he hadn't felt for a long time. He didn't know for certain what it was, but it was something. But was it a good thing? Part of him wanted it to be.

Rebecca sat and sipped her coffee, apparently untroubled by his silence. She had pulled a yellow legal pad from her briefcase and was positioning it on her lap when their eyes met. Without hesitation, she smiled again. Derek swallowed. *Calm down. She only wants information to help Tyler. There's nothing personal here. She's doing her job.* He took a deep breath and began to tell her the details of what had happened the day Jennifer Sampson had died.

* * *

Rebecca finished her notes and set her pen down so she could read what she had written.

"Is it okay?" he asked. "Was I clear enough with the medical stuff?"

"You did fine in explaining it all to me. I'm concerned about what the police and the McKennys said. There's already quite a bit of evidence against Tyler. If they obtain any more, they'll have a strong case."

"It doesn't matter. He's innocent."

She tilted her head. "You sound sure about that. How come? You know Tyler well?"

"He was the first person I met when I came to Stockton. I was on the outskirts of town when I got a flat on my Jeep. No big thing, except my spare was flat, too." He smiled.

Rebecca twirled a strand of hair around her finger. Realizing suddenly that she was staring, she let go of the hair and straightened, her own cheeks growing warm. Had Derek noticed? "What happened next?"

"Tyler showed up. Helped me get the tires fixed, showed me where the apartments were, and even helped me move in. The next Sunday morning, he invited me to church."

"You were close friends then?"

"Well, we were friends, but not really close. We kept it kind of superficial. Guy talk. I didn't even know he was married."

"So how can you be so confident that Tyler didn't do it?"

"I just know. I mean, I was watching him in the morgue when he first saw Jennifer. His grief was real. I know that he loved her."

"You're pretty definite about that."

He lifted his shoulders. "I guess I understand what he is going through."

"Uh-huh, Tyler mentioned that."

Derek stiffened. "Oh."

"I'm sorry," Rebecca said. "I didn't mean to over-step, but Tyler told me you lost your wife and daughter in a car accident. I'm sorry."

Derek stared out the window. Rebecca followed his gaze. Gray clouds slowly coalesced into a chill blanket, obscuring the sharp blue of the prairie sky. Drops of rain pelted the glass. When Derek spoke, Rebecca had to bend forward to hear him. "I loved them," he said.

Rebecca was afraid to breathe. It was as if he was speaking to someone else and not her, as if she was a distant observer overhearing vital testimony at a great trial. It wasn't really for her, but at the same time she didn't feel like an intruder. It seemed as though telling her his story was something he needed to do.

* * *

They had met in his final year of medicine. Derek had gotten up early to study but was distracted by the lithe blonde jogging through the park below his apartment window. He'd seen her every morning the previous week, and he'd finally worked up the courage to try to meet her.

His attempt to impress her with his athletic prowess was a disaster. He had barely started his run when he began to cramp up. Derek was limping when she passed him the first time, and by the time the woman lapped him, he was sitting on the grass in pain and embarrassment. She smiled as she ran past, and Derek watched her disappear through the trees at the end of the park. How stupid he'd felt as he sat there, wondering if he'd ever see her again. He needn't have worried.

That evening he sat staring at the tiny print of *The Principles of Internal Medicine*. When he realized that he'd read the same passage for the fifth time, he slammed the book shut. *This is pointless.* There had to be something better than another weekend of studying. Then he remembered that it was Friday night. Coffee and cake at the university's Christian student fellowship event. Derek shot a glance at the textbook. *Yeah, definitely better.* He'd limped into the hall and settled on a chair near the back. He had only been there a moment when someone took the seat beside him and Derek found himself staring into the bright blue eyes of the blonde runner. She smiled and asked how his leg was. Less than a year later, they were married.

Those first years were thrilling and frustrating. Adjusting to married life and the demands of an emergency medicine residency weren't always easy, but they stuck it out. They planned to wait until he was finished his training before having any children, but things happen, and Sarah was born near the end of his fourth year. With Derek's eyes and Cassie's hair, Sarah was perfect. And the rest of their life appeared to be as well.

Derek was offered positions at a number of different hospitals when he finished his residency and soon started at the ER of the Wexner Medical Center at OSU in Columbus, Ohio. He loved the work. It was exciting and challenging. It was easy to become totally engulfed in his career, to let it occupy all his time and energy. Derek wanted to put his family first, but he didn't always succeed.

The day of the crash, he was supposed to pick the girls up after his shift to take them to Sarah's preschool concert. She was so excited, she had barely slept the night before. Cassie even planned a celebration with cake and ice cream after, a four-year-old's version of an opening night reception. The ER was swamped. The waiting room was already packed with the usual assortment of infections and injuries when the ambulances began bringing in the victims of a large apartment fire. Then one arrived with a firefighter in full cardiac arrest. The other doctors asked Derek to stay. They needed him.

He'd been too busy to call Cassie himself and had asked the ward clerk do it. He would try to meet them at the school in about an hour, hopefully before Sarah went on. It had started raining. The other driver had been drinking, and, as Derek would find out later, not for the first time. In fact, he had a history of previous convictions for driving under the influence and was speeding when he ran the red light. Cassie probably never even saw him. She didn't have a chance. Neither of them did.

They told him later that they had to use the Jaws of Life to remove them from the wreckage. Cassie died at the scene. Sarah lived only a little longer, scarcely making it to Nationwide Children's. She never regained consciousness.

"Take time off," his boss told him. "Take as long as you need. Don't worry about the hospital." His co-workers tried to be sympathetic and understanding. But how could anyone really understand? He couldn't handle being in their old apartment. The emptiness ate at him. He had to do something. After only a few weeks, he went back to work. He needed something to fill the hours, to distract him. For a while, it worked.

There were lots of car accidents in the Columbus area. On any given shift in the ER, the doctors could expect to deal with a few of them. Most often, the trauma was fairly mild. Other victims never made it to Emergency, they went straight to the morgue. There were lots of reasons for accidents—road conditions, weather, speeding, even road rage.

Alcohol was often the cause. Derek managed to avoid any such cases for months, but it had to happen sooner or later.

The driver was young, early twenties. The EMT said he had been traveling at high speed the wrong way down a one-way street. The people in the minivan he plowed into probably never saw him coming. The ambulance crew reported that there was liquor in his vehicle, and that he smelled of alcohol. He went into respiratory arrest prior to arrival. The paramedic had managed an intubation but was having difficulty ventilating him. There was bruising on the right chest wall with no breath sounds, low blood pressure, and a shift of the trachea to the left. Derek recognized immediately that the man had a tension pneumothorax and had grabbed a large bore needle to decompress the right lung. But then, he hesitated.

* * *

Derek blinked as if coming out of a trance. "I don't know why I'm telling you all this. I don't, usually. I mean, I hardly know you."

"It's okay." Rebecca's eyes were moist. "I think I understand. At least a bit." She hesitated. "Maybe it helps to talk about it."

"That's what I've been told. I'm not sure." They sat in silence.

"What happened next?" Rebecca asked. "In the ER in Columbus? Did you save the guy?"

"No, I didn't. I couldn't move. Someone else took over. Put in the needle and drew off the air, saved the guy's life. I quit the next day. I couldn't go back, couldn't do it anymore. I moved out here a few months later."

"But why? After what you'd been through, anybody would understand. I mean, you're treating a drunk driver like the one that killed your family. It's natural that you might freeze up and hesitate, even not know what to do."

"I knew what to do." Derek met her gaze steadily. "I knew exactly what was needed. Only... I didn't want to do it. I didn't want to save him. I wanted him to die."

* * *

Paschek stalked to the front entrance of the police station and wrenched the door open. He stopped with a jerk and gritted his teeth before waving Detective Melansen to go ahead in a mock display of courtesy.

Melansen grasped his arm. "Keep it cool, Eugene. The case is coming together."

"Not fast enough for me." He tugged his arm from the detective's grasp and followed him inside, letting the door slam behind him. After Tyler Sampson and his newly-acquired lawyer had left the station, Paschek and Melansen had taken Tyler's computer to a local expert. None of them were capable of searching a hard drive. Paschek's man was.

On the way to his office, Paschek dropped his keys on the desk in front of Deputy Standingready. "Your shift almost over?"

"Yes, sir. Just finishing some paperwork."

"Leave it. Shooter's computer is in the trunk of my car. Get it and return it to the evidence locker. Make sure it's good and secure. What's on it is going to put the final nail in Shooter Sampson's coffin."

Standingready grabbed the keys and stood. Paschek grinned like a hungry wolf. "This could be your big day, Rookie. You've got a chance to be involved in arresting a murderer. You should be proud."

"Yes, sir, if you say so."

Paschek snorted. "I do say so. Take care of the computer, and then run down and get us a pot of coffee from the diner." He turned to follow Melansen and shouted over his shoulder, "And bring me back some M&M's."

* * *

It felt as if all the air had been sucked from the room. Derek lurched to his feet and stumbled to the kitchen.

Grabbing the carafe, he came back to stand in the doorway. "Uh, do you want any more coffee?" *Stupid. Of course she doesn't want more coffee.*

"No thanks."

Derek spun around, feeling her staring at his back. He set the coffee down and peered into its murky depths.

"I think I should be going. I mean, it's getting late, and I've got a lot of work to do." Rebecca's heels clicked on the linoleum and then the door opened. "Thanks for all your help, Dr. Kessler. I'll let you know how things go next with Tyler."

Dr. Kessler. So they were back to that. Derek leaned his head against the wall. A breath of air escaped through his lips. "I'm sorry."

The door closed.

He slapped his hand against the wall and groaned. Shaking his head, he took slow, deep breaths, trying to calm the staccato beat of his pulse. It wasn't supposed to be like this. Wasn't talking about it supposed to help? It had when he'd talked to Bert. But then, he'd held a few details back. Today, it was as though a floodgate had opened, and he'd let everything flow out. Now he felt worse. What could Rebecca be thinking?

Was that why he was upset? He barely knew her, and he was worried about what she might think? *I'm betraying Cassie.* Derek turned and leaned against the wall. The apartment pressed in on him as he slid to the floor and buried his face in his hands. The voice in his head was louder now, the accusations harsher. How could he forget his vows, forget her so soon? How could he be so faithless? How had he ended up so alone?

TWENTY-TWO

"Who steals my purse steals trash; 'tis something, nothing;
'twas mine, 'tis his, and has been slave to thousands; But he
that filches from me my good name robs me of that which
not enriches him, and makes me poor indeed."
Othello, Act III, Scene III

Paschek knew he was being difficult and didn't care. "We have enough evidence. We should go to the DA." He ceased his relentless pacing to lean over the desk.

"I don't agree," Melansen replied. He opened the file and peered at it over the top of his glasses. "There's more work to do first."

"What else do you want? You saw what our computer geek found. Shooter had been researching different poisons on his computer. He had even downloaded articles on ethylene glycol." Paschek rounded the desk and pointed at the file. "Then he went and bought some. There's the receipt. Who buys gas line antifreeze in August?"

Melansen slowly removed his glasses and rubbed his eyes. "It's not enough, not yet."

"How can you say that? He had the opportunity, and his alibi is shaky. I say he did it."

"Look, Eugene, you've got good instincts, always have. But sometimes you're like a dog with a bone. Don't get tunnel vision. We need to follow up on a few other things first. Tie up the loose ends, and then we can move on to Mr. Sampson."

Paschek opened his mouth to protest further but stopped and jerked his head to the side, listening with intensity. He sprang forward and snatched open the door. Deputy Standingready stumbled into the room with a tray of coffee in his hands. He hurried to set the tray on the desk and go, but Paschek blocked his passage. "How long were you listening?"

"Sir?"

"You heard me. I'm not wild about eavesdroppers, but I hate liars."

"Only a moment or two. I heard what you were saying about the evidence."

Paschek crossed his arms and leaned against the doorframe. "So, what do you think? What should we do?"

"Sir?" Standingready's mouth dropped open slightly. "You're asking me?"

"Why not? You've been in on it from the start. Surely, you've got an opinion."

"Well…"

"Come on, man, spit it out."

"Well, sir, it's like Detective Melansen said, you need something more. You need motive. Why would he—why would anyone—commit murder?"

Paschek stared at the deputy for an instant before walking over to the desk and peering down at the tray. Beside the carafe and the mugs were two bags of M&M candies. Paschek smiled and settled into a chair. "Thank you, Deputy. You may go now." He waited until the office door closed before turning to Melansen. "What more do you want?"

Melansen poured himself a cup of coffee. "Your deputy's right. We need a motive."

Paschek grunted and poked through the papers on his desk. "I thought I saw something. Yeah, here it is, a life insurance policy on Jennifer Sampson. Shooter's listed as the beneficiary."

"Could be something. How much is it for?"

"Not a lot—fifty thousand."

Melansen rubbed a hand over his chin. "You're right, not that much."

"People have killed for a lot less, Oliver. You know that."

"Okay, I'll concede that point. Was Tyler Sampson hard up for cash? Gambling debts, anything like that?"

Paschek stirred through the papers and frowned. "Actually, Shooter's pretty flush. Good money working the rigs these days, and his old man left him the house and around six hundred acres of land. Not rich by any stretch, but not struggling either. Doesn't look like money fits."

"Okay, we'll look elsewhere. To start with, I want to know what the victim was seeing this doctor in Helena about. What is he, a counselor or something?"

"A psychologist."

"Right. So, if he comes out and says she was depressed and suicidal it kind of makes a murder charge more difficult to stick, doesn't it, Eugene?"

"I suppose."

"Let's wait for that then. I talked to the Helena police earlier. They spoke to this doctor and he wants to help but wants to be sure he's not violating any confidentiality laws first. So…"

"We have to wait for a judge to issue a court order opening his files."

"Exactly. That'll happen tomorrow morning. In the meantime, I think we need to make sure that we've eliminated any other suspects. What have you got?"

"All right, Detective. Simply put, there are no other suspects. The victim got along well with her neighbors and the rest of the community. There's no evidence she was having an affair and there aren't any big debts. Nothing was stolen from the house, and there's no sign of drug use. She hadn't argued or fought with anyone except her husband."

"What about her father? What did you call him, a religious fanatic?"

"Yeah, McKenny is that all right." Paschek stretched and sipped his coffee. "He's never been violent that I'm aware of, although I'm sure he's capable of it. He claims he was home working on his sermon from early Friday morning on, and his wife vouches for him. Besides, I don't think he'd use poison to kill someone. I swear there have been a few times he would've tried to strangle Shooter if we hadn't been there."

Melansen nodded and refilled his cup. "Looking over everything, I'd say I agree with you, Eugene. The evidence is definitely pointing at Tyler Sampson. Let's make sure we can wrap it up with a bow before we hand it off to the DA, though."

Paschek set his coffee down and pocketed the candy. "All right, let's do that."

* * *

The apartment had darkened in the early evening light by the time Derek stirred. His appetite was meager, but he needed to eat. His ER shift would be starting in a few hours, and he'd regret it if he didn't have a good meal beforehand. He should go shopping for groceries, but that thought was overwhelming. The prospect of another fast-food burger made him gag. There was the restaurant downtown, The Homestead Café. The name might be hokey, but at least the food was good. He grabbed his keys and headed for the door.

The vinyl countertops and red leatherette booths likely hadn't been in style in a few decades, but everything was clean. And busy. Every booth and table was full. Derek scanned the room. A couple of the stools at the main counter were empty. He hesitated. He wasn't in the mood for company or conversation. Maybe he should go. The smell of homestyle cooking overcame his caution, and he trudged to one of the stools, hoping he could get through his meal without anyone noticing him.

"Evening, Doc," the waitress said as she wiped down the counter in front of him. "Coffee?"

So much for anonymity. "Uh, no thanks… Nancy." Her name tag was bright blue, which matched her hair. "Just water, please."

"You want a menu?"

"Thanks." Derek took the laminated page while Nancy set a glass in front of him. "Is there a special tonight?"

Her blue hair waved from side to side. "Honey, Harvey's cooking tonight. Ain't nothing special when he's on the grill." She laughed and headed down the counter to serve another customer. Derek perused the menu, searching for something to pique his appetite. He spun about sharply on the stool when a horn blasted from the street. Two teenage boys in a rusted pickup truck hooted at a group of girls on the sidewalk. Derek shook his head and turned around. As he did, he knocked over the glass and sent water cascading over the counter.

The man beside him jumped up in a futile attempt to escape the deluge. While Nancy threw a stack of napkins on the puddle, Derek lunged to right the glass. "Oh crap, I'm sorry."

"Hey, no problem, it's only water." The other customer grabbed a handful of napkins and blotted his trousers before wiping down his stool. Then he straightened and held out his hand. "I'm Joseph Standingready, a deputy with the sheriff's office."

"I could tell." Derek returned the handshake. "The uniform kind of gives it away."

"I suppose so." Standingready settled back onto his stool. "I didn't catch your name."

"It's Kessler, Derek Kessler."

"Kessler? Are you the doc from the hospital ER?"

Derek shrugged, resigned. "Yep."

"The one who treated the Sampson girl?"

He hesitated. Jennifer was the last thing he wanted to talk about tonight. "Yes, she was my patient. Are you working on her case?"

It was Standingready's turn to pause. "I guess you could say that. I'm only a rookie, though. They don't tell me much." Nancy replaced Derek's water and Standingready's coffee. The deputy cleared his throat. "What say we steer away from that stuff for now? I'm off duty."

Derek grinned. "Sounds good to me."

* * *

Rebecca's drive from Dr. Kessler's apartment had been slow and meandering. She needed time to think. Staying out of the chill isolation of her condominium was a bonus. What to make of this doctor? He barely knew Tyler Sampson but offered to cover his legal expenses. He knew nothing about court or the law but was absolutely convinced that Tyler was innocent. He seemed shy and private but then opened up about real and deep hurts from his past. Maybe he needed to talk. Maybe her being a stranger willing to listen made the difference, made it easier somehow. Or maybe it was something else.

Rebecca let the car roll to a stop. She frowned as she peered into the growing darkness. Where was she? A sign caught her eye. Stockton Community Fellowship. A church. *Wait a minute, this is where Dr. Kessler—no, Derek—said he attends, where he'd met Tyler.* Rebecca continued to read. *Jesus died for you.* She pursed her lips. *One of those kinds of churches.* Funny, Derek didn't act like some religious nut. He was a nice guy, the type of guy she could really go for. He was even single. Well, widowed and still not over it. Which kind of made him more attractive, vulnerable even. She grimaced. Different from her usual.

Rebecca studied the unpretentious building. When had she last been in a church? If she didn't count weddings and funerals, then never. No, there was one time. At Christmas when she was fourteen. Her father was off on one of his "business trips", and Mother suddenly announced they were going out. Then she dragged them to some big church downtown.

From the little Rebecca could remember, it was kind of boring at first, but then got really strange. About halfway through, her mother started to cry. Rebecca tried to burrow down in the pew while her mom sniffled and sobbed beside her, but it was too much. She grabbed the car keys and ran outside. Rebecca had glanced over her shoulder, expecting her mother to follow, but she didn't. A couple of old people had gone and sat beside her. Her mom kept crying. She didn't even look up. Rebecca couldn't get to the car fast enough.

By the time her mother came out of the church, Rebecca wasn't mad anymore. She was just cold. At least her mother wasn't still bawling, but she was with the old couple. Then she did something even stranger. She hugged those two elderly strangers. In public. For a long time. It made absolutely no sense.

It still didn't. Rebecca hadn't thought about that day in a long time. Her mother had seemed different for a while. More calm, peaceful even. It hadn't lasted. How could it? The fighting had started up again, and her father continued to stay out late or go off on trips. Then her mother had started drinking. Things had gotten worse after that, much worse.

Something was dripping on her hands. Rebecca glanced in the rearview mirror. Her mascara was smeared, and tears ran down her cheeks. She grabbed several tissues from the back seat and swiped at her face. She pounded on the steering wheel and then wrapped her arms tightly around herself. *Hold it in. Keep it down.* It was no use. Resting her forehead on the steering wheel, she shuddered. The tears came in spasms.

A light tapping on her window jolted her upright.

"Are you all right, Miss?"

Rebecca hit the button to lower the glass. Paulina would have had a fit. Sitting alone on the street and then opening her window to answer a stranger? Somehow, it seemed okay. She quickly wiped her face before replying, "I'm fine. Really, I am."

"Are you sure? I'm Josh Bucknell, the pastor of the church here. Do you need to talk to someone?"

"No, thank you. I'll be okay. I have to go." Rebecca shifted the car into drive and pulled away. In the rearview mirror she could see the pastor standing in the street watching her. Great. She could see tomorrow's headline: "Local Lawyer Cracks Up Outside Holy Roller Church." Exactly the kind of publicity she needed.

What was wrong with her?

* * *

Derek winced when he glanced at the dark stain on the deputy's khaki trousers. "Sorry about that."

"Hey, like I said, don't worry about it. I've been wet before, and it'll dry up quick enough." Standingready grinned and flipped open a menu. "You can make it up to me by telling me what's good to eat here."

"The fried chicken is to die for. And I mean that literally. It's loaded with enough cholesterol to clog up a dozen arteries."

"All right, Doctor, I'll hold off on the chicken for the time being. What else?"

"The meatloaf is good, but the real hidden gem is the Greek salad. Who'd have thought that you could get an authentic Greek salad in a small-town Montana diner? No lettuce, Kalamata olives, real Feta cheese. It's great."

"Um, I think I'll stick to the meatloaf."

"Your loss."

Nancy wrote their orders on a notepad and hightailed it to the kitchen. Derek took a sip of his water. "So, how long have you been a deputy?"

"This is my first job. Fresh out of the Academy in Helena."

"The Academy?"

"Montana Law Enforcement Academy. Did my basic training there and a couple of professional courses."

"And then you moved to Stockton?"

"Yep. The county had already hired me before I took the course, so when I finished, I came right here. How about you? How long have you been in town?"

"Less than six months."

"Still trying to fit in, then? Man, I feel the same way. It's been three months since I joined the Sheriff's Office, and I still feel like an outsider."

"I understand."

"It can be rough at first. Don't get me wrong, the other deputies are a great bunch—well, most of them—but sometimes it's hard to figure things out."

"I guess so."

Standingready rambled on. After a few minutes, the police officer stopped and shook his head. "Hey man, I'm sorry," he said, "I'm not usually like this. It's weird, but it's like I've known you a long time."

Derek's shoulders tensed up. "Don't worry about it." He glanced at the clock on the wall and then at the exit. Maybe he could get his salad to go. Turning back, he found himself staring into the deputy's face. The gentleness there melted the tightness in his chest, and a smile eased into existence. "I think I know what you mean."

Their meals arrived, and Standingready clasped his hands in front of him and bowed his head. Somehow, the silence that followed was not uncomfortable. After a moment or two, the deputy looked up and smiled. "Sorry, but I always pray before eating. Usually just saying thanks to Jesus, but this time I felt I had to do more—pray for the case and for everyone involved. Including you."

Derek stared at the deputy. "I appreciate it." He folded and unfolded his hands. "But why would you do that? And why take a chance and tell me?"

The deputy lifted his shoulders. "What chance am I taking? God told me what to do, and I obeyed."

"What if I had gotten angry? What if I didn't want your prayers? What if I'm offended?"

"Then I'd apologize. Not for praying or for obeying God, but for offending you. And then I'd ask you why my relationship with Christ would bother you."

"You sound pretty sure of yourself."

"Why not? I know who I am and where my value comes from. Not from anything I've done, but because Christ loves me. I believe in that. I believe in Him. What about you?"

"I used to." Derek rubbed his eyes. "Lately, it seems so hard."

Deputy Standingready rested a hand on the Derek's shoulder. "Christ said He would never leave us. Never give up on us. And He never will."

"I wish I had your faith."

"It only takes a mustard seed."

Derek tilted his head. "Pardon me?"

"The Bible says that's all we need. Faith the size of a mustard seed. I used to have a lot less."

"Really?"

"Yeah," Standingready said. "Buy me a piece of pie, and I'll tell you all about it."

* * *

Rebecca strode up the walk to her doorway. Her fingers trembled as she fumbled with her keys. *Get inside. It's safer inside.* Her breathing was ragged, and a muscle in her forehead twitched. *Stop it. Think about something else.* The echo of her heels on the cold tile floors seemed to mock her as she hurried into the kitchen. *Lights. Get the lights on.* At least the power company liked these little panic attacks. Maybe they should try to induce anxiety in the rest of their customers. Be a good way to increase profits.

She smiled slightly and let her breath out slowly. *That's better.* After grabbing a diet cola from the fridge, she wandered into the living area. The message light flashed on the telephone. Good news or bad? Might be business, or Paulina, or Judge Farr. It could even be Derek. She pushed the play button.

The first two messages were offers for another credit card, and the third was a reminder from the movie outlet that she had not yet returned the extended version of the blockbuster movie everyone had raved about. She hadn't watched it yet, either. When would this hick town get a streaming service? The fourth message was from Philip.

"Hey, babe," the voice from the machine said, "I hadn't heard from you yet, so I thought I'd give you a call. Hope you're busy packing for our date. I've cleared the whole weekend for you. I'll even leave my cell at the office. Say you'll come. Call me."

Rebecca turned off the answering machine and stretched out on the sofa, rubbing her temples with her fingers. The stress was giving her another headache. Minutes passed as she lay motionless. The only sound was the pulse in her ears. All light had faded from her windows before she stirred and reached for her purse so she could grab a pill and ward off the pending attack.

She had a choice. Go back to Philip and keep things the same. Continue coasting through life. Or do something different. Maybe take a chance on a real relationship. She glanced over at her briefcase. The notes from the Sampson case were in it. She pressed her eyes shut. She'd gotten involved after vowing not to let that happen again. Derek's face as he told her about his wife and child, about their deaths, flashed through her mind. *Careful.* Things could get dangerous. The telephone beckoned. Philip was safe. *Safe is good. Safe is easy. Derek? That was risky.* Her heart might actually be on the line with him.

Rebecca sat up and reached for the phone. Time to make a decision.

TWENTY-THREE

"Thus conscience does make cowards of us all."
Hamlet, Act III, Scene I

Paschek was on his third cup of coffee before the day shift arrived. His stomach and his temper had both started a slow burn. He drummed his fingers on his desktop. The burn intensified. He swiveled to glare out the window. Most folks were happy this time of year. The local harvest was progressing well, and the oil patch remained in high gear. Paschek didn't like it.

A good harvest meant money in people's pockets. A busy oil field meant money in other people's pockets. Excess cash meant celebrations. That meant more drinking, more fights, more reckless driving—in short, more work for him. He snorted. Of course, a lousy harvest and a shutdown in the oil business meant the same thing, only for different reasons. Whether people were drowning their sorrows or reveling in their good fortune, it was always the same. Trouble for the sheriff.

The sound of a loud cough yanked him out of his musing. Marsh stood over his desk with a paper in his hand. "Don't you know better than to come in without knocking first?"

"I did. Twice." Marsh squirmed under the sheriff's scowl. "Sorry. I've got the court order for that psych guy's records in the Sampson case. I was waiting outside the courthouse when Judge Farr arrived, like you asked."

"So, what are you waiting for? No medals for doing your job. Get it off to the Helena police."

"I already did. Faxed it to them and followed up with a phone call. They said they'd get to it as soon as they could, but it might be a day or two."

"Why?"

"They said they're swamped. Had some gang thing over the weekend and now everyone's too busy."

The burn became a full-fledged blaze. Paschek's comments on the parentage and competence of the members of the other police force were loud and profane. He surged to his feet and snatched the court order out of Marsh's hand. "Wipe that smirk off your face and go make sure my cruiser is full of gas."

"You going to Helena?"

Paschek swore again. "What do you think I'm doing? Let Melansen know, and try not to screw up anything else while I'm gone." The deputy slunk out of the office and Paschek reached down and opened his desk drawer. The Mason jar with its cargo of green M&M's was waiting. Might as well make the trip worthwhile.

* * *

It was a better Monday morning than most. Rebecca set her pen down and rose to walk over to the doorway of her office. "These papers are ready for the realtor. Can you let him know?"

Paulina looked up from her computer. "No problem. By the way, Isabel Vermette is here."

"Excellent. Show her in." Rebecca waited by the door as the woman entered her office. Isabel looked tired. Her eyes were reddened and her face pale. The brown hair touching her shoulders was limp. She smiled weakly at the lawyer and crumpled onto the chair across from her desk.

"Thanks for coming, Ms. Vermette. Would you like coffee? Tea? Water?"

"Tea would be nice, thank you."

"Paulina," Rebecca called, "would you bring us tea, please?" She closed the office door and rounded her desk, studying her guest as she did. Casually but neatly dressed in a plaid Western shirt and blue jeans, the woman matched the stereotype expected for a lady rancher. A little makeup, maybe some sleep, and she'd be quite pretty. "How are you doing, Ms. Vermette?"

"Please, it's Isabel."

"All right, Isabel. Are you okay?"

"It's been rough. Jennifer was a friend, and our girls adored each other. My heart breaks every time I look at that little one. Her mother's dead, and now the police seem to think Tyler had something to do with it?"

"What do you think?"

"Tyler couldn't have. He loved Jenn so much. He'd never hurt her."

"That's what I'm trying to prove. Maybe you can help."

"I'll do anything. What do you need to know?"

Rebecca straightened a few papers on her desk and set out a yellow legal pad as Paulina entered the office with two mugs of tea. "Thank you, Paulina." When her assistant had left the room and closed the door, Rebecca folded her hands on top of the legal pad. "For starters, did you often babysit Olivia Sampson?"

"Two or three times a month. Jenn used her mother more though."

"Tabitha McKenny?"

"That's right. Tabitha would go over to Jenn's house at least a couple of times a week."

Rebecca unclasped her hands and reached for a pen. "So Jennifer got on well with her mother?"

"Well enough, I suppose. They were never very affectionate."

"How about her father, Samuel McKenny?"

The woman blanched slightly. *Interesting.* "I think she was a bit scared of him. I know I was."

"Why?"

Isabel wiped her hands on her jeans and chewed on her bottom lip. "I don't know. I just was. He seemed so angry all the time. And some of the things he'd say."

"Like what?" Rebecca scribbled notes on the pad.

"Like we're going to burn in hell if we don't believe what he does."

"So you're not religious?"

Isabel met Rebecca's gaze. "Religion doesn't have anything to do with it." She pushed her shoulders back. "My faith in God is strong. Samuel McKenny doesn't think it's enough to believe in Jesus. You have to believe in Samuel McKenny."

"Oh. Okay. I'm not sure what that implies, but let's leave it for now. What about Tyler? How did he get along with the McKennys?"

"I think Tabitha tolerated him, but Samuel hated him, pure and simple."

"Enough to try to do him harm? Enough to harm them both?"

"Oh, yeah, he tried to run Tyler off more than once before they were married. One time Anton—that's my husband—heard him threaten both of them."

"What happened?"

"We were hosting a small engagement party for Rebecca and Tyler. The McKennys weren't supposed to be there. We'd invited them, but they'd refused. Anyway, Samuel showed up and started to shout at Tyler. Anton pulled him aside and tried to calm him down. McKenny said some nasty things. Then Jenn came over and tried to smooth things over, and McKenny said if they went through with the marriage they'd both regret it."

Rebecca wrote down McKenny's words and underlined *they'd both regret it*. "Anything specific? Did he threaten physical harm?"

"No, just that they would regret it. And that he'd make sure of it."

"That was quite a few years ago. Anything happen since?"

"Nothing that dramatic. Things seemed to have settled between Jenn and her parents. Having Olivia helped."

"What about with Tyler?"

"Mostly he'd stay away from them. Like I said, Tabitha appeared to accept him—at least a bit. I think they'd even talk some when she was at Jenn's place. Samuel was a different story. Tyler figured it was best to simply avoid him. Out of sight, out of mind, he hoped. I'm not sure if it worked."

Rebecca set her pen down and skimmed over her notes. "Did you have Olivia for a sleepover very often?"

"No, not really. Jenn wasn't too keen to have Olivia spend the night anywhere except at her place or at the McKennys'."

"Why did you have her this time?"

"Jenn said her mother was feeling kinda sick and wasn't up to having her. Abby and Livy loved it. They played and laughed and giggled all night." Isabel had wrapped her fingers around the mug but hadn't taken a sip of tea. "I haven't heard her laugh since."

Rebecca waited. Isabel swiped a tear off her cheek. "Sorry."

"It's okay." Rebecca handed her a tissue from the box on her desk. "Do you know what Jenn was doing while Olivia was with you?"

"I'm not sure. Jenn didn't always say what she was up to. I know Tyler was away on the oil patch. I thought maybe she had another appointment in Helena."

"Helena?"

She was seeing some sort of counselor or therapist there."

"Do you know the therapist's name?"

"I should know it. Grange? No, something with an 'A.' Ainge. That's it, Ainge."

Rebecca leaned forward and pushed the button for her office intercom. "Paulina, I need you to do a couple of things for me. First, call Tyler Sampson and get him to run down here right away. I need him to sign a couple of release of information forms on Jennifer, and then I need you to do an Internet search, find out what you can about a therapist in Helena, last name Ainge."

Standing, she reached across the desk to take Isabel's hand. "Thank you so much. I may have more questions for you later. Is it okay if I call you again?"

For the first time, Isabel smiled. "Of course. I truly want to help. Olivia and Tyler deserve to know the truth."

"That's what we all want. We just have to find out what that is."

* * *

Derek jerked upright and blinked. What was that noise? He frowned and squinted. He was seated at his kitchen table with a half-eaten breakfast and an open Bible before him. *Must have fallen asleep.* His phone rang. The harsh ring tone assaulted his ears. Likely the noise that had woken him. He stabbed at the button to stop the offending sound. "Hello?"

"Derek? It's Rebecca."

"Rebecca?"

"Andrychuk, remember? The lawyer. You okay? Did I wake you up?"

"No, I mean, yeah." Derek struck his forehead with his open palm. *Idiot.* "I'm really sorry, Rebecca. I must've fallen asleep over breakfast. Guess I was kinda out of it."

"It's a bit late for breakfast." Her voice held laughter. "Do you always sleep this late on a Monday?"

"Actually, I was on duty last night. Just got off at seven thirty."

"Oh, I'm sorry. I could call back later."

"No, it's okay. It was pretty quiet last night, and I grabbed four or five hours' sleep in the staff room. I'm good." Silence. "Really."

"Well, if you're sure… I've been checking a few things on the Sampson case, and I just finished talking to Isabel Vermette."

"Was she any help?"

"Maybe. I learned a bit and have another lead to check into." She sighed. "If I was a big-city criminal lawyer, I'd have someone else doing this. A legal assistant or maybe even a private detective. But I'm not. I'll do the best I can, but you know, you might want to get someone else, someone with more experience in criminal law."

"Tyler has confidence in you." Derek chewed his bottom lip. "He told me how things went at the police station. Said you handled everything." He waited through a pause.

"What about you? Do you have confidence in me?"

"Well, yeah. I do."

"Look," she said, "I have a little free time after lunch. I want to check out a few things, and I need to ask the McKennys some questions."

"You sure? I mean, I guess you know what you're doing, but the man seems like a loose cannon to me."

"He is. That's why I'm calling. I'm not comfortable going out there alone and was wondering if you would come with me."

Derek ran his fingers through his already-disheveled hair. "I'm not sure I'm the best one to take. McKenny wasn't very pleasant the last time we talked. He blames me for letting his daughter die."

"Maybe he's cooled off. Or, maybe he'll get so angry at you, he'll give something away. Regardless, I need to try and get information from him. Will you come?"

"Am I there as a bodyguard or as bait?"

Rebecca laughed. "I admit that you'd be a bit of both. What do you say? Pick you up in an hour?"

"All right. I'll be waiting out in front." As he set the phone back on its cradle, a thought passed through his mind. It had been a long time since a woman had picked him up for anything. It was kind of nice.

* * *

"Everything's in order." Paschek drummed his hands on his thighs as the psychologist started to read the court order for the third time. "You see where the district court judge signed it? Dated it, too." He gritted his teeth. *Don't push too hard. We need this idiot on our side.* He uncrossed his arms and leaned back in the chair. He felt like a spring unwinding and about to snap.

"Yes, yes, I see that, Officer… What did you say your name was again?"

"Paschek, and it's Sheriff." He was starting to get a headache. "Are you satisfied with the court order, Dr. Ainge?"

"Oh, yes, of course, Officer… Sheriff, whatever it was again. I'm quite clear. This document requires that I open my files on Jennifer Sampson and discuss her case with the police, that being you." Ainge pulled a file from his desk drawer and set it before the sheriff. "I'll have my secretary make a copy of the file as requested. I will, of course, keep the original for myself."

"Thank you, Doctor. I have a few questions. Are you a medical doctor?"

"No. I have a PhD in clinical psychology from Cornell."

"What was your relationship with the victim, Jennifer Sampson?"

"Ms. Sampson had been coming to see me for about seven months for counseling."

"What sort of counseling?"

"About her relationships, mostly. She was unhappy in her marriage, unfulfilled as a mother, resentful of her parents. A veritable host of social anxieties."

"A lot of problems, then."

"Oh, my goodness, yes. Most related to a poor self-esteem and unanswered dreams and desires. Ms. Sampson was a lot like a lost child. She knew what she wanted but was too frightened to try to obtain it."

"What did she want?"

"I don't believe that she had fully realized what it was, but of course I could see it. She wanted to be a free and independent woman with no one else controlling her life. She was beginning to gain enough courage to achieve that."

"I see." Paschek scanned the open file before him and scratched his head. He shouldn't say what he was thinking, but it was too hard to resist. "You really believe all that crap?"

The psychologist stiffened, a red flush spreading from his starched white shirt collar to his cheeks. He clenched and unclenched his jaw. "Yes, I do." He started to reach across the desk to retrieve the file but stopped and laced his fingers together. "You see, Officer, the human mind is extremely complex. Very few laypersons could possibly begin to understand how complex. It can take years, even decades, of intense study and experience before one can begin to grasp it all."

"If you say so. Jennifer Sampson wanted to be—what was it—free?"

"Yes, I believe that is correct."

"Free from what?"

"A multitude of things. She felt she had no control over her own life, that she never had. First her father had controlled her, and then her husband. Jennifer Sampson wanted to be free to run her own life."

"Enough to kill herself?"

"No." Ainge leaned back in his chair. "No, I do not believe she would ever contemplate suicide. While some might say suicide is the ultimate expression of control of one's self, Ms. Sampson was not the type. She would be too worried about the aftermath, that things would get…well… messy."

"Meaning?"

"Ms. Sampson was obsessive compulsive when it came to neatness. It was the one area of her life she was in control of. She had to keep everything orderly and precise. Everything in perfect order. No, she would never commit suicide."

"Okay. You said she was getting brave enough to do something about her life. What did you mean?"

"She had indicated that she was planning to file for divorce from her husband. From what she told me, he's an alcoholic and had more than one affair during their marriage. Moreover, he repeatedly refused to accept any counseling for his drinking or for their marriage."

"I see. Had she told him about the divorce?"

Dr. Ainge unclasped his hands and stroked his goatee. "I don't know about that. I do know she wanted to make certain of a few things first. Ms. Sampson was gaining courage, but had not achieved all that she needed yet. Though she had decided to leave her husband, she was not fully independent and was planning to return to her parents' house. We were going to discuss that further this week, but now…" The psychologist spread his hands and shrugged.

Paschek rose. "Thanks for your assistance. Anything else you can think of that might be significant?"

The counselor pursed his lips. "There was something. It's probably nothing, but it did seem odd. Ms. Sampson had on a couple of occasions asked about the long-term effects of child abuse. She denied any real concerns about this, and when I pressed her on why she needed to know, she said it was for a friend. She hadn't brought it up recently, so I thought it was no longer an issue."

"Do you still feel that way?"

"No, I'm afraid that now, I'm not so sure."

TWENTY-FOUR

"Villainy, villainy, villainy!"
Othello, Act V, Scene II

"Is that it?" Derek pointed out the passenger window at a farm.

Rebecca shook her head. "No, that's the Hendry place." *Nice to be the one who knows her way around for once.* "The McKennys live another mile or two down the road. If I have my bearings right, the Sampson house is a couple miles east of here. We would have passed it if we'd driven straight out from town, but I prefer coming this way. More paved roads."

Moments later, they turned into a different yard and drove past a row of poplar trees. The small two-story house was spotless but somber. The exterior had been painted a dull gray, and every window was obscured by curtains of the same uncompromising shade. The lawn was meticulously trimmed, but the flower beds were devoid of color. Instead of daisies or pansies, they were filled with a thick, low shrub with a silver tint to its leaves. Even the car parked in front of the house was gray.

"Not very cheerful," Derek said.

"I'm guessing that means we're at the right place." She shot him a wry grin as she pushed open her car door. They were starting to walk toward the house when the door opened and the McKennys stepped out onto the porch. Samuel McKenny stood with his hands on his hips. Tabitha McKenny stayed behind her husband.

McKenny's face was grim. "What do you want?"

Rebecca smiled and stepped forward, her hand outstretched. "Mr. McKenny, I'm Rebecca Andrychuk, a lawyer from town."

"I know who you are," McKenny said, ignoring her hand. "I asked what you wanted."

"Father," Tabitha whispered, "Shouldn't we offer them tea?"

"No. I don't think we should." He sent a heated look at Derek. "I also know who and what you are. Helping me get her body doesn't change anything. You're still the one who let Jennifer die."

"Mr. McKenny, I'm sorry for—" Derek started to reply.

Jennifer's father threw up a hand to stop him. "I don't want to hear any more excuses. You let her die and then you desecrated her body with your science."

"The autopsy was necessary."

"What was necessary was that you give her to me right away. Instead you cut her up. By the time we got her back, it was too late. If you had given her to me when I first asked, I could have done something. We wouldn't have lost her."

Derek cocked his head. "What do you mean? I don't understand."

"Of course you don't understand. How could you? Such mysteries are only revealed to the select."

Time to get this conversation under control. "Mr. McKenny," Rebecca said, stepping forward, "I'd like to ask you a few questions, if I might?" When the old man didn't respond, she tugged a notebook from the bag she'd slung over her shoulder. "I'll take that as a yes. How was your relationship with Jennifer?"

McKenny scowled down at her from the porch. "She was my daughter. I was her father. What more is there to say?"

"Did you get along well?"

"When she wasn't in rebellion."

"Ah." Rebecca made a note of his wording. "Do you think she was depressed?"

"Absolutely not."

"You sound very sure."

"I am. Jennifer had finally come to her senses. She was returning to us." When Rebecca raised one eyebrow, he continued. "She was going to leave that criminal and come back home at last."

"Criminal? Do you mean Tyler Sampson?"

"Who else? He seduced her away from us, and when she finally realized the truth about him, he killed her." McKenny kicked at a small stool and it clattered across the porch. "That's why you're here, isn't it? You're trying to protect him."

"Everyone is entitled to legal representation."

"We're done here. I have nothing more to say."

"Please, Mr. McKenny, a couple more questions."

"No." He thrust out an arm in the direction of Rebecca's car. "Get off my land. Now."

* * *

Paschek slapped the psychologist's files down on the passenger seat of his police cruiser and grabbed his cell phone. This whole thing was getting dirty now. Murder was bad enough, but child abuse? *It's in the blood.* Shooter's Uncle Billie had gone to federal prison. He'd still be there if he hadn't somehow faked his way out of solitary and wound up getting shanked in the exercise yard. Even cons hate child abusers.

Someone at the station answered on the third ring and Paschek demanded to speak to Marsh. When whoever it was informed him Marsh was out, Paschek snatched his hat off and smacked it against the dash. "Forget it, give me Melansen or, if he's gone, then Standingready. I don't care if he's a rookie, he's up on the case." Paschek drummed his fingers in the dashboard until the deputy came on the line. "Rookie? Listen up, get hold of Melansen and tell him I've got the files from the psychologist. All the motive we need. Have him call me ASAP, and tell him I'll be back in three…" He glanced over his shoulder. The Mason jar of green M&M's lay in the backseat. "Make that four hours. You got that?"

"Yes, sir."

"Good."

He snapped off the cell phone and shoved the transmission into drive. Real good.

* * *

"I said get off my property." Samuel McKenny clenched his fists and started down the porch stairs. Derek moved to block his path to Rebecca, but Tabitha stepped between them.

"Please, Father," she said, placing one hand on his chest and raising the other to ward off Derek, "Don't let them anger you." She cast a pleading look at Derek. "Please leave us alone. We have lost so much already."

He stared into her pale blue eyes. *Pain. And sadness.* He nodded. The medical side of his brain couldn't help but notice something else—a hint of yellow in those eyes. As he turned away, a heavy scent reached him. *A strange perfume?* Derek glanced at Rebecca, but she didn't seem to notice. She opened her mouth to speak, but when Derek touched her arm lightly, she shrugged and fell into step beside him as they retreated to her car.

"That wasn't very helpful." She snapped on her seat belt.

"I guess not." Derek watched the McKennys as they trudged into the house. Tabitha seemed overcome with weakness and stumbled on the threshold. Her husband reached out to steady her and as he did, turned and locked his eyes on Derek's. The look struck him like a wave buffeting the shore. *Anger and something worse.* Derek looked away.

Something behind a large shed caught his gaze. There, partially obscured by a grove of trees, was a vehicle.

A black truck.

* * *

Sheriff Paschek scrutinized the low brick building, hoping someone would appear at one of the care home's windows. No one did. He slumped against the side of his car, his teeth clenched and his eyes screwed shut. He barely breathed.

He slammed his fist against his bad leg and sucked in air through his teeth as the jolt of pain coursed up his spine. He raised his hand for another blow, but stopped. *Enough.* There was work to do.

Sliding onto the driver's seat of the police cruiser, he tossed another Mason jar onto the back seat, identical to the one he had brought with him from Stockton, except for one thing.

This one was empty.

* * *

Rebecca was quiet as she drove. She'd hoped to get more out of the McKennys, but it was hard to see past the old man's anger. She replayed every line of their conversation in her mind, searching for any hidden meaning. Glancing over at Derek, she caught him watching her closely. He blushed and looked away. Rebecca smiled.

"Sorry I wasn't more help," he said.

"No worries. McKenny wasn't going to give us anything, at least not intentionally."

"What do you mean?"

"He doesn't trust us. He doesn't trust many people. I didn't expect him to tell us much, but I was hoping he'd let something slip."

"I guess I wasn't very good bait."

Rebecca laughed. "You did manage to bait him into nearly socking you."

"Which definitely was not my intention."

She stared out the front windshield. A sign informed her that Stockton was a mile away. "Thanks, by the way."

"For what?"

"For stepping in when McKenny got threatening. I appreciated it." She bit her bottom lip and glanced over at Derek. "It felt good to be protected."

"My pleasure."

Their eyes locked, and they both smiled.

The remainder of their drive was quiet. As she pulled up to Derek's apartment building and stopped the car, he cleared his throat. "Thanks for including me in this. I'm glad to be doing something—to help Tyler, I mean."

Rebecca propped an elbow on the console, leaned a bit closer to him. "You're welcome."

"Uh, yeah." He coughed and shifted on his seat. "Can you tell me anything else about the McKennys? Is Tabitha sick?"

"Not that I know of, although I really don't know them well. Most of what I've heard is town gossip." Rebecca straightened. "Old Sam and Tabitha are quite the couple, that's for sure. Weird how she calls him Father all the time. The old guy inherited a few square miles of ranch land north of here from his grandfather. Too dry for wheat and too small for cattle, and McKenny didn't know anything about either. So, he opened a small church. Struggled along for a few years until they found oil on his land. He used some of the proceeds from that to build a bigger church in town. That was before I came to Stockton. I guess it did pretty well for a while, but it's died off the last couple of years."

"How come?"

"Who knows? Maybe because McKenny likes to run everything himself. I don't know a lot about churches."

"I should ask my pastor. He might know."

"Pastor Josh?"

"You know him?"

Rebecca twisted her fingers together. "I might have met him once—or maybe heard his name. I don't know." She took hold of the steering wheel. "I better get going. I have work to do."

"Sure, I understand." Derek climbed out of the car. "I'll talk to you later."

He started down the sidewalk. *Don't let him go.* Blowing out a breath, Rebecca lowered her window. "Hey, do you want to get together this evening? For coffee, maybe? To discuss the case, I mean?"

Derek stopped and faced her. "I'd like to but…" He ran a hand over his dark hair. "I have to work at eight. I really should get some sleep."

She waved a hand through the air. "Hey, don't worry. Maybe some other time." Should she suggest they go somewhere now and have supper? That might still give him enough time to sleep. *No, don't push it. Give it time.* "I'll call you tomorrow."

Derek smiled. "That would be fine."

As Rebecca drove away, she contemplated him in her rearview mirror. *Fine? It won't just be fine, Doctor Kessler. It'll be a lot better than that.*

* * *

"We've got plenty now," Paschek said as he slapped the file down on the desk.

Detective Melansen sipped his tea calmly. Outside the station, the Monday-evening traffic was light, the town quiet and peaceful. "Give it to me again. I want to be sure there's no loose ends."

"Okay, if you insist, we'll go over it once more." Paschek clasped his hands behind his back. "Jennifer Sampson was murdered. Forensics confirmed the presence of ethylene glycol in her system. It was also in her glass of lemonade, but not in the pitcher. Nasty stuff. Odorless, colorless, but really sweet-tasting."

"Which the sourness of the lemonade would counteract."

"Exactly."

"How would that affect someone who ingested it?"

"I've done a little research on that. Initially the victim would act drunk and then pass out. The poison starts shutting down organs. The lungs, the kidneys, then the heart. Messes up the blood somehow. If you don't get treatment immediately, you're dead."

"And in Stockton…"

"There's no way to detect the stuff, let alone treat it."

"Still, it could have been suicide. Or an accident."

"No note, no evidence of depression, and it would be difficult to add gas line antifreeze to your glass by mistake."

"Agreed. But why the husband?"

"It all fits." Paschek continued striding across the office. Three steps to the door. Three steps back. "He had motive. Their marriage was falling apart, and Jennifer was leaving him. The psychologist and her parents confirmed that. She'd be taking the little girl. Good thing, too. Especially with the hints that Ainge joker dropped about possible abuse. More motive."

Melansen clasped his hands behind his head. "Means?"

"The gas line antifreeze was in his garage. I don't buy that cock-and-bull story of him having trouble last winter with his truck and then bumping into the stuff at the hardware store and spontaneously picking it up."

"That is weak, for sure. And what about opportunity?"

"No credible alibi or witnesses, and lots of time to drive home and back to the hotel. The info Standingready extracted from the kid who cut their grass confirms it. His truck was there that morning." Paschek stopped pacing and slammed his hand down on the file. "And then, there's the letter. Jennifer Sampson's own words. She knew he was planning to kill her."

Melansen drained the last of his tea. "That should be enough. Go ahead and pick up Tyler Sampson." He pulled a folded piece of paper from his shirt pocket and tossed it onto the desk. "You'll want this."

Paschek took the document and shook his head. "A warrant. When did you get this?"

"This afternoon, while you were strolling back from Helena. I know you, Eugene. You say you've got the motive, I believe you. So did the DA."

"Then why put me through this song and dance?"

"Shoot, you know I like everything neat and tidy." Melansen stood and headed for the door. "Besides, I like to hear you talk."

* * *

Derek sat up on the couch and grabbed his phone to check the time. Sleep wasn't coming, and he had a few hours before his shift. He glanced toward his kitchen and grunted. He needed to eat something, but there was no way he was cooking. Might as well go grab something. As he reached for his keys, his mind wandered to Tyler Sampson. Why not make it takeout for two? With a kid's meal.

He texted Tyler and was glad when the young man accepted his offer. Tyler wasn't at the Vermettes' anymore but had returned to his own place. The police had finished with the house late Sunday, and he was happy to get Olivia back in her own room. The whole thing had been rough on the little girl, and a treat like a burger and fries might cheer her up. Derek assured him the address he had texted would be enough to make sure his GPS got him there.

When Derek pulled into the yard, Tyler was sitting on the front steps watching his daughter play on the front lawn. Grabbing the bags of fast food, Derek brandished them high in the air as he stepped from the car. Tyler laughed and lifted his hand to wave. The smile vanished from Tyler's face and the hand froze in midair. Derek looked over his shoulder. A second vehicle had followed him in. It was Sheriff Paschek.

* * *

Paschek adjusted his gun belt as he stepped from the cruiser. Motioning Deputy Standingready to follow, he narrowed his eyes slightly and moved toward the house. He ignored the ER physician and stopped in front of Tyler. Olivia Sampson ran up the stairs from the yard and wrapped her arms around her father's leg.

"It's time, Shooter."

"What do you want this time, Sheriff?" Tyler lifted his daughter into his arms. The little girl whimpered and buried her face in his neck.

"Okay, we'll be formal about it," Paschek said. "Tyler Sampson, you are under arrest for the murder of Jennifer Sampson."

The color drained from Tyler's face, and he slowly closed his eyes. He seemed to be holding his breath. He hugged Olivia closer and opened his eyes. "My daughter…?"

"Child and Family Services will be here in a minute. They will determine the best place for her."

Tyler's shoulders slumped. "The McKennys?"

"Likely. They're the kid's grandparents."

"Couldn't she go to Isabel's?"

"Not my call. Or yours." Paschek touched his gun belt again. "Now we're going to put the cuffs on you and wait for the social worker." The sheriff took a step back. Tyler came down the stairs and set Olivia on the ground.

Keeping his right hand on his gun, Paschek motioned with his left. "Come on, Shooter, you know the drill. Turn around. Feet apart. Hands behind your back."

Once Tyler had assumed the position, Standingready stepped forward and snapped the handcuffs in place. The deputy turned Tyler back around as Olivia clutched at him and began to cry. "This is wrong," Derek said from behind Paschek. "He didn't do it."

Paschek turned. "Is that so?"

"He's innocent. I know it."

"Oh, you know it." Paschek jabbed a finger into the center of Derek's chest. "You. You know. That he's innocent. And how is that, doc? You a great detective? Sherlock Holmes? Maybe Miss Marple?"

Derek was forced to take a step backward. "I just know."

"Maybe you do know something." Paschek moved closer to Derek and lowered his voice. "Maybe you knew beforehand. Was it a coincidence that you were working the ER on Thursday? Or did your friend Tyler know you'd be there?" The sheriff leaned in, his voice a harsh whisper in Derek's ear. "How hard did you really try to save Jennifer?"

"What?" Derek recoiled but was trapped against the hood of his car. "That's ridiculous. I had nothing to do with it."

Paschek stepped back and raised his palms toward the physician. "Never said you did, Doc. Never said you did." His smile was feral. "Now, why don't you stay out of my way?" Paschek spun around and strode forward to loom over Tyler. "You're going to jail, Shooter. As soon as the social worker's here for the girl." He clapped a hand down on Tyler's shoulder. "And, you know what, you ain't never getting out." The sheriff straightened and looked over his shoulder. He caught Derek's eye. "Never."

TWENTY-FIVE

*"For, as thou urgest justice, be assured thou shalt
have justice, more than thou desirest."*
The Merchant of Venice, Act IV, Scene I

The staff from Child and Family Services had arrived. Derek remained frozen to the hood of his car, watching as Tyler tried to calm his daughter before sending her into the house with the social workers. As the door closed, Paschek motioned for Tyler to stand.

"Time to go."

Standingready helped Tyler to his feet and the trio moved to the police cruiser. As they passed, Derek pushed away from the vehicle. "I'm sorry, Tyler."

The younger man glanced at Derek as he shuffled by. "Keep praying for me."

Paschek placed a hand on Tyler's upper back and pushed, hard enough to make him stumble. "Get in the car." Standingready steadied the prisoner and then eased Tyler into the back seat. Paschek's face was hard when he glared at Derek. "You know something? He's going to need all the prayers he can get, so you keep at it." He spat on the ground and reached for the car door. "Not that it's going to do any good."

* * *

Rebecca was locking her office door when her cell phone rang. Call display was working just fine, and she smiled as she walked to her car. "Hi, Derek, I thought you'd be sleeping. Night shift and all that."

"I would be, except I had to let you know that Tyler's been arrested."

Rebecca set her briefcase on the hood of her car. "You've got to be kidding me." She exhaled loudly. "Actually, I believe it. That's typical of Paschek. Doesn't surprise me at all. Nothing I can do tonight, but I'll contact the court first thing in the morning to see when we can get a bail hearing."

"Will they let him out? The sheriff seemed pretty certain."

"Don't worry. I think most of the evidence is pretty shaky. I'll have to call the DA to find out what else they have. Full disclosure and all that."

"I hope you're right."

"Where'd they send the little girl?"

"Child and Family Services took her. I'm not sure where she'll end up. Maybe with the McKennys?"

"Okay, I'll try to check on that, too. If Tyler calls, I'll let him know. You can do the same if he rings you. When does your shift start?"

"Pretty soon. I have to be at the hospital in an hour."

"Okay, I'll be reviewing the file tonight, but there won't be a lot to do until I find out what Paschek's got."

"Will you need money for Tyler's bail?"

"Depends what the judge sets it at. If the charge is a murder one, could be a bit steep. I'll try to find a good bondsman to deal with."

"As long as they let him out. I still believe he's innocent."

"I do as well. Okay, talk to you later. Bye." She slumped against the side of her car. Was she up to this? A capital murder case? The air suddenly felt hot and stale.

Her cell phone rang again, but this time her smile vanished when she saw the name.

Philip.

* * *

Work was a relief. Mind-numbing and repetitive, but a relief. It was past midnight when Derek released the last patient with a simple head cold into the night. He propped his feet on the desk and had just started to lean back when Maggie LaPerriere appeared over him.

"Sorry, Dr. Kessler, but I need you to come with me to the pharmacy."

"Now? What's up?"

"A cancer patient has delirium. He tore off his fentanyl patch. The ward needs a new one, or he'll be in severe pain before morning."

"Can't they just tape the old one back on?"

"Afraid not. He dropped it in the toilet."

The pharmacy wasn't far from the ER. Maggie unlocked the door and strode to the narcotics cabinet. She or one of the other nursing supervisors could take anything else from the night cupboard, but narcotics required a witness and two signatures. She unlocked the cabinet and pulled out the record book as a nurse appeared in the doorway.

"Maggie, we need you. Carol's doing a delivery, and another girl's come in. The baby's starting to crown."

"Where's Dr. Jamison?"

"Flat tire. We need you now."

Maggie glanced at Derek, but he quickly raised both hands. "Hey, you've delivered a lot more babies than I have. Go ahead. I'll take care of things here."

Fentanyl patch, 50 micrograms, one patch. Derek signed the ledger and slid it back into the cabinet. He'd have to get Maggie to counter sign it later. Closing the doors, he headed out of the pharmacy and stopped to double check that the door was locked.

Can't be too careful.

* * *

The condo was dark. Rebecca sat unmoving on the sofa, staring into nothingness. The phone rang again. She had muted her cell phone, but he hadn't stopped calling. She gritted her teeth and watched as it went to voice mail. Her hand moved on its own. It hit the playback button, daring her to give in.

"C'mon, babe, I know you're there. Pick up the phone. Damn it, you think I'm going to keep calling forever? Last chance, babe."

The call light flashed again. She grabbed the cell phone, almost knocking the end table over. It was a struggle to control her breathing.

"Philip?"

* * *

It wasn't quiet for long. A carload of teenagers had missed a curve and spun into a tree. The injuries were all minor, but they kept him busy. Maggie was still tied up delivering that baby and not likely to appear anytime soon. The girl he was suturing gave a yelp.

"Sorry. I'll put in more freezing."

She started to cry.

"Is it still hurting?" Derek reached for the syringe.

"I'm in so much trouble. What am I going to tell my dad?"

"It was an accident. I'm sure he'll understand."

"No, you don't get it. I was already grounded. I'm in so much trouble."

Derek thought about Tyler. *You know what? You're not the only one.*

* * *

His pager vibrated and Derek's eyes snapped open. He checked his watch as he trudged back to the ER. He'd lain down in the call room only thirty minutes before. *Hang in there, shift's almost over.*

Maggie hovered over a middle-aged man on a stretcher.

"What's up, Maggie?"

"Forty-four-year-old male with central chest pain into his jaw for about an hour. We're running a twelve lead right now."

"Any meds?"

"The paramedics gave him sub-ling nitro and a couple ASA to chew. Pain's decreased but still 6 out of 10."

"Okay, start a nitro drip, and give 5 of morphine." He placed a hand on the man's arm and smiled. "You'll feel better soon, sir."

"Don't kid me, Doc," the man replied with a grimace. "My dad died at forty-two. I've been waiting for this. It's my heart, ain't it?"

Derek took the electrocardiogram from Maggie and studied it. "Looks like it. But things are different now. We can dissolve the clot and prevent damage. You got yourself in here quick enough."

The man grabbed Derek's hand. "I got three kids, Doc. I don't wanna die."

"I'll do everything I can." He hesitated before squeezing the man's hand. "Would it be all right if I prayed for you?"

"Yeah. Thanks, Doc, that'd mean a lot."

* * *

The sun was up, and Rebecca was awake. No alarm had assaulted her with its harsh noise. No pager had annoyed her with its false cheerfulness. She was simply awake. She blinked in the morning sun and stretched. *What day is it? Tuesday.* It promised to be a good day. She smiled and sat up. Picking up her phone, she scrolled to her day planner and reviewed the schedule. She needed to find out when Tyler's bail hearing would be, but it shouldn't be a problem. Tyler had no record of criminal activity, and the evidence against him was all circumstantial. Piece of cake. She'd have to go over everything with him in more detail and make sure she hadn't missed anything. Maybe talk to Derek again.

Laughter bubbled up. First she had something more important to do. Switching to her contact list, she highlighted Philip's name and number, and then hit the erase button.

* * *

The patient was feeling better. Whether it was the morphine, the nitro drip, or the prayer, Derek couldn't say, but as he took the chart and headed out of the exam room, he smiled. Whatever it was, it felt good. As he reached the doorway, a commotion from the hallway snapped his head around. The young ward clerk stood with her eyes wide and mouth open in the midst of a pile of charts scattered around the floor at her feet. Farther down the hallway, Derek caught a glimpse of a rapidly departing figure in a long white coat. Derek shifted his attention back to the clerk. She looked as if she might burst into tears.

"You all right? Let me help." He crouched and started gathering up the papers.

"It was Dr. Cudworth." The young woman's face flushed red. "He almost ran me over." Her hue deepened to crimson. "And what he said."

Derek straightened and handed her the last few charts. "Cudworth? What was he doing in the ER? There are no surgical cases I'm aware of."

"I saw him come in the ambulance entrance. I think he parks around the corner. You know, where all the trees are? He sometimes cuts through the ER to the wards."

"So why the hurry?"

"He didn't seem in a rush at first. I saw him pulling on his white coat as he came in, and then he stood outside one of the exam rooms for a couple of minutes. As if he was watching something. Then all of sudden, he took off like his tail was on fire. Did he ever look mad. Knocked the charts right out of my arms and kept going."

"Which room was he standing by?"

"I think it was the one you came out of, Dr. Kessler."

Derek crossed his arms and stared at the doors leading to the rest of the hospital, until Maggie's approach broke into his troubled thoughts.

"Labs are back," she said. "They confirm an MI."

"Okay, let's start running the clot buster and get him into ICU. Once he's stable, we'll get a transfer to Great Falls for angioplasty. I'm hoping he's a good candidate for ballooning and a stent." He glanced back at the door Cudworth had run through and shook his head. Couldn't worry about that now. He had enough to do and more than enough problems already.

* * *

The spasm caught him as he stepped from his police cruiser. Paschek winced and reached down to rub his thigh. When he looked up, Detective Melansen stood by the door of the station.

The detective folded his newspaper under one arm. "How's the leg?"

Paschek gritted his teeth. "It only hurts when I laugh."

"Not very much, then."

"Sounds about right."

"Seriously, are the bullet fragments still in there?"

"Yes." Paschek limped toward him.

Melansen reached out and squeezed his arm. "Why don't you get them removed? I'm sure it'd hurt a lot less."

"Maybe I want them there. Maybe I deserve the pain."

"You weren't to blame. No one was."

Paschek stared into the other man's eyes and then down at the hand still holding his arm. "That's your opinion." Melansen dropped his hand and followed him into the building. Paschek strode toward his office, stopping to glare at the deputy manning the front desk. "Where's Marsh? Where's the rookie?"

The man bolted upright. "Deputy Marsh is off duty today, Sheriff."

"And…?"

The man swallowed hard. "Uh… that is, Deputy Standingready went to get coffee for you, sir."

Paschek grunted. "All right, then. Tell him to bring it to my office right away. You hear?" Without waiting for an answer, he pulled open his door and waved Melansen in.

"Are you going to Sampson's bail hearing?" Melansen asked as he settled onto one of the chairs.

"No need. Everything's been handled."

"Do you think he'll make bail?"

For the first time that morning, Sheriff Paschek smiled. "Not a chance. Our friend Shooter is not going anywhere."

* * *

The morning sun was harsh on his eyes, and he could already feel the heat rising from the pavement. Derek yawned and strode away from the hospital exit. The only thing he wanted and needed right now was sleep.

"Dr. Kessler?"

He groaned and gritted his teeth. Another voice calling him back to purgatory. What order had he forgotten to sign, or what form did he need to finish? He stopped and turned with an effort. It wasn't a nurse.

"Dr. Kessler, may I speak to you, please?"

Who was she? Medical records? Therapies? No uniform, no white coat. He rubbed his eyes. "What's this about?"

"I'd rather not discuss that here, Doctor. Would you be able to come up to my office?"

Office? Maybe admin, then. "Now? Look, Ms...."

"Antosh. I know we haven't spoken in a while, and I've been meaning to make the effort to have more contact with the medical staff, but, well, you know how hectic things get around here."

Antosh? Julia Antosh? The CEO of the health district? *Ooops.* "I'm sorry, Ms. Antosh. I'm coming off a heavy night shift, and I've had virtually no sleep for the past couple of days. Could this wait until a little later? This afternoon, maybe?"

The woman frowned. "I suppose, but be at my office by three. I don't want to have to refer this to the Medical Liaison Committee. I'd rather try to deal with the complaint myself."

That woke him up. "Complaint?"

She had already spun around and strutted back into the hospital. Derek could only watch her go as the thought echoed through his mind. *Complaint?*

TWENTY-SIX

"Men at some times are masters of their fate: The fault, dear
Brutus, is not in our stars, but in ourselves."
Julius Caesar, Act I, Scene II

She was the first one at the office. Rebecca couldn't remember when
that had happened last. No, she could remember. It had never
happened. Having even thought to pick up muffins and start the coffee
brewing, she was feeling pretty proud of herself. Rebecca leaned back in
her chair and smiled.

"Okay, who are you, and what have you done with my boss?"

Paulina stood in the doorway, her hands on her hips.

"Ha ha, very funny. Just eat your muffin." Rebecca straightened the
files on her desk. "Did you get Tyler to sign that release of information
form?"

"Did it right after lunch yesterday. I've got it right here."

"Excellent. Fax it off to that psychologist, Ainge or whatever his
name is, and then get him on the line. I want to talk to him before he
hears that Tyler's been charged and starts getting cold feet."

"Anything else?"

"Yeah, what time is Tyler's bail hearing?"

"It should be early. I don't think much else happened over the weekend. I'll call the courthouse to find out."

Rebecca powered up her desktop and logged into the state law library so she could review case files and articles on bail hearings involving capital crimes. Jotting notes on a legal pad, she nodded. *Tyler should be out of jail within a day or two.* She reached out and flicked on the intercom. "Paulina, I need names and numbers for a couple of bail bondsmen. Have you got hold of Ainge yet? When's the bail hearing? And who…"

"I'm right here."

Rebecca looked up as Paulina handed her a cup of coffee. "Oops, sorry. Did you get through to Ainge?"

"No, not yet. His answering machine says he won't be in until nine. I'll keep trying. In the meantime, I've brought you a list of all the bail bondsmen in the county. I underlined the two with the best reputations."

"That's fantastic, Paulina." Rebecca took a long sip of her coffee. "How do you know which ones are good?"

"Let's just say that I love my husband dearly, but I could do without his relatives."

"Got you. When's Tyler's hearing?"

"That's a bit of a problem. The hearing is at half past nine in Judge Winslow's court. Do you want to me to wait and contact the psychologist afterward?"

Rebecca grimaced. "No, if the DA or Paschek calls him before I do, he might not talk to me. I need that information." She glanced at her watch. Ten to nine. "Give me his number, and I'll keep trying on my cell. I'll reach him before court." She set her coffee down and rubbed her eyes. "I hope."

* * *

Derek felt as though he were swimming through oatmeal. His movements seemed to be getting slower by the minute. His mouth was full of cotton balls, and his eyes had been scrubbed with sandpaper. The fatigue hung over him, weighing his body down like an iron shroud, but his mind wouldn't stop.

The hot shower hadn't helped, and the breakfast burrito he had grabbed on the way home was making things worse. Derek sat up on the edge of his bed, yawned and stretched, then laid back down and rolled over. With an effort, he focused his eyes on the clock. It was almost nine, and he still couldn't stop thinking.

Tyler. Olivia. Paschek. Their faces rolled through his mind like boulders down a steep hill. One other face crashed against his psyche with even greater regularity. Rebecca. He buried his face in the pillow and groaned. What was he supposed to do? What would Cassie do?

Give it to God. Trust in the Lord.

He stiffened and then relaxed. A mumbled prayer slipped from his lips. His joints began to unlock, his muscles to unwind. He let out a slow, deep breath.

And drifted off.

* * *

"Dr. Ainge? This is Rebecca Andrychuk. I'm a lawyer from Stockton. I'm calling on behalf of my client, Tyler Sampson, to ask you a few questions about his late wife, Jennifer. Do you have a minute?"

"I already went over all this with that policeman. The sheriff was here yesterday." His tone of voice made it clear what he'd thought of the man.

"I understand." Rebecca jotted down a note. *Didn't like Paschek. Good.* "However, I would appreciate it if you could answer a couple more questions for me. It's quite important to my client."

"Does it have to be right now? I have a very busy schedule."

"Please, Dr. Ainge. I really need this information."

He blew out a breath. "Very well. Before we begin, the police had a court order for my files. What do you have? I'm sure you are aware of the need for me to have legal protection."

"Oh yes," Rebecca said. "My secretary faxed a document to you earlier signed by Jennifer Sampson's next of kin, her husband Tyler. It gives you permission to release your information to me. I assure you it is all quite legal."

Ainge sniffed loudly. "Yes, yes, here it is. Perhaps I could fax my notes to you?"

"That would be helpful, but I do need to ask you a few things as well." Rebecca kept her voice warm and friendly. *Don't push him too hard or he'll clam up.* This guy needed a little encouragement. "You will, of course, send me a bill for your time and effort. I realize that as a professional your time is valuable, and we want to show our appreciation."

"I suppose that would be acceptable," Ainge said. Rebecca smiled. *That got his attention.* "What would you like to know?"

"Thank you, Doctor. Can you tell me about Jennifer Sampson's relationship with the men in her life? Her husband and her father?"

"Certainly. Jennifer was quite conflicted over her relationship with her husband. On one hand, she felt that he was a good provider and seemed to care for her, on the other she felt stifled in the relationship."

"How so?"

"Jennifer had come to recognize that she had never developed and grown into her own person. She was always under someone else, first her father and then her husband. She needed to exercise independence so that she could fully find herself."

"Meaning?"

"She needed to be on her own. To stand on her own two feet."

"I see. Was she contemplating a divorce?"

"Yes, she was. Jennifer had finally worked up enough courage to leave her husband. She no longer had any deep feelings for him and was ready to break away. Unfortunately, she still lacked the strength of will to embrace her own independence."

"Can you explain?"

"She was contemplating a move back in with her parents. Jennifer believed it would be temporary, but I feared she might fall back under the influence of her father."

"And that would be bad because…?"

"It was obvious to me that Samuel McKenny had previously tried to exert total control and dominance over his daughter. I felt that he would try to again, which would stifle her growth." He was silent for a few seconds. When he spoke again, his voice was softer. "There was something else."

"Go on."

"I could never quite put my finger on it, and Jennifer wasn't forthcoming, but I had the impression that something was off."

"Off?"

"Wrong. Sinister, even."

"Sinister? That's pretty dramatic, isn't it?"

"Perhaps. Maybe I'm overstating it, but it troubled me. Something about Jennifer's relationship with her father or her husband. Possibly involving her daughter, I couldn't tell." His voice changed again, regaining its authoritative tone. "As her therapist, I could only take her so far. I believe that she was beginning to find herself, but she had not—how to put it—arrived yet."

Rebecca finished her notes and underlined the word sinister. "Thank you for your assistance, Dr. Ainge. It's been helpful."

"Oh, but surely you want to know the rest?"

"The rest?"

"Yes. You had asked about Jennifer's relationship with the men in her life. I assumed you meant all of them."

"Excuse me?"

"There was one more. Jennifer Sampson had a relationship with another man."

* * *

She was late. Rebecca's conversation with Ainge had taken longer than expected, but it had been worth it. Rebecca hurried into the courtroom to take her place beside Tyler.

Judge Winslow scowled down at her. "You're late, Miss Andrychuk."

"I'm sorry, Your Honor. It won't happen again."

"I suppose you want to confer with your client."

"Yes, Your Honor, if I may."

"Two minutes." The judge pulled his bifocals off and began polishing the lenses. "Not a second more."

"Thank you, Your Honor." She sank onto the chair and leaned close to Tyler. He looked pale and drawn in the orange prison garb. Dark shadows underlined his eyes, and coarse stubble covered his chin. "How are you holding up?"

It seemed to take Tyler a moment to focus on her face. "Where's Livy?"

"She's with Child and Family Services. They'll rule on where she goes once we're done here."

"Will they let her come home?"

"I don't know. They're a kingdom unto themselves. No way to predict what they will do."

"I need to make sure she's safe."

Rebecca covered his pale hand with hers and squeezed it. "I understand. First, let's get you out of jail. I have a bail bondsman lined up. As soon as the judge sets the amount, I'll set everything up."

His nod was barely perceptible. "Okay."

"Miss Andrychuk." Winslow's voice was strident. "Are you ready to proceed?"

Rebecca stood and smoothed her skirt. "Yes, Your Honor."

"Very well. In the case of the People vs. Tyler Sampson, the charge is first degree murder. I've reviewed the facts of the case, and I'm prepared to rule on bail. Any questions? Comments?"

That was quick. "Yes, Your Honor. Mr. Sampson is regularly employed with Black Steel Oil. He has a home to maintain and a young daughter to support. He has no history of violence and does not pose a threat to the community. I request that bail be set at a reasonable amount."

Winslow turned to the District Attorney. "You have anything to add, Mr. Chartrand?"

"No, George—I mean, Your Honor. Nothing more than what I presented to you while we were waiting for my esteemed colleague." He offered Rebecca an oily smile. She gritted her teeth and looked back at Winslow.

"Don't worry, Miss Andrychuk, I'll explain," the judge said. "Your client does have a history of petty theft and driving while under the influence. There have been several episodes of violence, though I will grant, no charges resulted. I have a bigger concern, however." He picked up a sheet of paper and peered over the top of his glasses. "The DA has provided me with this affidavit, signed by witnesses, testifying that three days ago your client was overheard stating that, given the chance, he would flee to Canada."

Rebecca blinked. "Are you certain?"

"The bailiff will give you a copy of the statement. As you will see, on Friday Mr. Sampson was heard saying that he would go to Canada."

Not good. She touched Tyler's shoulder as the bailiff walked over. "What's that about?"

The young man stared at the paper. "I don't get it. Wait, at the snack bar downtown? I was with Derek. We were talking about stuff."

"Did you say something about Canada?"

Tyler scratched his head. "No. No, I didn't. Nothing like that."

"Your Honor, I object." Rebecca faced the bench. "Surely, this is hearsay."

"Perhaps, but this is a bail hearing and not a trial. I am convinced that Mr. Sampson is a flight risk." He slammed his gavel down. "Bail is denied."

"Your Honor!"

Winslow rapped the bench with his gavel again and then pointed it at Rebecca. "Watch your tone, Counselor. Mr. Sampson will be transferred to the Glacier County Jail, pending trial."

Although she wanted to scream, Rebecca worked to keep her voice level. "Your Honor, I would request that Mr. Sampson be held here in Stockton, so I can confer with him regularly. I need to build my case."

"Cut Bank is only forty-five minutes away, Miss Andrychuk."

"I know, Your Honor, but I will need to speak with my client frequently over the next few days."

The District Attorney cleared his throat. "Your Honor, the State has no objection to this. The local cells are less comfortable than County, but if that's what Ms. Andrychuk wants, I'm okay with it."

"Very well, I'll let you make the arrangements with the sheriff. Court is adjourned. Bailiff, bring me the file on the next case."

Rebecca gripped Tyler's arm. "Don't worry, we'll appeal. This is just wrong."

A county deputy took Tyler by the elbow and pulled him to his feet. Tyler grabbed Rebecca's sleeve as the police officer started to lead him away. "Donuts," he said. "We were talking about donuts."

Rebecca lifted her hand. "It'll be all right. Just a few days. I'm sure once I launch an appeal, they'll have to grant bail."

Tyler nodded as the deputy jerked him toward the side exit. His gaze drifted to the back of the courtroom and the color drained from his face. Rebecca pivoted in her chair. The McKennys were seated in the last row, their faces hard and cold. Granite and ice. Samuel McKenny's finger was a gnarled dart that he stabbed at Tyler's retreating form.

His heated glare found Rebecca. The anger blew around her like a desert wind. McKenny jabbed his finger again, aiming at her heart this time. Rebecca swallowed hard and looked away, struggling to slow her breathing. When she looked back, the McKennys were gone.

* * *

Derek bolted upright and wiped his face with his hands in a vain attempt to push the cobwebs from his mind. Why had he set his alarm? He'd only been asleep a few hours and his next shift wasn't until late. He peered at his phone through hooded eyes. Two fifteen. What was so important? The memory was slow but persistent. A meeting with administration. Something about a complaint.

No getting out of this one. He uncoiled from the bed and headed to the bathroom. A quick shower and a cup of coffee and he might be awake enough to face the health district's CEO. What else could go wrong?

Moments later, he thought he heard his phone ringing. He turned off the shower and listened intently. *Nothing. Must have been mistaken.* He turned the water back on.

* * *

He must be sleeping. If so, he'd likely turned the ringer off on his phone. Rebecca disconnected the call. She'd been waiting to phone Derek since she'd gotten back from the courthouse. Her failure to get Tyler bail had gnawed at her through the mundane legal matters that had filled her appointment book. She needed to do something.

She had spent as much time as she could between appointments preparing a draft for the appeal. Now she needed Derek to confirm the context of Tyler's comments. Surely they had not been planning an escape route north. The appeal court would believe her. She hoped.

She had a lot more to do to prepare Tyler's defence. Ainge had said Jennifer was involved with another man. Rebecca ran a hand over the faxed copy of Jennifer Sampson's file. Dr. Ainge's notes were all neatly typed. Clear and concise, they covered everything the two of them had discussed. Almost everything. There was no mention of another man in the reports. Rebecca tapped a finger on the report. When she had asked him if he had told the police about it, he'd said no, they hadn't asked. Besides, the sheriff had not appreciated the intricacies of his analysis. *What a piece of work.* She did appreciate him telling her about this mystery man. Once she'd found out Jennifer's friend existed, it wasn't hard to find out his name. At least it hadn't been hard for Paulina. Gossip was the official language of Stockton, and Paulina was a master of it.

Now Rebecca needed to check the man out. She felt the need to confront the McKennys again, but after the way the old man had looked at her in the courtroom, she didn't want to go alone. Derek could wait in the car. Backup, so to speak. That way he'd be there if she needed him.

But now he wasn't available. Rebecca wasn't sure of his schedule and didn't know when he worked again. Besides, was it really fair to expect him to be her bodyguard? He was a busy doctor, not a bouncer. How could she ask him to put up with another of Samuel McKenny's tirades? Time for her to buck up and do what needed to be done.

She stuck her head out the office door. "Anything more today, Paulina?"

"You were supposed to finish the new will for Tony Mendoza."

"Again? Didn't we do a rewrite three months ago?"

"He's got a new sweetheart at the nursing home. And you promised the Braydons you'd have their real estate package done."

"Yes, by the end of the week."

"Also, the town clerk has an appointment to see you in an hour."

"Not more stuff on parking ordinances."

Paulina wagged her finger. "You took the contract. You need to do the work."

Rebecca closed her eyes and leaned her forehead against the door frame. "You gotta be kidding me. Really not in the mood for that today." She rubbed her eyes and then peeked through her fingers at her secretary.

Paulina had crossed her arms and was tapping her foot. "All right," she said, "I'll have the real estate paperwork ready for you tomorrow, and I'll reschedule the guy from city hall. Tony can wait. He's only 87."

Rebecca grinned and grabbed her car keys. "Thanks, Paulina. Don't worry. It's all going to work out fine."

As she hurried toward the front door, Paulina flung a hand in the air. "Careful, boss. Don't do anything you might regret."

Rebecca turned the knob and shoved open the door with her hip. "I'll try. This time, I'll really try."

TWENTY-SEVEN

"He thinks too much. Such men are dangerous."
Julius Caesar, Act I, Scene II

After driving past his usual parking spot outside the ER entrance, Derek pulled into the visitor lot. Walking through the department would elicit questions from the staff he wasn't sure he wanted to answer—at least not until he knew what this complaint was about.

Administration was on the top floor of the hospital. As soon as Derek exited the stairwell, the difference from the rest of the building was obvious. The air conditioning was quieter and more efficient. The industrial linoleum gave way to plush carpet, and the decor shifted from institutional to postmodern.

The receptionist looked up as he approached. "Good afternoon, Dr. Kessler. May I help you?"

"I have a meeting scheduled with Ms. Antosh."

"Oh my, she didn't tell me. I'll see if she is available."

Derek waited until she had disappeared into the back offices before turning to study the space around him. A couple chairs had been pushed against the far wall beside a large display encouraging visitors to consider donations and bequests to the hospital foundation. A smiling photo of Simon Cudworth hovered over plans for a proposed endoscopy suite. Derek leaned in for a closer look. Cudworth's smile did not even approach his eyes.

He was so deep in thought he jumped when a voice broke the hushed silence of the office.

"Dr. Kessler? The CEO will see you now."

* * *

The house was an older split-level on the east side of Stockton. Situated on a small rise overlooking the narrow river valley, it had quite a nice view—not as good as on the west side of town, with the mountains in the distance, but nice nonetheless. Rebecca parked her Mustang and headed up the walkway to the door. It opened on the second knock to reveal a thin, dark-haired man in his late twenties. He wore a nondescript gray sweatshirt and blue jeans, and a carpenter's apron was slung over his shoulder. To the right of the doorway sat a large toolbox.

"Can I help you?"

"Are you Austin Thornwell?"

"Yeah, but I'm not taking on any new jobs right now."

Rebecca's eyebrows drew together. "Excuse me?"

"I'm sorry, but I'm swamped. I can give you the name of a couple of other tradesmen, though. What do you need? Electrical or plumbing?"

"I'm not here about anything like that. I'm Rebecca Andrychuk, a lawyer here in Stockton."

"Whoa." Thornwell held up both hands. "I know I'm a few weeks late finishing the job, but like I said, I'm swamped. There was no need for them to call a lawyer."

"Them?"

"The Dubrowskys. Isn't that who sent you? I'm about to head out to one other work site. I'll finish that job tonight and be at their place in the morning."

"I'm not here on behalf of the Dubrowskys."

"Well, that's a relief." Thornwell grabbed his toolbox and stepped out of the house. Rebecca had to move a pace back as he closed the door. "Who *are* you here for then?"

She was forced to follow as he strode toward a pickup in the driveway. Thornwell swung the toolbox into the back of the truck and tossed the carpenter's apron in after it. He leaned against the side of the vehicle, crossed his arms, and grinned. Dimples beckoned from each cheek.

"Did you know Jennifer Sampson?" Rebecca said.

The smile faded and his hands dropped to his sides. "Yeah, I knew Jennifer. I heard what happened."

"How did you know her?"

"We were friends." His jaw worked. "I used to attend her father's church. We were even in youth Bible study together."

"Did you date?"

"Ha." He waggled a finger in her face. "No dating allowed. Not that I didn't want to. Jennifer was special, but nothing happened between us back then."

"Back then? How about now?"

"Nothing then. Nothing now."

"When was the last time you saw her?"

"A few weeks ago. She phoned me up and wanted to meet. I wasn't sure if that was a good idea. She kept pushing."

"What did she want?"

"I think she was trying to reconnect. I did my best to put her off."

"You weren't interested? I thought you said she was special."

"She was. But I've moved on. I've got a girlfriend in Browning and a thriving business. I don't need any more headaches. Anyway, we only met once for coffee. Nothing else."

"Where did you met?"

"Does it matter? Nothing happened. We talked a bit, and no, I'm not getting into it. Not here. Not now."

"You said you used to attend McKenny's church. Why not anymore?"

Thornwell pushed away from the truck. "Who did you say you represented?"

"I didn't. My client is Tyler Sampson, Jennifer's husband."

"Well, I don't know him at all," he said as he moved around to the driver's side of the truck, "but I do know about his reputation. He used to be pretty wild. That was what Jennifer wanted, though."

"About the McKennys…"

"Look, I need to go to work. And there are things I'd rather not talk about. Let sleeping dogs lie, you know what I mean?" He yanked open the door to his truck and slid onto the seat.

Rebecca gripped the door frame. "I really need to ask you a few more questions."

Thornwell exhaled slowly and reached across the seat to open the glove compartment. He pulled out a business card and handed it to Rebecca. "That's my cell number. Call me later this evening, and I'll see what I can do." He started to swing the door shut, but Rebecca stood her ground.

"One more thing," she asked. "Where were you on Friday morning?"

Thornwell's eyes went hard. "Later," he said and pushed Rebecca's hand away. "I mean that. Not now. Later."

Rebecca stepped back and he slammed the door. She glanced at the card. Thornwell's Plumbing and Electrical. She studied the vehicle as he backed it out of the driveway. It was a Dodge Ram pickup with a two-tone paint job, tan on the bottom and black on the top.

* * *

The office surprised him. Derek had expected something plush and luxurious. Instead, it was designed to be efficient and workmanlike. The desk was covered with papers and dominated by a pair of computer screens while both of the visitors' chairs were weighed down by stacks of files. The wall to his right was filled with bookshelves and filing cabinets, while the left displayed a scattering of family photos and a few neutral pieces of artwork. The window behind Julia Antosh's desk overlooked the staff parking lot but did have a view of the distant mountains.

Antosh grabbed the files from one of the chairs. "Please have a seat, Dr. Kessler. Would you like coffee?"

Derek shook his head. "No, thanks. I appreciate you letting me put this off until now, but I've got to say I'm still pretty tired. I don't want to be rude or anything, but maybe we could deal with this complaint thing quickly?" He waved his hand over the desk. "I mean, I can see you're pretty busy."

Antosh shifted a pile of papers and sat down on the corner of her desk. "You're right. Things can get hectic around here." She sighed and shoved her short hair behind her ears. The chestnut waves were frosted with a touch of silver. "It's not an easy job, but I love it. Most of the time."

Derek grimaced. "I take it this is the part you don't like."

"That's right. I don't enjoy getting involved in disagreements between colleagues."

"Colleagues?"

"I'm afraid so, Doctor." Antosh took a deep breath. "We've had a complaint. From Dr. Cudworth."

His forehead wrinkled. "From Cudworth? What about?"

"Your religious activities."

Derek rolled his eyes. "You mean my praying for patients?"

"I'm afraid so. It's not that I'm opposed to it, or that there is any specific policy against it, but…"

"But Cudworth doesn't like it."

Antosh bit her lip. "I know it's been a rough time for you, Doctor. I'm sure it hasn't been easy coming here. I mean, after your family…" She clasped her manicured fingers in her lap. "Please understand, there's been trouble in the past over prayer."

"What kind of trouble?"

"A few years ago, Dr. Simon Cudworth lost a patient. He ordered an autopsy. Some religious group had been holding a prayer vigil in the patient's room, and when the orderlies came to get the body, they wouldn't let them in. We had to call the police, and there was almost a riot. The leader of the group claimed he could bring the man back to life."

Red flags popped up in his mind. "Who was it? The leader, I mean?"

"I think his name was Samuel something."

"McKenny?"

Her blue eyes widened. "Yes. That was him. It was a bad situation, and Dr. Cudworth was very upset. He threatened to press charges and McKenny threatened right back." She unclasped her fingers and picked a piece of lint off of her wool skirt. "The hospital was going through a financial crisis, and the last thing we wanted was negative publicity. We managed to quiet things down, but Dr. Cudworth has never forgotten the incident."

"Sounds like Cudworth."

She slid off the desk and stood. "Anyway, I need to ask you to let things calm down. Maybe don't be so obvious with your actions."

"Actions? Like praying for my patients?"

"Please, Dr. Kessler, you're a valuable member of our team. We'd hate to lose you."

"Meaning?"

She lifted her chin. "Dr. Cudworth is very influential around here. He is also on the committee that will recommend whether to extend your contract, or not."

Derek shifted his gaze to the window. In the distance, the mountains were shrouded in dark clouds. He rose stiffly to his feet. "I get the message."

* * *

The Mustang's engine pinged as it cooled. Rebecca had been sitting on the side of the road for more than ten minutes, going over the plan in her mind. Was it a good idea or not to visit the McKennys? Maybe she should have brought Paulina with her. Maybe she should wait for Derek. Maybe she should just forget the whole thing.

She adjusted the rear-view mirror to look herself in the eye. "Suck it up, princess." She started the car and turned down the lane to the old farmhouse.

As the Mustang rolled to a stop in front of the house, Rebecca peered through the windshield. The car she had seen earlier was missing. Was it possible no one was home? She wasn't sure whether to be disappointed or relieved. Then a curtain in the front window moved. Taking a deep breath, Rebecca pushed open the door of the car and climbed out. When she reached the door, she rapped firmly on the wood. All was quiet. She knocked again, harder this time. "Mr. McKenny? Are you there?" A rustling sound came from within the house. "I know you're there. I need to talk to you."

The door opened an inch. "You shouldn't be here," Tabitha McKenny hissed. "Father isn't here. Go away."

Rebecca shoved her foot in the crack of the door. "Please, Mrs. McKenny, I only have a couple of questions. It won't take long." The door eased open an inch farther. "We both want the same thing, don't we?"

The old woman lowered her gaze to the glossy pump wedged against her front door and blew out a breath. "I suppose you'll want tea."

The inside of the house wasn't any more colorful than the outside. Rebecca wrinkled her nose. It smelled funny. She managed a smile when Tabitha McKenny set a teacup on the table in front of her. "Thank you."

"It's Earl Grey," Tabitha said. "I don't like any of those herbal concoctions."

"This is fine." Rebecca took a sip and set the cup down. "I'd like to talk to you about your daughter."

Tabitha sat down on the hard kitchen chair across from Rebecca, her back ramrod straight. "What do you want to know?"

"I never met Jennifer. What was she like?"

"She was a strong-willed child. Rebellious. She never wanted to obey, to do what was right. She fought against Father all the time."

"Did that make Mr. McKenny angry?"

The old woman narrowed her eyes. "I know what you're trying to do. You're wrong. Father is a good man. He only does what is right. What needs to be done."

Rebecca bit her lip. "I'm sorry; I didn't mean to imply anything."

"I understand more than you think. You're a lawyer, Miss Andrychuk. I know what lawyers are like." She leaned forward and lowered her voice. "I know what you're like."

Rebecca's fingers tightened around her cup. "Excuse me?"

"Stockton's a small town, isn't it, Miss Andrychuk? One hears things. You're not married, are you? Never have been is what I've heard."

"I don't see what that has to do with anything."

"Did you think you could keep it secret? How many men you have been with? How many of them were married?"

Rebecca sucked in a deep breath through clenched teeth. "That's none of your…"

Tabitha pulled back, her face softening. "More tea, dear? Oh, you've hardly touched what you have. Don't you like tea?"

"Uh, no, I mean, yes, of course I like tea." Rebecca forced her fingers to unclench. "I'm sorry if I offended you, Mrs. McKenny. It was not my intent." A scattering of tea leaves swirled in a slow circle in her tea cup. She swallowed and met the old woman's eyes. "Please, tell me more about Jennifer. How was your relationship?"

Tabitha sipped her tea. The cup rattled against the saucer when she set it down. The silence stretched into awkwardness. Tabitha's voice was just above a whisper when she spoke at last. "It wasn't easy. She did what she wanted, no matter what I said. She hurt Father so much when she went with that boy."

"Tyler?"

"Yes. Him." She spat the word. "He was bad from the start. I knew no good would come from it."

"Do you think he did it? Killed her?"

Tabitha pushed back her shoulders. "Of course he did it. Who else could have?"

"I don't know. Was there anyone else who didn't get along with Jennifer? Who might have been angry with her? Besides Mr. McKenny, I mean."

Tabitha stood suddenly and carried the teacups to the sink. The frailty Rebecca had noted earlier seemed gone. The old woman glanced at the kitchen clock before turning. "You need to go now. Father will be home soon. You should not be here."

"Why is that such a problem? Will he be angry? Might I be in danger if he found me here?"

Tabitha folded her arms. "You should always remember, Miss Andrychuk, the world can be a dangerous place." She shuffled to the front door. "That's why it is vital to be careful, to protect the things that are important."

"Are you protecting someone, Mrs. McKenny?"

The old woman held the door open. "Goodbye, Miss Andrychuk."

TWENTY-EIGHT

"Reputation is an idle and most false imposition: oft got without merit, and lost without deserving."
Othello, Act II, Scene III

His cell phone was ringing again. Derek wanted nothing more than to grab a few hours of rest before his next shift, but it didn't seem meant to be. He grabbed the device and scowled. Some one-eight-hundred number. Likely another survey or a telemarketer trying to sell him cruise tickets. He let it ring and was about to toss the phone on the table when he noticed he'd missed a call earlier. He recognized the number. Rebecca.

Derek set the phone down and then picked it up again. She'd phoned before he had gone to see Julia Antosh. Must have been while he was in the shower. What was she calling about? Tyler's case? Or something else? He picked up his photo of Cassie and gazed at her face. She had been so beautiful. He stared at the phone and then back at the photograph. He let the phone slip from his hand and traced the crack in the photo frame's glass with his finger. A tremor moved from his hands to his shoulders.

The first tear splashed down onto the photograph.

* * *

The small window of reinforced glass in the steel door looked out over the corridor that ran past the holding cells. Two cells lined each side of the corridor, and all four were identical—six-by-eight rooms with a single cot, a small steel sink, and a toilet. There were no outside windows, nothing to break the gray sterility. All the cells were empty except one.

Standing in the corridor, Paschek peered through the glass. Through the wall of bars that fronted Tyler Sampson's cell, he could just make out the man's form lying on a cot. Of course, if he wanted a better look, he only had to study the bank of monitors outside the holding area. Every move Tyler made was watched and recorded on closed-circuit television. Nothing would be missed.

Paschek turned to the duty officer and grunted. "Open it up. Me and Shooter need to have a talk."

The buzz from the door was shrill and loud, but Tyler didn't move. Paschek strode to the cell and leaned against the bars. "Shooter. Hey, Shooter, I want to talk to you."

Tyler lay facing the wall. When he didn't respond, Paschek rapped his handcuffs against the bars. "Come on, Tyler. Don't make me come in there."

The prisoner rolled over and dropped his feet to the floor. He kept his head down.

"That's better," the sheriff said. "I've got a couple of questions for you." He pressed his lips into a grim line. "Look at me when I'm talking to you."

Tyler raised his head. The right side of his face was raw beef steak, the eye almost swollen shut, a pearl of blood clotted by his nostril.

Paschek cursed. "What happened to you?"

"I fell."

"Don't give me that crap. Who did this?"

"I got nothing to say." Tyler lowered himself back down on the cot and turned to the wall. "Nothing at all."

Paschek stalked back down the corridor and pounded on the door until it buzzed open. He shoved through the opening and leapt to tower over the duty officer. "Show me the tapes of everything since Sampson's been back in the cells." He fisted the front of the man's uniform shirt and yanked him closer. "And if anything is missing, you are going to regret it. Do I make myself clear?"

The officer blanched and nodded. "Yes, sir, Sheriff."

It didn't take long. Paschek had not been Tyler's first visitor. Someone else had already been in the holding area. The sheriff stood and clenched his fists. The visitor had even looked up and grinned at the camera as he was leaving the cell. Deputy Marsh.

* * *

Rebecca pulled the business card from her purse and dialed the number. Thornwell answered on the second ring.

"I said to call me later."

"It is later, Mr. Thornwell. You can talk to me now, or I can pass your name onto Sheriff Paschek. I think he'd be interested." She held her breath and waited.

"Fifteen minutes," he said at last. "Meet me behind the Conoco station south of town."

"Thank you, Mr. Thornwell, I'll be—" The line went dead.

* * *

She was early. Sitting in her car behind an isolated gas station waiting for someone Rebecca knew nothing about didn't seem like such a good idea once she had actually arrived. No customers were around, and she wasn't even sure if anyone was working at the gas station. Rebecca rolled down her window a couple of inches to let a little of the cool evening air waft into her vehicle. She was starting to reconsider the whole thing when Thornwell drove up in his truck.

He reached over and pushed open the passenger-side door. "Get in."

Rebecca contemplated him. *Do I really want to do this?*

"I said, get in. You wanted to talk, so let's talk." When she didn't move, he added, "Look, I can't risk being seen talking to you. This is the only way."

Rebecca sighed and climbed out of her car, dragging her purse with her. As she walked over to the truck, she slipped her hand inside the leather bag. *Good.* Her pepper spray was right there if she needed it. As soon as she closed the door, Thornwell sped out of the lot and onto a gravel road.

"Where are we going?"

"Just driving. Anywhere we won't be seen."

"You mentioned that already. Who are you afraid might see us?"

"Let's just say I wanna play it safe." He turned off onto another road. "You have questions. Ask them."

"All right, you and Jennifer were friends. Tell me about that."

Thornwell stared straight ahead and squeezed the steering wheel. "We knew each other a long time. My folks went to McKenny's church back then, and Jenn and I were in the youth group together. She hated it. It was never much fun. Sitting around singing old hymns and reading out of the Bible. I loved it 'cause Jenn was there.

"Like I said, she was special. Prettiest girl in church. Shoot, she was the prettiest girl in the county. Her smile lit up the whole room, and when she talked to you, you felt like you were the most important person around." He slowed the truck as they went over a rail crossing and then sped up again. "There was always something else there, though. Like she was sad, or scared, or something."

"Scared of what?"

"I don't know. She'd never say. I kinda thought she was scared of her dad. I know the rest of us were."

"Why?"

"McKenny's over the top. Real hellfire and brimstone kinda guy. Back then, he had a lot of influence, though. If he didn't like you, he could get a lot of people to shun you."

"Shun you?"

"If McKenny told the church to stay away from you, they did. He would ruin your business and wreck your social life. Some folks thought he could curse you and that would be the end. It ain't like that anymore."

"What happened?"

"He started getting too full of himself. Handling snakes, predicting miracles, claiming he could heal people. He even said he could raise the dead. The worst part was he started saying only he could do it. That no one else could talk to God but him. Leastways, that's what I heard."

"You weren't there anymore?"

"Nah, the snake thing kinda freaked my folks out, and we stopped going. Most other folks quit after a while when none of his claims actually came true."

"What about Jennifer?"

"I guess she was the typical PK—preacher's kid, I mean. She wanted something else. She acted as though she wanted something wild and crazy, but I think she just wanted a way out."

"Was that when she met Tyler?"

"I guess so." The truck vibrated with a brief rumble as Thornwell turned off the road and through a Texas gate. The gravel road morphed into a dirt trail, and Rebecca gripped her pepper spray more tightly.

"Where are we going?" she said.

"I wanted to avoid the highway." He reached out and tapped a small black box mounted on his dashboard. "Radar detector. Was starting to pick up a signal."

"So? You weren't speeding."

"I still wanted to avoid any cops, okay? Anyway, you were asking about Sampson. I don't really know him, but he used to have a reputation. I think Jenn went after him because of that."

"Jennifer pursued him?"

"Oh, yeah. Course, he didn't really try to escape. Like I said, Jenn was the prettiest girl around, and she knew how to get what she wanted. Seemed that what she wanted was someone the opposite of her dad."

"How did McKenny react?"

"He went ballistic. Tried to lock her in the house, keep her away from Sampson. Didn't work."

"What about after they got married?"

"The old man still hated it. He kept trying to get her to leave Sampson and come back home. I think he got worse after the little girl was born."

"Olivia?"

"Uh-huh. Funny thing is, I heard that Sampson turned out to be a good dad. Better parent than Jenn, anyway."

Rebecca cocked her head. "Really?"

"Now, look. I liked Jenn, I really cared about her, but she was full of herself. Wanted everything perfect and neat and clean. Thought her house should be like some magazine cover and that her daughter should be some perfect little princess. Jenn would throw a hissy fit if everything wasn't just so."

"You said she had gotten in touch with you recently?"

"She had. I think she wanted me to tell her that it was okay if she left her husband. She didn't like it when I told her she shouldn't, that she should make it work."

"What did she say?"

"That I didn't know the truth of it. That if I did I'd tell her to leave." The truck shuddered as they passed over another gate. "She told me others were encouraging her to go."

"What others?"

"I don't know, but I had a few ideas."

"What do you mean?"

"Let's just say that after Jenn and I met that one time, I started having troubles." Thornwell glanced at Rebecca and then back at the road. "Things like parking tickets. Getting pulled over for speeding when I wasn't. Charged with driving with a tail light that wasn't broken until after I got stopped."

"The cops were harassing you?"

"Not all the cops. One of them." The truck rolled to a stop. They were back behind the Conoco station. Thornwell pointed to Rebecca's car. "Time's up."

"Wait, who was it? Who was harassing you?"

He shifted to face her. "I gotta work in this town."

"I won't say anything to anyone, but I need to know. For Tyler's sake. For Olivia's."

Thornwell scanned the lot. When he spoke, his voice was hoarse and low. "It was Deputy Marsh."

* * *

Maybe he'd leave the door the way it was. A sheet of plywood held in place with cellophane packing tape might not be as professional-looking as glass, but at least it wouldn't shatter as easily. Paschek hadn't really slammed it that hard. At least, not the first time. A hesitant knocking came from his battered entryway. The sheriff wrenched the door open and scowled at the deputy standing before him. "You'd better be here to tell me that you've finally found Marsh."

"Uh, no. Sorry, sir, no word yet." The man stepped to the side and allowed Rebecca Andrychuk to peer in.

Paschek cursed under his breath and waved her in. "I should have been expecting you."

"I think you missed a piece." Rebecca stepped forward and pointed at a shard of glass with the toe of her high heels. "Rough day?"

"Bad enough." Paschek closed the door with forced restraint and turned to face the lawyer. "Look, I don't know what you heard, but it's not that bad. We're dealing with this, and believe me, it will not happen again."

"What are you talking about?"

"Shooter, I mean, Tyler's injuries are not that serious."

"Injuries?" Her eyes narrowed. "What injuries?"

"You don't know?" Paschek swore again. "One of the deputies got a little rough with Mr. Sampson. Gave him a couple of bruises, that's all. Like I said, nothing serious."

She jammed her fists into her hips. "I'll be the judge of what's serious and what's not. Has he seen a doctor?"

"No." The sheriff lifted both hands and sank onto his desk chair.. "We offered, but he refused. Said he was okay and asked to be left alone."

"Who did it?"

The sheriff hesitated. "Deputy Marsh."

Her jaw tightened. "I want to see my client. Now."

"Of course. Another deputy will take you to the holding area right…"

Rebecca marched through what was left of the door and hurled it shut. The plywood quivered in its frame and then tumbled to the floor.

The sheriff lowered his head and banged it once, twice on the top of his desk.

* * *

"Right this way, Ms. Andrychuk."

Rebecca gritted her teeth and counted down from ten. *I can't believe they actually beat my client.* She swore under her breath as a deputy led her through the front office and down a corridor to the holding cells. As he approached the first doorway, her cell phone chirped from her handbag. She was tempted to ignore it but relented. It was Derek. "I need to take this." She waited until the man had moved a discreet distance away before answering. "Hey."

"Hi, sorry I missed your call earlier."

"Me, too." She took a deep breath, forcing a calmness she did not feel. "It's been quite the afternoon."

"Do you want to talk about it?"

"I do. But not right now. I have to check on Tyler. He got roughed up a bit in jail."

"Oh, no. Is he okay? You want me to take a look at him?"

"I'm not sure. Paschek claims that he refused to see a doctor. I'll talk to him in a minute and call you back if I think he needs anything." She chewed her bottom lip. "It would help, though, to see you later—to talk things over. About the case, I mean."

"Okay." He sounded hesitant.

"Have you eaten? If you'd like to come to my place, I could make us something, or we could order in. Whatever you'd like."

"Uh, I don't, I mean, maybe we could meet somewhere else? There's that little coffee shop."

"No thanks. That place is what's keeping Tyler in here." She took another deep breath. "Look, I get it. This isn't a date." *At least, not yet.* "It's a business meeting. Like I said, I need your help with this case. Tell you what, there's a park down by the town hall. Picnic tables and everything. Meet me there in an hour, and I'll bring the food. The weather's nice, and there's sure to be a few people around." *Safer that way.*

"All right," Derek said. "That sounds good. See you there."

Rebecca slipped the cell phone back in her purse and nodded to the waiting officer. "I'm ready now, Deputy...?"

"Standingready, ma'am. Glad to be of assistance."

* * *

"How was Tyler?"

Rebecca opened the trunk of her car before answering. "He'll be okay." She handed Derek a picnic basket and then pulled out a blanket. "He's pretty sore. His face is a mess but should be okay with time. He thanked you for the offer but doesn't think he needs to see anyone. I couldn't see anything that looked like it needed stitches, but I'm no expert."

"Did he say what happened?"

Rebecca kicked a stone out of their path as they walked into the downtown park. "He wouldn't give me any details. Wouldn't even say who did it, although I know it was Marsh because Paschek told me. Anyway, Tyler was adamant that he doesn't want to press charges."

"Would it help his case if he did?"

"Not really. If—I mean, when—we get him off on the murder charge, we could sue for police brutality. I don't think Tyler would interested in that, either. I'm still going to look into it further." *If only to keep Paschek sweating.* She stopped and surveyed the park. All three picnic tables were occupied. With a brisk stride, she led the way to a patch of lawn beneath a burr oak and spread out the blanket. Taking the basket from Derek, she set out their meal as he settled onto the blanket cross-legged.

"This looks great," he said as he accepted a thick sandwich of pumpernickel and corned beef. "The potato salad looks homemade. How did you manage to prepare all this?"

Rebecca crinkled up her nose. "I didn't." Setting the last of the meal down, she placed one hand over her heart and raised the other. "As an officer of the court, I do solemnly swear that I had my secretary Paulina make this up for me." She laughed and grabbed a sandwich for herself.

"I don't do a lot of cooking that doesn't involve a microwave or a take-out menu."

"Well, this is still a treat. Thanks for inviting me." Derek took another bite and carefully wiped his mouth with a napkin. "You wanted to tell me about your afternoon?"

Rebecca nodded and between mouthfuls told Derek about her meetings with Austin Thornwell and Tabitha McKenny.

"I don't trust Samuel McKenny," Derek said after she had finished. "Something about him is off, somehow."

"Maybe, but I'm more concerned about Deputy Marsh. He starts harassing Thornwell after he met with Jennifer, and then assaults Tyler in the jail. I'm starting to suspect that Marsh and Jennifer were somehow involved. Maybe even that he killed her."

"I don't know. From what you've told me, poison sounds a bit too subtle for Deputy Marsh."

Rebecca packed the leftovers in the basket. "I suppose that could be. I just know that Marsh is a real creep." She hesitated before putting the last container away. "He's smart, though. Knows police procedure and how criminals usually act. Maybe he chose poison simply because it would seem out of character."

"I guess that's possible." Derek stood and reached for Rebecca's hand to help her to her feet.

She smiled. Her fingers felt good in his. His skin was warm, and she could sense his strength and his gentleness. She liked the feeling. Maintaining her hold on his hand, their eyes locked, she edged closer.

Then his cell phone rang.

* * *

If you want something done right, you better do it yourself. None of the other deputies had been able track Marsh down. Paschek didn't care that the man was off duty. He didn't care that every time they tried his cell phone all they got was a message that it was outside of the service area. And he didn't care that his rogue deputy could be anywhere from Colorado to Canada. He wanted Marsh found.

It had taken several phone calls and a lot of legwork, including a visit to an angry rancher who advised the sheriff that if a certain deputy continued to harass his daughter, he would demonstrate to said deputy how they turned a bull calf into a steer. Paschek thought that might not be a bad idea. He exchanged his police cruiser for a four-wheel-drive pickup and followed an old dirt road into the foothills.

As he'd suspected, Marsh's black SUV was parked by a grove of aspens at the head of the trail. Paschek jumped out of his truck, slammed his cap down on his head, and followed a footpath up between the trees. There was a trout stream over the next rise, and that was where he expected to find Deputy Marsh. He was halfway up the path when the silence of the hillside was fractured by a gunshot.

Paschek cursed softly as he dropped into a crouch. Drawing his Glock, he edged to the top of the rise and peered down at the creek bed. Standing beside the stream, Marsh raised his arm to sight down the barrel of a pistol he clutched in both hands. Even from that distance, Paschek recognized the weapon—a cap and ball Colt Navy revolver. Marsh fired again, and farther upstream a beer can flipped into the air. The sheriff cursed once more, louder this time, and rose to his feet. "Marsh, you idiot, what do you think you're doing?"

The deputy whirled and stooped into a gunfighter's pose, the Colt down by his hip. His face was grim and hard for an instant, and then a broad smile broke across it. "Dang it, Sheriff, I could have shot you, sneaking up on me like that." He straightened and dropped the Colt into its holster.

Paschek sauntered down the gentle slope of the hillside. "Can I take a look at your pistol?"

"Sure thing, Sheriff. It was my granddad's."

Paschek took the revolver in his left hand. The barrel was still warm from being fired, although, unlike the sheriff, it was starting to cool off. Paschek's free hand darted out, an open handed cobra strike that left a bright red hand print on Marsh's cheek and a spot of blood on his upper lip.

"What the..."

The Sheriff's hand snapped out again, this time to grab Marsh by the collar and yank him close. "You ever do something that stupid again, and the next time it won't be a slap on the face—it'll be my boot."

"What are you talking about?"

"Shooter Sampson, you moron." Paschek pushed the man away and spat on the ground at his feet. "Roughing him up while he's in custody? In front of video cameras? You gotta be kidding me."

Marsh slowly wiped the blood from his lip and smiled. "Is that all? I had a little talk with Tyler. Nothing more. No need to get upset."

"Upset? You think this is upset? If Sampson's lawyer uses this to get him off on a technicality, you'll see how upset I get. You won't like it."

"Don't worry about it. Tyler won't say anything. He knows the score."

"Yeah? Well, he won't have to talk if that lady lawyer gets hold of the security tapes." Paschek's eyes were cold as they sliced into the deputy's. Marsh held Paschek's gaze for a moment and then lowered his head.

"Tapes can be erased," he muttered.

"That would be tampering with evidence." Paschek transferred the Navy Colt to his right hand and aimed at the fallen beer can. With each gunshot, the can bounced and skittered farther down the creek bed. Only when the hammer clicked on a spent cylinder did he pause to let the black powder smoke swirl away. He flipped the weapon over and handed it butt-first to Marsh. "Nice pistol."

He gazed westward at the peaks of the Lewis Range. "The good news for you is that the jail security system has been having… technical difficulties. Whole week of recordings lost." Paschek's smile was grim. "The better news is that we're going to do an exchange of sorts with another police agency. You'll be spending the next couple of weeks working with the tribal police on the Flathead Reserve."

"You're not serious."

Paschek's smiled widened as he started up the hill. "Old friend of mine's in charge there. He promised to make sure you enjoyed yourself."

"You can't do that."

Marsh's curses drifted away in the wind as the sheriff reached the top of the rise. He shouted back over his shoulder before he continued on to his truck. "It's already done. See you in few weeks." As he opened the door to the vehicle, he shook his head. If only all of his problems could be solved that easily.

* * *

Rebecca had never liked hospitals, and she was beginning to really hate the local one. She slammed the trunk down on the remnants of their picnic while Derek sped off to assist with the latest crisis in Emergency. *So much for a romantic interlude.* She slumped down in the driver's seat and thought nasty thoughts about the health care system. Catching herself with a mental slap in the face, she straightened up. *Really, you're that selfish?* A school bus had collided with a semi-truck, which is what had pulled Derek back to work. *Those kids could be badly hurt.* That was far more pressing than her date with him, but still… She sighed. Between her pager going off and his, they might always struggle to spend time together. She pictured him caring for his patients and smiled. *Still might be worth another shot.*

Drumming her fingers on the steering wheel, she surveyed the park. The other picnickers were packing up to leave. They'd either be heading home or off to start an evening shift wherever they worked. She should do the same. She took the file she had left on the passenger seat and began leafing through the pages. When she looked up again, only a few young couples were left in the park. A hot spasm shot across her chest when one of them walked by, holding hands and laughing.

Rebecca snorted and slapped the papers back down. She could sit there and watch kids snuggling on a park bench, or she could go do something. The thought of returning to her condo made her shiver. Dark, quiet, and empty—not at all what she needed. She turned the key in the ignition and revved the engine on the Mustang. The jail's holding cells weren't far. Tyler might be more interested in talking now, and Deputy Marsh might be there as well. She had questions for both of them.

She squealed out of her parking spot and headed for the road. Right now, she had more questions than answers.

TWENTY-NINE

"Our doubts are traitors, and make us lose the good
we oft might win by fearing to attempt."
Measure for Measure Act I, Scene IV

Sometimes it was the sheer volume of patients in the ER that caused the problem. Other times it was the complexity or seriousness of the cases, and sometimes it was both. Derek merely smiled when Dr. Chandra Naidu kept saying how much she hated having to call him in early. They both knew she needed help, but she still apparently felt the need to apologize repeatedly for interrupting his supper.

"It's okay, really." Derek grabbed a handful of clipboards and scanned the charts. "Any of the kids in danger?"

Chandra shook her head. "I don't think so. I did a quick ABC survey on all of them while we were getting the worst into the rooms."

"Airway, breathing, and circulation—excellent. Any spinal injuries?"

"Most of them walked in. Two kids in neck braces and one on a spine board. I've sent them to X-ray already."

"Sounds good. Anything else before I get started?"

"I'm worried about the bus driver, Mrs. Williamson. I think she may have had an MI. In fact, I think that's what caused the accident."

"Okay, you look after her, and I'll see to these." He spread the charts out on the desk and quickly ran through them. The nursing staff always did a good job of triaging patients, but he liked to make sure. The stack of emergent and urgent cases was high, exactly what he'd expect from a collision between a school bus and semi, even if it had been at low speed. Throw in a possible heart attack and one of the kids having a severe asthma attack, and they had a crisis in the ER that was too much for one doctor.

A non-urgent case caught his eye. Fifty-four-year-old woman complaining of being tired. Derek rolled his eyes. It never failed—fill the waiting room with serious cases and someone was sure to come in with something trivial. He glanced over the rest of the woman's file. Complaints of fatigue, weakness, and numbness in the feet. Derek tapped a pen on the clipboard. Something about the case bothered him. He set the chart aside and made a mental note to look into it later.

Derek reviewed the remaining charts: three limb injuries, a concussion, four lacerations, and two with complaints of chest or abdominal pain. Chandra was checking the bus driver for cardiac issues, and Derek had already ordered medications for the child with the asthma attack. He decided to check on the other kids who had come in and rule out any internal injuries or significant head trauma first. The triage nurse hurried in from the waiting room and Derek held up a hand. "Any problems out there?"

"A bunch of scared kids with scrapes and bruises and a group of upset parents." She pushed the door shut and leaned against it. "Nothing I can't handle." She made a face as she jerked her head in the direction of the waiting room. "Really."

Derek grinned and handed her half of the charts. "Let's get to it."

* * *

The police station was quiet, almost deserted, when Rebecca stepped through the front door. Spotting the new deputy at the front desk, she summoned forth her best smile. "I'd like to talk to Deputy Marsh."

"I'm sorry, ma'am. He's not here."

"Ma'am? No one ever calls me ma'am." He shifted on his seat and she smiled again at his discomfort. "Call me Rebecca or Miss Andrychuk, Deputy… I'm sorry, I've forgotten your name."

"It's Standingready, ma'am—I mean, Miss."

Rebecca held out her hand. "I'm pleased to meet you again, Deputy Standingready. I really need to talk to Deputy Marsh. Can you tell me how I can reach him?"

"I'm afraid I don't know, Miss."

"When's he back on duty?"

"I really couldn't say." A muscle twitched below Standingready's eye. "I don't think he'll be back for quite a while."

"Oh, really? And why would that be?" When he lifted his shoulders, she blew out a breath. "Never mind. Is the sheriff in?"

"No, he's not here, either."

Rebecca set her briefcase on the desk and raised one eyebrow. "Interesting. I assume the sheriff will be back soon?"

"Oh yes, Miss, he will be."

"Today? Tomorrow?" Rebecca allowed another smile, smaller this time, to touch her lips as she studied Deputy Standingready. He refused to meet her eyes, concentrating instead on straightening a pile of papers on his desk, his fingers trembling slightly. *Hmm. Was he nervous? Scared?* Either way, she could work with it. She patted his arm. "Don't worry, Deputy, I understand. The sheriff probably doesn't tell you what he's doing."

His head jerked. "It's not that. He just said not to mention he was going after Marsh—I mean, uh, that is…" Standingready froze.

She held up both hands. "Don't worry, Officer, I won't say a word." She looked at her watch and then back at the deputy. "He might be back soon, then? I think I'll wait." She picked her briefcase up off the desk. "In the meantime, I'd like to see my client, if I may?"

* * *

Derek finished wrapping an elastic bandage around a splint and turned to the boy's mother. "There could be some swelling, so try to keep his arm up on a couple of pillows. If you come back in a couple of days, we should be able to take the splint off and put a cast on."

"How long will it take for the break to heal?"

"Both bones in Sean's arm were fractured and had to be reduced, so I'd say a full six weeks."

"Wanna go swimmin'." The boy's voice was slurred, and his eyelids continued to droop. "Wanna go."

"Hush, Sean, don't be rude."

Derek reached for the boy's file. "Don't worry, ma'am, it's the meds we gave him. He'll be pretty sleepy for a while. When he wakes up, tell him that when you bring him back I'll give him a special cast that he can go swimming with."

"Thank you, Doctor."

As Derek stepped from the treatment room, he spotted Chandra hurrying toward the stairwell. "Something wrong?"

"Maybe. I confirmed an MI in the bus driver and gave her a clot buster. She seemed stable when I transferred her to ICU, but now she's experiencing arrhythmias."

"Hey, you're one of the top docs in the county. You can handle it. Page me if you need any help." Derek watched her go before trudging to the nursing station. He rubbed the back of his neck and stretched, waiting for the nurse behind the desk to finish talking on the phone. The clock in the ER glared at him with rabid intensity. His shift was only technically starting now, which meant he had a long way to go. Leaning over the desk, he glanced into the staff room. With any luck, someone would make a pot of coffee. He was going to need it. The nurse disconnected her call. "Okay," Derek said, straightening up. "What's next?"

The semi-truck driver sat up when Derek and the triage nurse entered the room. "Hey, Doc, I said I was okay. Don't want nothin' done till them kids all been seen to."

"They all have been, so why don't you lie down and let me look at that leg."

The man grunted but settled back as instructed. "Don't know what that lady was thinkin'. Rolled out right in front of me. Good thing I'd been climbin' that hill. If I'd a been goin' full speed, I think I'd a killed them all."

"But you didn't. In fact, most of the kids have only minor injuries. Now lie still. X-rays were okay. Nothing broken. You've got some big cuts, though. We'll clean your leg up and put in a few sutures."

"Ain't no worry, Doc, I'll be okay. Hey, that stuff stings. There gonna be any scars? What's that? That's a big needle, Doc. Whatcha doin' with…?"

The truck driver's eyes rolled up in his head, and he fell back on the stretcher. Derek felt the man's pulse. Nice and regular.

"Did he just pass out?" the nurse asked.

"He sure did. Get me fresh gloves, please, and some 4-0 suture. If I hurry, I can be done before he wakes up."

* * *

Tyler's face looked better, but his movements were still slow and stiff as he shuffled into the interrogation room. Rebecca joined him at the table as Deputy Standingready shackled Tyler's left wrist to the table.

"Is that really necessary?"

"Afraid so, Miss. Procedure."

"What about that?" Rebecca pointed at the camera blinking red from above the doorway.

"That too, but don't worry. The microphones are all disconnected."

Rebecca waited for the deputy to leave before sitting. Tyler stared at her through eyes narrowed to slits before leaning back in the chair and crossing his arms. Rebecca tilted her head. "I'm on your side, you know. You need to talk to me."

Tyler's shoulders drooped, the defiance fading from his eyes. His voice was low and hesitant. "I don't know what to say. Everything's gone so bad."

"It's not over. We're only getting started."

"I've lost Jenn and now Livy. I'm stuck in here, and I don't see any way out." He rubbed his eyes. "I hear they kill you by injecting poison in Montana."

"Don't be ridiculous. No way you're getting the death penalty. There's only been two or three executions in the past forty years." Rebecca pressed her palms to the table. "More importantly, you're innocent, and I'm going to prove it. Tomorrow, I start the appeal to get you bail."

Tyler sighed. "Thanks. I needed to hear that. What can I do to help?"

"I know it was Marsh who beat you. Let's start there."

Tyler's cheeks paled, and he shot a look at the camera. Bending forward, he lowered his voice. "All right, yeah, he did it. Real brave when he knew I couldn't fight back."

"What was it about?"

"Jenn. Marsh was ragging me about her, telling me she'd always been too good for me. That he knew she wanted out." Tyler took a deep breath and studied his fingernails. "Said that was why I killed her." He gritted his teeth. "I told him what he could do to himself, and that's when he lit into me. Coulda been worse."

"It's bad enough as it is. I can bring him up on charges and—"

Tyler shook his head emphatically. "Absolutely not."

She exhaled loudly. "Fine. At least tell me why you think he hit you. Was there something going on between him and Jenn?"

His face darkened. "Not on her part, I don't think. But Marsh was sweet on Jenn. She told me he'd let her off for speeding and stuff like that a couple times. Then he started coming by the house when I was away."

"Jennifer tell you that, too?"

"Yeah, she laughed about it. Said she told him he'd have to be more than a deputy for her to look his way. She liked to tease sometimes."

"Teasing can be dangerous."

Tyler wiggled a loose tooth and winced. "Tell me about it."

"So you know, Marsh won't bother you again. Apparently Sheriff Paschek has gotten rid of him for a while." Rebecca pulled a notebook and pen out of her briefcase. "Let's move on. Do you know Austin Thornwell?"

"Heard of him but never met him. I think Jenn mentioned his name once or twice."

"Do you think she could have been having an affair with him?"

Tyler ran a hand over his chin. The stubble rasped beneath his fingers. "No, I don't. You've got to understand, for all the ways Jennifer rebelled against her father, she still believed in God and tried to do the right thing. She was a virgin when we got married, and she was pretty hard on anyone who was fooling around. No, she wouldn't do that."

Rebecca tapped the pen on the notebook. "If you say so. I still want to know where you were the morning of Jennifer's death, your relationship with her, how you got on with the McKennys, everything." She stopped tapping the pen and held it over the notebook, ready to write. "Let's get started."

* * *

Something about the final case worried him. Derek had finished with the accident victims, admitting four for observation and discharging most of the rest. Only the asthmatic child had needed to be sent to the ward and even she had responded well to treatment. Chandra had been able to stabilize the bus driver and was making arrangements to transfer her to Kalispell in the morning for angiography. That only left the woman with fatigue.

Derek walked into the woman's room, still studying her chart. He stopped by the side of the bed and greeted her before lowering the file. "How long have you been experiencing these symptoms?" He studied her, assessing any symptoms he could observe. She was middle-aged, a bit overweight, pale, and played with the blanket on her bed as though she was feeling anxious.

"Over a week, Doctor." She spoke slowly, pausing after every few words. "Got no energy. Feet feeling numb. Shouldn't bother you... but my husband Earl... made me come. My doc's away. Holidays. Could have waited. Probably just nerves."

Derek watched her closely as she spoke. Her face stayed blank, almost expressionless, but her eyes darted back and forth. Her breathing seemed even and steady with no wheezing or tightness. He glanced back at the chart. Vitals were good, with normal heartbeat and breathing rate. "Any shortness of breath or chest pain?"

"No."

He noted that on the chart. "Abnormal bleeding?"

She shook her head.

"Black, tar-like stools?"

A little color flowed back into her cheeks. "No."

Hmm. No previous significant medical or surgical issues. He did have one idea about what it could be, but needed to make sure. Derek set the chart down on the small dinner table and lifted the bottom of the sheet.

From the way she responded when he poked and squeezed her foot, she definitely seemed to have a degree of numbness, but that was subjective. Her generalized weakness could be explained by overall poor fitness but not her difficulty speaking. Derek tugged the stethoscope off his neck. Heart and lungs were normal and her abdominal exam was unremarkable. Ear, nose, throat, and eye exams were normal. Her knee jerk reflex did seem diminished.

Derek leaned closer to examine her face. "Grit your teeth for me. Now open your eyes wide. Screw them shut. Tight as you can." Her facial muscles appeared slightly weak. He reached for her chart and flipped it open. "Did you have a cold or flu in the past month?"

"Well, yeah. Had a bad flu... about two weeks... ago. Got over that."

"Have you had any tick bites? Any cuts? Are your immunizations up to date?"

"I stay in town. Haven't had a... tick bite in a long time. Last time... I had a cut was... three or four years ago." She stopped and took a few shallow breaths. "Gave me a shot then. I've had all the rest. Even hepatitis... and that shingles one. Earl took me to Mexico for our anniversary. Six years ago."

"I'd like to run a few tests. Blood work, mainly, but I need to do a spinal tap as well."

"What's that?"

"We'll insert a needle into your back to draw fluid from around your spinal cord. It'll hurt a bit but it's quite safe."

"What's wrong... with me?"

"I'm not completely sure yet. That's why we need the tests."

"Will I… be okay?"

"We'll know soon."

A tear slid down the woman's cheek. "I'm scared."

Derek squeezed her hand. "No need. We're going to take good care of you. I'll make sure that you come through this fine."

"Promise?"

"Yes, I promise. Now, let's get the tests done so we know for sure what we're dealing with."

* * *

Rebecca huffed an exasperated breath as she studied what she'd written as Tyler spoke. Her notes on the case were extensive but somehow incomplete. She didn't like having doubts about a case. There was enough uncertainty in the rest of her life already. She set the pen down on the pad and smiled at Tyler, hoping the faint flicker of suspicion didn't show in her eyes. He was her client, and she had been hired to defend him. Guilt or innocence was not an issue. "That should do, for now. I'll finish the appeal, and we'll go over everything again after I get you out of here."

Tyler nodded. "Thanks. I'm not sure how much more I can take of this. Being away from Livy is the hardest part."

"Do you want me to check on her? Take her a message?"

"Could you? Oh, man, that would help."

"No problem." Rebecca nudged the notebook and pen closer to him. "Go ahead and write her a letter while I see if Paschek is back. I need to discuss a few things with the sheriff."

Leaving Tyler in the interrogation room, Rebecca marched down the corridor toward the front of the police station. Her thoughts on everything he had told her, she turned a corner and was forced to stutter to a halt when a disheveled man loomed before her.

"Whoa there, honey. Where you going so fast?" His dirty-blond hair hung in lank strands down to the shoulders of a plaid shirt stained with grease and blood. His grin displayed evidence of a recently-departed tooth while his breath slammed against her with a mixture of stale beer and vomit. Rebecca blanched and flattened herself against the wall.

"Shut up, Karlsen." The deputy behind the man grabbed him by the collar and shoved him down the corridor. "You've got nothing to say to Miss Andrychuk."

"Andrychuk?" Karlsen's voice echoed through the hallway. "The lawyer gal? Hey, I need a lawyer." He struggled to turn around, but the deputy held him firm. "I wanna talk to you."

Rebecca waved her hand in front of her face. "I'm busy. The court will appoint you a lawyer."

The deputy grunted and pushed the man toward the holding cells. "See, she doesn't want to talk to you."

Although he'd disappeared around the corner, Rebecca heard Karlsen shout, "You'd better talk to me. Just ask him. Ask Shooter."

Rebecca froze, until the solid thud of the door leading to the cells roused her. Slightly shaken from the encounter, she took a few deep breaths, replaying the exchange in her head. *Karlsen.* Although she'd like nothing better than to forget him, something told her she'd better remember that man's name.

THIRTY

"There is nothing either good or bad,
but thinking makes it so."
Hamlet Act II, Scene II

Derek slid the needle between the woman's vertebrae with practiced ease and advanced the four-inch shaft until he felt the pop the tip made when it pierced the fibrous sheath around the spinal cord. He removed the central wire from the needle and watched as a drop of clear grayish liquid appeared. He let the flow continue until he had collected enough to fill the small vial. He handed the spinal fluid to the lab tech and then withdrew the needle.

"All done." He covered the puncture wound with an adhesive dressing before helping the woman roll onto her back. "You may get a bit of a headache from the spinal tap, but it shouldn't be too bad."

"Didn't hurt," she said, fixing her eyes on Derek's face. "Please… tell me what… you think is wrong."

"I'd rather not say until I'm sure."

"Am I… going to die?"

Derek rested a hand on her gowned shoulder. "No, you're not. I'm fairly certain what the issue is, and as soon as we confirm the diagnosis we can start the treatment. It may take a while, but you're going to be fine."

The woman managed a weak smile. Derek strolled from the room and glanced around the ER before pausing to stare out the window. Should he be doing more? Like praying for her. Either he was guilty for not following orders, or he was guilty for not following God. It was strictly a no-win situation. His shoulders sagged in defeat. Could he keep his promise? He had sounded pretty certain when he was talking to the patient, but lately it seemed there wasn't much he was sure of. Derek touched the gold band on his finger. Not much at all.

* * *

Paschek hadn't shown up, and Rebecca was getting tired of waiting. She'd already scanned her notes twice and was starting through them a third time when Deputy Standingready informed her that Tyler wanted to see her again. Her client was still in the interrogation room, and when the deputy unlocked the door to let her in, Tyler handed her a small stack of pages, his shackles rattling when he moved.

Rebecca took them and smiled. "Quite the letter."

"I guess I had a lot to say."

"I'll get this to Olivia as soon as I can."

"Thanks." Deputy Standingready walked over to him, and Tyler's shoulders slumped. "Guess I have to go back to my cell now."

"Just one more day, I hope. Come on, I'll walk you."

As the deputy led them into the cell block, Rebecca shrank away when the only other prisoner stood and leaned against the bars of his cell. Karlsen whistled and stuck his hands through the bars. "Shooter. Buddy. Tell your lawyer lady she needs to talk to me."

Rebecca nudged Tyler in the ribs and whispered, "You know him?"

"Sort of."

"What's he on about?"

"Don't know." Tyler entered his own cell and turned as Standingready slid the door shut and locked it. "Really, I don't know."

Rebecca repressed a sigh and followed the Deputy back down the corridor. Karlsen grinned at her as she approached. "You'll be talking to me, lawyer lady." Dropping his voice to a hoarse whisper, he continued, "Or the sheriff will."

* * *

The results of the spinal tap were back. White count was normal. Glucose normal. No bacteria detected. No red blood cells. All the parameters were normal except one. Protein was elevated. Clutching the report, Derek walked back into the exam room. "The tests are here, and the results confirm my suspicions."

"What… do I have… Doc?"

"A condition called Guillain-Barré Syndrome. We're not sure what caused it, but it's likely related to that flu you had. The syndrome results in inflammation in the nerves, which causes weakness and numbness."

"Will I… get better?"

"Yes, you will. We'll need to watch you closely for a while, so we're going to admit you to ICU. There's a medication that can help. It's called immunoglobulin. We'll be giving you a dose tonight and then more as soon as we get a supply from Billings."

"Thank you." The woman's hand fluttered in the air, and Derek reached out to take it. "Thank you… so much."

Derek squeezed her hand. He opened his mouth to speak but then hesitated. When he continued, it was simply to tell her to rest while he arranged the transfer to ICU. Stepping from the room, he leaned against the wall and rubbed his eyes. He knew he had made the right diagnosis, but was that enough? He let his gaze inch upward.

The ward clerk approached him. "Call for you, Doctor," she said as she motioned to the front desk. "Line two." Derek slipped from the exam room and made his way to the front of the ER to take the call.

"I hope you're not too busy."

Rebecca's voice did strange things to his insides, and Derek wasn't sure how he felt about that. He pressed a palm to his abdomen. "No, the rush is over. It was crazy for a while though."

"I wanted to tell you that I enjoyed our picnic."

"Uh, me too."

"The only problem was you got called away before we could have dessert."

"Dessert?"

"I had two pieces of Paulina's blueberry cheesecake in a cooler in my car."

Two of the ER nurses were watching him. One of them whispered something to the other and they both giggled. Derek's neck warmed as he turned away and lowered his voice. "Oh. I'm sorry I missed that."

"I think I should make it up to you. How about breakfast at the diner downtown after you're finished work?"

"Breakfast? Are you sure? My shift ends at seven."

"No problem. I'm an early riser anyway."

"All right, I'll see you then." Derek dropped the receiver back on its cradle and leaned against the counter. The two nurses were still grinning at him, and he inclined his head toward the full room of waiting patients. "What is this, break time?" He tried to sound stern, but his lips twitched and they both laughed. Derek rolled his eyes and grabbed a stack of lab results.

"Uh, Doctor?" the ward clerk said. "Those are from this morning. They're ready to be filed in the charts."

"Just checking to make sure everything's okay. Can't be too careful." He dropped the stack back on the desk. The triage nurse strode toward him. *Saved.*

"Got three kids for you in Room Four," she said, handing him their papers. "Nothing serious. Looks like the whole family has a mild case of the stomach flu. I hate even having to bother you with this stuff."

"No, that's fine." Derek hurried off in the direction of the examination room. "No problem at all." He blew the air out of his lungs slowly. Maybe the clerk hadn't noticed anything. He glanced back and grimaced. The ward clerk and the triage nurse stood at the desk chatting with the ER nurses. All four of them looked over at him and smirked. *Great. Just great.*

* * *

Seven in the morning? What had she been thinking? Rebecca tugged an elastic from her coat pocket and pulled her long hair back into a sleek ponytail. She'd have to be up before six to get ready in time. Why hadn't she suggested a later breakfast? Why had she lied about being an early riser? *This guy better be worth it.* She tossed the ponytail back over her shoulder and smiled. *So far, it looks promising.*

More promising than her wait for Sheriff Paschek, anyway. She unfolded herself from the hard, plastic waiting room chair and trudged over to the station desk. The deputy lifted a hand before she could even ask. Rebecca snorted and stalked back to the chair to grab her briefcase. She'd had enough. Confronting Paschek would have to wait for another day. He'd have to show up sooner or later, and when he did…

"Miss Andrychuk?"

Rebecca spun around. "What?"

Deputy Standingready's eyes widened as he stepped back. "Sorry, I didn't mean to startle you."

"Don't tell me," she said, planting a hand on her hip. "Paschek is finally back on the job. Well, now he can wait for me. I'm going home."

"Ah, no, ma'am—that is, the sheriff isn't back yet. But Karlsen keeps demanding to talk to you. I said you'd refuse, but thought I should warn you that he'll be pestering your office come morning since he'll get his phone call then."

Rebecca gripped her briefcase tighter. *Might as well get this over with.* "I guess I'll need to use the interrogation room again."

* * *

Rebecca waited in the corridor until the deputy had deposited Karlsen in the interrogation room. "You'll follow *procedure* and shackle his wrist, too?"

"Every time, Miss. Every time."

Rebecca closed the door behind the deputy and then leaned back against it to study the prisoner. Karlsen was using the nail of his pinky finger to pick food from between his teeth. With a satisfied grunt, he pulled something out and flicked it across the room. He leered at Rebecca. "Ain't never had a lawyer as good-lookin' as you."

"And you don't have one now. You've got two minutes. Say what you've got to say."

"Oh, we'll be talking for a bit longer, seein' as how you're going to agree to be my lawyer—for free, that is."

"Now why would I do that?"

"'Cause of what I got to say about Shooter Sampson. I figure it's worth you takin' care of me. Unless, of course, you think I'd be better makin' a deal with the sheriff."

Rebecca lifted her arm to glance at her watch. "You have one minute left."

Karlsen snorted. "You're a tough one. I like that. Think we'll get along just fine." He leaned forward and licked his lips. "So, listen up, sweetie, 'cause I sure got me a story to tell."

* * *

No good deed went unpunished. At least, that was what Sheriff Paschek had come to believe. If he had left his radio off, he never would have heard about the accident on Highway 89. If he hadn't been so conscientious, he never would have headed over there to see if he could help. If the rookie state patrolman had displayed any sense, Paschek wouldn't have had to stick around to make sure things were done right. Instead, he'd waited until the paramedics had assured him that everyone would be okay, and the state police had finally sent someone out who knew how to process an accident scene. Served him right.

Paschek rolled to a stop on the hill overlooking Stockton. In the dwindling light of dusk, it was a phosphorescent stain on a patchwork of vermillion and indigo. The police station was down there. His work was down there. All his problems were down there. Paschek grunted and massaged his forehead. *Most of his problems.* He thumbed his radio. *Might as well check in.*

"Blackburn here. That you, Sheriff? Thought you'd be back before now."

"I got waylaid. What's the status?"

"Quiet. Me and the rookie got things under control. Mostly anyway."

"What do you mean 'mostly'?"

"That lawyer lady's here. She's been waiting for you for a long time, and she looks kind of pi... I mean, upset."

Paschek hit the mute button and let out a stream of expletives before thumbing the speaker back on. "Tell her I'm busy. Tell her I got called out on something. Tell her whatever you want, but make sure she knows I won't be back in tonight."

"Okay, Sheriff. She'll be asking if you'll be in tomorrow. What should I say?"

"The truth. You're only a deputy, and the sheriff don't tell you nothin'. Paschek over and out."

He slammed the radio receiver down and stared out into the gloom. He was off the hook for tonight. So why did he feel like he'd managed to make his problems a whole lot bigger?

* * *

The sun had etched a molten path above the horizon by the time Derek stepped from the hospital. He stretched and yawned before heading for his Jeep. His shift had been busy at first but had quieted down as the night wore on. He'd even been able to catch a couple of hours of sleep between three and five. Still, he could hardly wait to get back to his apartment and stretch out on a real bed. He was opening the door to the Wrangler when his cell phone vibrated and he pulled it from his pocket and checked the screen.

A text from Rebecca. His stomach did that funny little dance again as he read the words, hearing her voice in his head as he did. *Running late. Go ahead and order for me. Coffee and toast, or a muffin if they're fresh. See you soon. R.*

Derek stared at the silent phone. It smirked at him, scorning his befuddled brain. *Breakfast? Rebecca?* Slowly the lights came on. *Oh, no.* If he hustled he could still get there first. Could he phone ahead and place their orders? *Brilliant.* That was what he'd do.

He dialed as he hopped into the car, placed the order as he crossed the parking lot, and disconnected the call before he hit the street. Done.

The waitress had lied. The muffins weren't fresh, but it was too late to change the order by the time he realized it. Derek has barely gotten settled on his chair when Rebecca appeared at the door of the restaurant. She arrived at the table at the same time as their breakfast.

"I've got a lot to tell you," she said as she poked at the lump of baking on her plate.

"About the sheriff?"

"No, he never made it back to the station. I'd like to think it's because he's afraid of me, but somehow I doubt that. It's about Tyler."

"Good news, I hope. Is he getting out on bail?"

"Not yet. I'll present my appeal later today. We'll see then. I think he has a good chance of being released, although I'm not sure for how long."

"What do you mean?"

Rebecca took a slow swallow of her coffee. "I had a meeting with another prisoner last night. He told me a few things about our Mr. Sampson."

"What sort of things?"

"That he was lying about being asleep at the oil crew's motel at the time Jennifer was killed."

"Lying? Are you sure?" His mouth suddenly felt dry, and he set down his piece of toast.

"There's a witness. He was seen outside a bar in Shelby."

"A bar? That can't be. Tyler hasn't had a drink in months."

"Maybe he lied about that, too."

Derek's breath hissed out like a punctured balloon. "I can't believe it. What did Tyler say about this?"

"I haven't talked to him yet. I wanted to discuss it with you before bringing it up."

Derek squirmed in his chair. "Is there no end to this?" He drove his fingers through his hair. "What are you going to do? What if Tyler is lying?"

"It will weaken our case if the sheriff finds out about it, but that's not the real issue."

"What is, then?"

She methodically peeled back the cover of an individual creamer. "Look, I'm Tyler's lawyer, and I will defend him the best of my ability." She poured the creamer into her cup and grabbed another. "His guilt or innocence doesn't matter."

"Of course it matters."

Rebecca rested a hand on Derek's arm. "I know it matters to you. That's what I wanted to say. You hired me, and while Tyler can cover most of the fees, I will understand if you want put an end to that part of... things." She slid her hand along his arm until it covered his. "The court can appoint another lawyer. I'll pass on my files, and we can step away from it. If that's what you want."

The smell of burnt grease wafted to him from the diner's grill, intensifying the churning acid in his gut. The back of his hand tingled where Rebecca's touched it. "I... I don't know." Derek slipped his hand away. "I can't think right now. Maybe, uh, maybe you should keep at it. For now." Edging away from the table, he clambered to his feet. "I think I should go."

Her eyes widened and her jaw dropped slightly. "You haven't finished your breakfast. And there's more we need to talk about."

"I'm sorry, I can't right now." He could sense her eyes on him as the sounds of the diner faded into the background. He could barely hear the cry of a toddler, the crash of dishes in the kitchen, the dull hum of conversation. "I'm sorry."

Rebecca unfolded her arms with the reluctance of ice breaking free from a shoreline. "I see."

"I really need sleep right now, but maybe I could call you later. To go over the case. Or you could call me after you find out what Tyler has to say."

Rebecca sighed. A slight smile touched her lips as she gave him an almost imperceptible nod. "All right. We'll talk later."

"That'd be good." He dropped enough cash on the table to cover the bill and headed for the exit. The morning sun dazzled him as he marched to his car. A chill knot settled between his shoulder blades.

What if Tyler was playing them for a fool and actually was guilty? And was Derek ready for whatever it was that was happening with Rebecca? He suppressed a groan as he yanked open his door. Doubts and obstacles appeared to be popping up everywhere. He was starting to feel like Daniel, facing an entire pride of lions, ready to pounce. *The question is, am I stepping into the lion's den or out of it?*

* * *

Rebecca toyed with the remnants of her muffin and listened as a pair of siblings at the next table argued over who was touching whom. She hadn't expected breakfast to end so soon, and she definitely hadn't expected to finish it on her own. Now she had time to fill. The appeal hearing wasn't scheduled until eleven. The fact that it was at the district court in Shelby was a happy coincidence. She could check out the story about Tyler being in a bar at the same time.

She stood and slung her bag over her shoulder. Probably best for her to put Derek out of her mind anyway and concentrate on the case. Maneuvering her way around the tables, she paused at the door near a couple seated in a pool of bright sunlight. The man was watching intently as the woman laughed and cupped his face. What would that be like, sitting and enjoying a meal with someone she cared for? Not worrying about whether he was judging her, or attracted to her, or thinking about his wife. Rebecca kicked an empty paper coffee cup out of her way with the toe of her heeled boot. Could she do it? Completely be herself, no pretensions, no hidden agendas? Have that be good enough for whoever she was with?

Enough wallowing. Rebecca jumped into her car and slammed the door. Popping the Mustang into drive, she spun out of the diner's parking lot. She had just turned onto Main Street when she noticed flashing lights in her rearview mirror. She gritted her teeth. Sheriff Paschek.

He rapped on her window with his knuckles and she lowered the glass. "Licence and registration please, Miss."

"I was on my way to talk to you, Paschek. Nice to see that you're not dodging out on me like yesterday."

"Licence and registration."

"Why don't we talk about Tyler Sampson and Deputy Marsh first? Where is Deputy Marsh?"

Sheriff Paschek gripped the top of the window and leaned in until his mirrored sunglasses were inches from her face. "I said, licence and registration. Now."

"You know who I am. And you know you had no reason to pull me over."

"There's a stop sign back there, Miss Andrychuk. Or didn't you see it?"

"Yeah, I saw it. And I stopped at it, too."

"Not at the right spot, you didn't. Any good lawyer would know that you have to stop at the line. Not six inches past it." Paschek straightened up and finished writing the ticket. He handed it to her and smirked. "Are you a good lawyer, Miss Andrychuk?"

"This is crap, Paschek, and you know it."

Paschek pulled off his sunglasses. "I'll tell what's crap. You and your new boyfriend thinking you can handle a murder case. You can't."

Rebecca gripped the steering wheel. "I don't know what you're talking about."

"Oh, I'm sorry." Paschek slipped the sunglasses back on. "I forgot. You've got so many guys, they're hard to keep straight, aren't they? I meant the latest one. He's different from the rest, isn't he, Rebecca? Not married, at least not anymore."

"You bastard," she whispered.

"You have a nice day now, Miss Andrychuk."

Heat flooded Rebecca's face. She shoved open the door and lurched from the car. "Just a minute, Paschek."

"We're through here, Miss Andrychuk."

"No, we're not." She jabbed a finger toward the center of his chest. "Not by a long shot."

Paschek knocked her finger away with his arm. "Be careful who you poke, girl." His voice was a low growl. "The bears around here wake up mean."

"Are you threatening me, Sheriff? What you going to do? Beat me up like you did my client? Are you ready to talk to a judge about police brutality?"

Paschek's features relaxed into something vaguely amused. "Funny. Shooter never complained about police brutality. He refused medical care and declined to make any kind of formal statement. As far as I'm concerned, we're finished with that. Don't see how you can complain to a judge when your client denies anything happened."

"I want to talk to Marsh."

"Ah, well, that'll be a problem. Deputy Marsh has been assigned to liaison with another police agency. He'll be out of the county for a while."

"How long is *a while*?"

"Can't say for sure. Three, maybe six months."

"This is a load of bull. Why are you protecting Marsh?"

"Protecting him?" Paschek snorted. "I could care less about that stupid hillbilly."

"Then what are you hiding?"

He adjusted his hat. "Good day, Miss Andrychuk. This time, we are really and truly finished. I have work to do, and I'm sure you have something else to occupy your time." Paschek spun around, gravel flying into the ditch beneath his heavy boots. He slid behind the wheel of his police cruiser and slammed the door.

Rebecca stalked to the open window and gripped the glass with both hands. "You're right about the bears around here, Sheriff, but even you should know which ones are the meanest. It's the mama bears that'll give you the most trouble. I'll be talking to you again soon." She whirled around and marched back to her own car. When Paschek pulled away, she collapsed against the door, breathing heavily. Her hand was trembling when she lifted it to her face. Was that fear or anger? She wasn't sure.

* * *

She didn't want another run-in with Paschek, but Rebecca needed to talk to her client. she'd keep her head down and hurry through the front office of the police station to the holding cells. Seemed like a good plan, until she reached the station and almost ran over someone exiting the building.

"Sorry," the man said, stepping aside. He tilted his head. "Wait, aren't you the young woman who was outside the church the other night?"

Rebecca squinted, trying to make out his face in the bright sunlight. She had hoped he would forget that incident. "I don't think…"

"You were in the red Mustang. Remember me? I'm the pastor there. Josh Bucknell." He grinned and stuck out his hand.

Rebecca hesitated and then shook his hand. A nervous smile touched her lips.

Bucknell let the door to the station swing shut. "Are you all right? Is anything wrong? Anything you need the police for?"

"No, everything's fine. I'm a lawyer, and I'm going in to meet with a client."

"I see." Bucknell paused. "Is it Tyler Sampson, by any chance? He's part of my congregation, and I was here visiting him." He shoved his hands into the pockets of his jeans. "He's very discouraged. He didn't say so, but I could tell. I hope you'll be able help him."

"I really can't comment on that."

"I understand. Confidentiality is vital." He tugged a business card out of his pocket. "If there's anything I can do to help, please give me a call."

Mumbling her thanks, Rebecca stuffed the card into her bag and hurried into the station. If someone from a church did help her, it would certainly be the first time.

* * *

Paschek wasn't there. Rebecca was relieved to have at least escaped that problem as she trailed behind Tyler. He stumbled down the corridor toward the interrogation room and winced as the deputy chained his wrist to the table.

The officer grunted softly. "Sorry, man. You need some Advil?"

Tyler shook his head. "No, thanks."

The deputy inclined his head toward Rebecca. "Would you like anything, Miss? Coffee? Water? A soda?"

Rebecca contemplated him. His uniform looked as though it had once been snug across his shoulders but now was taut only around the middle. She glanced at his name tag. "Coffee would be nice, Deputy Blackburn. Two creams please, and thank you." She settled onto the chair across from Tyler. "Did you get any sleep? You look tired."

"It's hard in here. They keep the lights on all the time, and it's always noisy. How much longer will I be here?"

"Not much longer, I hope. I'll be heading over to Shelby from here, and I'm hoping you will be out this afternoon." She drummed her fingers on the table top. "I need to ask you something."

"All I do these days is answer questions." He waved his free hand through the air. "Go ahead."

A light tap on the door interrupted them, and Rebecca paused as Blackburn entered the room to set a mug of coffee on the table. Nodding her thanks, she waited until he had left the room before she spoke. "You told me that the day Jennifer died, you spent the whole day at the motel."

Tyler shifted on his chair. "Yeah."

"I need you to tell me the truth. All of it."

His eyes narrowed. "I did."

"I can't do a good job of defending you unless you're completely honest with me."

"What are you talking about?"

Rebecca studied his face. Even the best poker player had a tell when he wasn't being honest. "How do you know Karlsen?"

"Sven? He works the rigs sometimes. I guess I met him there."

"Anywhere else?"

Tyler clenched his fists and leaned back as far as his shackled wrist would allow him. "Yeah, I partied with him a few times in the past." He looked as though he had just tasted something foul. "Like in the distant past."

"Karlsen says he saw you on the day Jennifer died, outside a bar in Shelby." She stared at her client. "Tell me he's lying, and we move on. However, I would prefer you tell me the truth."

Tyler drooped in his chair, his face suddenly ashen. "I didn't mean to. I didn't want to."

Rebecca inhaled sharply. "What did you do?"

THIRTY-ONE

"Then must you speak of one that lov'd not wisely
but too well."
Othello Act V, Scene II

The drive to Shelby was slower than Rebecca had anticipated. After her run-in with Paschek and Tyler's revelation, Rebecca feared attracting more police attention too much to go even a few miles over the speed limit. After the third cattle truck passed her when they weren't even on a downhill grade, she sped up a bit. She spent the next few minutes watching her rear-view mirror for flashing lights. When none appeared, she swore under her breath and pushed down on the accelerator.

Passing the last cattle truck made her feel a lot better. Getting a speeding ticket from a state highway patrolman did not. Even with that, she arrived at the courthouse early.

The appellate judge lacked the good-old-boy nature of the judge who had heard the initial bail hearing, in more ways than one. Judge Hollister was strict, unsmiling, and by the book. She was also a she. Rebecca was careful to keep her face blank and serious as she presented her case. The evidence against her client was all circumstantial. He'd never been charged with a violent crime. He regularly attended Alcoholics

Anonymous and church and had been sober for over six months. He had a good job and a young child to care for. He was not a flight risk. The incident in the diner had been misread and misunderstood. He should be granted bail.

The judge listened with studied care to both sides. She interrupted the prosecutor, Carl Chartrand, and Rebecca on a number of occasions to ask pointed questions and was quick to cut them off if they were too long-winded or overly dramatic. At last, she signaled for quiet. The hum of the air conditioner was the only sound as Judge Hollister reviewed her notes. Finally, she looked up. "Ms. Andrychuk, are you aware that in most cases with a charge of first degree murder, bail is not granted?"

"Yes, Your Honor."

"Why should I make an exception in your case?"

"The prosecution's case relies completely on circumstantial evidence and worse."

"Worse?" The judge raised her eyebrows. "What do you mean, Counselor?"

"Hearsay, Your Honor. The case is based entirely on a letter reputed to be written by the victim sometime prior to her death."

Chartrand surged to his feet. "I object."

"May I remind you, Mr. Chartrand, this is a bail appeal hearing and not a trial? Save your showmanship for the jury. Proceed, Ms. Andrychuk."

"Thank you, Your Honor. I am confident the letter will not be ruled admissible. The Supreme Court ruled against such evidence in the case of Giles versus California in 2008. I have the citation, if you wish."

"I am familiar with the case, Ms. Andrychuk, but thank you."

"Very well. Without this letter, the prosecution simply does not have a case. I would therefore request that my client be granted bail."

"Anything else, Ms. Andrychuk? Mr. Chartrand?"

Both of them shook their heads and the judge nodded. "In that case, we will have a short recess while I consider the details of the case."

Rebecca shoved papers into her briefcase as the judge left the courtroom. She started to chew on a fingernail but forced her hands to her lap. Was it enough? Had she done a good enough job? The hairs on the back of her neck stiffened. Something cold wormed its way down her spine. She jerked around and scanned the back of the courtroom.

There, in the last row, someone sat watching her. The man narrowed his eyes to harsh slits and raised a gnarled hand. He pointed a finger like a knife blade and stabbed it in her direction. Samuel McKenny.

* * *

Paschek slammed the phone down and cursed loudly.

"Something wrong, Eugene?" Detective Melansen rescued his tea from the still-vibrating desk and slid his chair back a few inches.

"Tyler Sampson made bail. That hotshot lawyer convinced the judge that our letter could be thrown out, and now Shooter gets to walk."

"That's unfortunate. If the trial judge agrees, our case will be significantly weakened."

"It's not over. No way Shooter's smart enough to keep out of trouble. Give him some rope, and he'll hang himself."

"Maybe."

"No maybe about it. First off, the judge put in strict bail conditions. The little girl stays with the grandparents, and Sampson can only see her under police supervision. He's got to stay away from the McKennys and report to the station daily. Of course, no alcohol or drugs."

"You think he won't stay in line?"

Paschek's grin was as sharp as a wolf's. "No chance. And there's more. Here, watch this." He turned his monitor and punched a button. "It's the tape of our interrogation. Here's where I'm asking him where he was the day of the murder. He pauses and looks away. He's being careful to remember exactly what he told me in the hospital. But then I ask him if he left the motel for any reason. There. Right there." Paschek stabbed the screen with his finger. "He looks me straight in the eye and answers the question the same way he did earlier, word for word."

"You think he's lying."

"Of course he's lying. Rigid repetition—giving me exactly the same answer because he memorized it and practiced it. And then watching to see if I believe him. He's hiding something."

Melansen sipped his tea and nodded. "I agree. But what?"

"That's what I'm going to find out."

The detective set his mug down. "I'm afraid you'll have to do that on your own. There's a case down in Big Sky that needs oversight, and I've been reassigned. The CDI was going to send a junior detective up, but I told them you could handle things."

"Thanks for that, Ollie, but I'd still prefer to have you riding shotgun."

Melansen rose and shook Paschek's hand. "I'll see if I can get back later, but no promises."

Paschek fell into step beside him as they walked to the front of the station. "It's been good to—"

Raucous laughter interrupted him. Sven Karlsen strutted out the entrance, making a crude gesture with both hands as he did. The sheriff stalked to the front desk and jabbed a cocked thumb at the door. "Where in blazes is that idiot going? Don't tell me he made bail too."

"Karlsen?" Deputy Blackburn swallowed. "No, sir, the charges were dropped."

"How did that happen?"

"The DA called. His lawyer got him off on a technicality."

"What are you talking about? The public defender couldn't find a technicality if it came up and bit him on the rear end."

"Wasn't him. It was that lawyer, Andrychuk."

"How could Karlsen afford her? When did he even talk to her?"

"Uh, Sheriff?" Joseph Standingready eased forward. "She was here yesterday waiting for you. Karlsen was pestering her, and she talked to him after she met with Tyler Sampson."

Paschek stroked his jaw. "So Karlsen wanted her to get him out. But why on earth would she help him?" He pushed open the door and held it for Melansen. "Something's going on. Possibly the break we need."

"I don't know, Eugene." Melansen exited the building. "Like I said, I'll return if I can. Call me if something comes up."

"Yeah, yeah." Paschek lifted a hand before going back inside and letting the door close. *Karlsen.* His head jerked. "Go get him back."

Standingready started. "Karlsen? But the charges were dropped."

"I don't care about that. I want him in for questioning. About Shooter Sampson and his dead wife." He shoved the door open again and waved the deputy outside. "One more piece of evidence. One more nail in the coffin."

* * *

As a resident, Derek had never been able to get enough sleep. Some things never changed. That afternoon, he awoke groggy and confused. It was later than he intended, and by the time he called Rebecca she was heading to court for another client and had little time to talk. She quickly filled him in on the appellate court ruling. The conditions were strict, but at least at least Tyler was out of jail. He'd had to use the house and his father's land as surety, but he'd been able to post the bond.

Derek wanted to ask about the rest of her trip to Shelby, but Rebecca had to run, as her case was being called. He dropped the cell phone on his couch and flopped down beside it. He still hadn't decided what to do about Tyler's case. If what the other prisoner had said was true, Tyler's alibi was ruined. Worse, it meant he had lied to them all. Derek raked his scalp with both hands. He wasn't sure what to believe anymore.

From what Tyler had told him, it seemed he had really loved Jennifer, that he would never do anything to hurt her, but what if Derek had read him wrong? If Tyler had lied about staying in the motel, what else had he lied about? Derek pressed the heels of his palms against his forehead. He had no idea. Lifting his head, he glanced at the end table and the things on it. The photo of Cassie. His Bible. There was a lot he wasn't sure of anymore. *Too much.*

Guillain-Barré.

He glanced around the room. Where had that thought come from? *Guillain-Barré.*

It had to mean something. Derek jerked to his feet. He'd guessed what that patient had as soon as he saw her, although he'd needed the tests to confirm it. Cudworth would call it instinct. Others, intuition maybe. His attention shifted back to the Bible on the end table, the photo. Cassie would have called it something else. He used to trust that voice. Did he still?

His mouth felt as if it were full of dust. He lurched to the sink and wrenched the tap open. The water did not seem to quench his thirst. He clenched his jaw. "I have to get out of here."

* * *

Derek's stomach led him to the Homestead Cafe. As his gaze passed over the lunch counter and moved toward the booths on the far side of the restaurant, he revised that theory. Maybe something—or someone—else had led him. Tyler was here.

Derek walked across the room and stopped at the end of the booth. "Hey."

Tyler looked up and grinned. He was pale, and the bruises on his face shone like overripe plums, but his eyes were bright and dancing. He jumped up and grabbed Derek in a bear hug. "It's great to see you, man." He waved at the opposite bench and settled back down. "I was going to call you later."

"No problem," Derek said. "I'm glad you were able to make bail."

"That makes two of us." Tyler glanced at his watch. "At least I get to see Livy. She's supposed to be here any minute."

"Maybe I should go? I don't want to intrude."

"No, it's okay. I've got time. Besides, I wanted to thank you for all you've done. I really mean that, man."

"I'm glad I could help." Derek slid onto the bench and lowered his voice. "I did need to ask you something, though. About what Karlsen said." Tyler's smile faded and Derek lifted both hands. "I have to know. That's all."

Tyler blew out his breath. "Yeah, I guess you deserve that." He tugged a napkin from the metal holder and twisted it around his fingers. "Karlsen was right about what he saw." He tossed the napkin onto the table. "But he didn't see everything." He picked up his glass of water and took a long, slow drink before setting the glass down hard enough for the liquid to slosh around. "I hated the long breaks on the rigs. Things were bad with Jenn, so I couldn't go home. I knew all the other guys were off drinking... or worse. I tried keeping to myself, but it was hard. Sometimes, I wanted a drink so bad." His voice shook and he wiped his mouth with the back of his hand. "I'm sorry."

"No problem. Take your time."

Tyler swallowed hard. "I did leave the motel late that morning. I was going to the bar. Just one drink—that was all. I got there, too. Sat outside it for almost an hour." When his eyes met Derek's, they were rimmed with red. "But I didn't go in. I swear it."

"I believe you."

Tyler banged a fist against his forehead. "I should have gone home. I might have saved her. Instead, I went back to my room and fell asleep. I didn't know. She needed me, and I just went to sleep."

Derek reached across the table and grasped his forearm. "It's not your fault. There's no way you could have known."

Tyler unclenched his fist. When he spoke, his voice was soft but steady. "Yeah, we have to keep telling ourselves that. Don't we?"

The two men stared at each other before Derek replied, "Yes, yes, we do."

"Now, ain't this cozy?"

Derek snapped his head around. Sheriff Paschek towered over them. Bile rose in the back of Derek's throat. He started to rise, but Tyler lifted his hand and he sank back down.

"What do you want, Paschek?" Tyler said.

"Who, me? Nothing at all, Shooter—oh, sorry, I mean, Tyler. I'm only the messenger this time. But I'm afraid the message isn't good."

Tyler's jaw tightened. "What do you mean? What is it?"

Paschek stuck his thumbs under his gun belt. "I'm sorry to say that your daughter isn't going to make it to your little family reunion. Sent the rookie out to pick her up for you, but she's not feeling up to it."

"What does that mean?" Tyler surged to his feet, forcing Paschek to take a sharp step backward.

"Easy there, Tyler." He touched his weapon. "It's just a cold. A little fever. But the McKennys felt that she was too sick to go out."

"So that's it? That old man says something and you simply accept it? She's my daughter. I have the right to see her. I want to see her."

"Hey, hey, hey. Keep it down. All you gotta do is reschedule. You can see her tomorrow."

"Tomorrow? Tomorrow McKenny comes up with another excuse, and you dance to his tune. I'm seeing my daughter." Tyler took a step forward.

Paschek stopped him with a hand on his chest. "I said take it easy." His voice had hardened. "Don't do anything stupid."

"Or what? You'll beat me up? No wait, I forgot, you get Marsh to do your dirty work."

Derek slipped from the booth and took the young man by the arm. "Tyler, let's get out of here. We'll go talk to Rebecca. Maybe have her complain to the judge."

Tyler's head jerked. "You don't get it, do you? I thought you'd understand, but you don't. They won't let up. The McKennys. Paschek. This whole town. They won't stop until they've taken everything." He shook off Derek's hand. "They already took Jennifer. They're not getting Livy." He shoved Paschek aside and stumbled from the diner. An uncomfortable hush fell over the restaurant. Derek glanced around. The other patrons had been watching, but they quickly looked away.

"Why did you do that?" Derek moved closer to the sheriff.

"Do what?"

"Give him the news like that. Provoke him."

Paschek pursed his lips into a half smile. "Just doing my job."

"No, it's more than that. I think I'm starting to understand you, Sheriff. What is it you really want?"

Paschek's breath smelled of stale coffee. "What I want is real simple. I want Shooter Sampson to take all the rope we give him and hang himself with it."

"What if you're wrong? What if he's innocent?" Paschek's eyes flickered. Derek studied him. Something was there. Something in the sheriff he hadn't seen before.

"Innocent? He's not innocent." Paschek turned away and muttered, so low that Derek barely caught what he said. "None of us are."

* * *

Rebecca turned her phone on as she left the courtroom. Three missed calls, one every half hour that she'd been in court. Before she could check on the numbers, her phone rang again and she pressed it to her ear.

"Rebecca Andrychuk."

The man on the other end let loose with a string of words she could barely make out. "Tyler? Slow down. Tell me everything."

He took a breath and then relayed what had happened in the diner.

Rebecca grimaced. "Paschek." She spit the word out of her mouth like a cherry pit. "What a jerk. Okay look, I'll speak to the judge. I won't be able to do anything about it today, but I can make sure it doesn't happen again."

"Never mind." Tyler's voice had gone calm. Too calm. "I'll take care of this myself."

Her eyes widened. "What does that mean? Don't do anything stupid. Tyler? Tyler?"

Rebecca stared at the dead phone in her hand and gritted her teeth. This was bad. Very bad. She needed to do something fast, before it got a lot worse. She shoved the phone into her pocket and hurried to her car. She had to get to Tyler. She only hoped it wouldn't be too late.

THIRTY-TWO

"If you have tears, prepare to shed them now."
Julius Caesar Act III, Scene II

After receiving her frantic phone call, Derek had caught up with Rebecca on the edge of town. He had to speed to keep her car in sight, and even at that, was only barely able to do so. By the time he pulled into the farmyard, she had jumped out of the car and was headed for the house. He ran to catch up.

A lone figure stood in the yard. A few feet from the front door, the man waved his arms and screamed at the house. As Derek raced forward, the curtains were shoved aside and two faces appeared in the window. Samuel and Tabitha McKenny. The old man's face was stark and red, his eyes wild, and his lips twisted in anger. He shook his fist at the figure in the yard before Tabitha pulled him away.

"Tyler!" Rebecca's voice was shrill as she raced forward to grasp the young man's arm. He yanked free and staggered backwards.

"Don't touch me. Leave me alone." The words were slurred.

"Are you crazy? You know you can't be here. You want to go back to jail?"

"Gotta see my daughter. Gotta see Livy." He spun back toward the house, swayed, and almost fell.

Derek pulled Tyler to his feet. "Careful now. I've got you." Tyler tried to shake him off, but Derek tightened his grip and dragged him away from the house.

"Lemme go. Livy needs me."

"Rebecca's right. You can't be here."

Tyler tried once more to lurch back toward the McKennys' front door, but Rebecca grabbed his free arm. He stared at her for a moment as a wave of confusion crashed over his face. Then he sank to the ground and began to cry.

Rebecca shot a look at Derek. "How much do you think he's had to drink?"

"Too much, for sure. Let's get him to my car. Maybe we can get him out of here before any more damage is done." Halfway across the yard, the wail of a police siren snatched that hope away.

The three of them froze next to Derek's car when the police vehicle wheeled into the yard, lights flashing. Sheriff Paschek and Deputy Standingready climbed out of the police car and stalked toward the trio. "We'll take it from here," Paschek said.

"It's just a misunderstanding, Sheriff." Rebecca let go of Tyler's arm and moved to stand in front of him. "Mr. Sampson was upset about not seeing his daughter. It won't happen again."

"You're absolutely right it won't happen again." Paschek curled his lip into a sneer. "'Cause Shooter here is going back to jail."

Keeping his grip on Tyler's arm, Derek lifted his other hand. "Come on, Sheriff, can't you let this one go? He didn't hurt anyone."

"Let it go? Drunk and disorderly. Disturbing the peace. Trespassing. Oh, and of course, breaking almost every one of his bail conditions. Let it go? I don't think so." Paschek jerked his chin in Tyler's direction. "Deputy, put the cuffs on Mr. Sampson."

Standingready eased past Rebecca. She and Derek let go of Tyler as the deputy pulled his arms behind his back. As he slipped the cuffs on, he gave a minute shake of his head and whispered, "Sorry about this."

Derek watched as the deputy led his friend to the patrol car and then whirled on Paschek. "You planned this, didn't you? The whole thing. McKenny claiming that Olivia was sick. The show at the diner. You set Tyler up."

"Careful, Doctor," Paschek said through gritted teeth, "This ain't your world. It's mine. You keep sticking your nose where it don't belong, and it might get clipped off."

"You're threatening me now? I've encountered bullies before, and it seems to me most of them are cowards."

Resting a hand on Derek's arm, Rebecca stepped forward. "I will be talking to Judge Hollister about this. I'll make sure she finds out about everything."

"You go ahead and do that, Miss Andrychuk." Paschek grinned and touched the bill of his hat. "You have a nice day now."

Derek stood rigid as the sheriff slid into the patrol car and pulled out of the farmyard. Rebecca leaned against him as if for support. His arm moved automatically to circle her waist. She tilted her head to look up at him.

"Thanks for being here with me," she said. "I'm sorry it turned out like this."

Her eyes were green, flecked with gold. His gaze lingered on her lips as they eased slowly into a slight smile. Something warm spread through Derek's chest.

"Hey!" The voice was harsh and angry. Rebecca straightened as Derek jerked around. Samuel and Tabitha McKenny stood in the open doorway of their house. The old man shook his fist at them. "Get off my land right now, or I'll call the police. Again."

Derek dropped his hand and stepped away from Rebecca. It was time to go.

* * *

The drive back into town was a lot slower than the one out and seemed even farther. Rebecca wanted nothing more than to go with Derek somewhere, to talk things over, simply to be with him. But that wasn't to be. They had both agreed that she needed to get to her office and see what she could do about Tyler. In reality, she didn't have much hope, at least not when it came to getting her client out of jail again. She glanced in her rearview mirror and smiled as Derek waved before turning off toward his apartment. She still had hope for other things, even if they would have to wait.

* * *

For a moment, Derek was tempted to keep following the Mustang back to Rebecca's office. *Yeah, like that would make things less complicated.* Moments later, he collapsed on the couch in his apartment and sat staring at his hands. The late afternoon had drained away into evening before he leaned back and squinted at the ceiling. "What else am I supposed to do?"

Silence.

"I'm not really helping Tyler that much, am I? Okay, I believe he's innocent, but what good is that?"

Silence.

"And what about Rebecca? I'm not sure I'm ready for that." He glanced at the photo of Cassie and a needle of ice pierced his chest. The glass was still broken. He'd forgotten to replace it. "It's too soon." He stumbled to his feet, a marionette with half its strings severed. His breathing was harsh and ragged as he lifted his voice to the ceiling. "What do you want me to do? Tell me."

His voice echoed through the small apartment. There was no reply.

* * *

The cell door thudded shut with dull clang. Paschek stood on the other side of the bars, his arms crossed in grim satisfaction. Tyler slumped down on the cot. "Why you doing this to me?"

"'Cause you're guilty, that's why."

"I didn't do it. I never hurt Jenn. I swear."

"The evidence says otherwise."

"But what if you don't have it all? What about Marsh? Rebecca told me he'd been bird dogging Jenn. Maybe *he* killed her."

Paschek smirked. "That all she's come up with? What a joke. Marsh had nothing to do with it. I know for a fact he was nowhere near Stockton when your wife was murdered. He's got something you don't." He unfolded his arms and gripped two of the cell bars. "An alibi."

"I told you already." The young man's voice held a tremor. "I was sleeping. At the motel."

"Yeah, right. Except for when you stepped out for a drink. Oh yeah, I know all about that. Your fancy lawyer got Sven Karlsen off on a technicality, but it didn't take much to get him to spill his guts about what he saw. He'll testify that on the morning of the murder you were sitting in your truck outside a bar in Shelby. Not a long drive from there to your house. Plenty of time." Paschek waved his hand with a flourish. "Take a look around, Shooter. This is going to be your home from now on. Get used to it."

Paschek started to walk away then stopped. "Why don't you confess? Save us all a lot of hassle?"

Tyler stiffened. "Because I'm innocent. I didn't do it." He shoved to his feet and made a desperate lunge at the door to the cell. "I need to see Livy. Let me see her."

"Don't think that's gonna happen."

"Please." Tears flooded the young man's eyes.

The sheriff's predatory grin wavered for a moment.. "It's not up to me. You'll have to talk to your lawyer about that. Maybe she can do something." He smacked the bars with the palm of his hand. "I wouldn't count on it, though."

* * *

The angry tone of his cell phone scraped its way into his consciousness. Derek wrenched his eyes open and sat up. He couldn't remember falling asleep. What time was it? The first red rays of dawn gleamed through the window. *Shepherd's warning.* The phone was insistent and he snatched it off the end table. "Hello?"

"Dr. Kessler? It's the ER calling. I know you're not working today but could you come back in?"

"What is it?"

"It's Bert Cavanaugh, Doctor. He's in bad shape. He's asking for you, and the nurse supervisor thought you'd want to know."

"I'll be right there."

* * *

The fill-in physician, Dr. Stadler, waited for Derek at the entrance to the ER.

"What happened, Art?"

"He was in his kitchen making breakfast when he took another fall. Right through a plate glass window. Neighbor saw him and called the ambulance."

"How bad is it?"

"Pretty bad. He severed the brachial artery. Lost a lot of blood."

"How many units has he had?"

"None."

"How can that be? You must have done something."

"Hey, take it easy. I tried, but Bert refused a transfusion."

Derek rubbed his forehead. Was Bert giving up?

"That's not all," Stadler said. "It's, well, it's his heart. He had an MI on the way in. Big one. He's refusing any treatment. Wanted to see you. I didn't know what else to do."

"It's okay, Art. I think I understand." Derek made his way to the casualty room. Bert lay on a gurney, his arm wrapped in a thick layer of gauze. Half of it was damp and red. His friend's face was pale, his breaths slow and shallow. When Derek laid a hand on his shoulder, Bert's eyelids flickered, and his eyes focused on Derek's. They both smiled.

"Sorry to wake you, Bert."

"Ah, 'To sleep, perchance to dream.'"

"Hamlet?"

"Yes. Only I haven't been dreaming. More of a vision. 'I saw the Lord, high and lifted up, and His train filled the temple.' That's Isaiah."

Bert's face glowed. "I've been there. With Him. With Marie." He closed his eyes, and a soft smile touched his lips. "I want to stand up."

"I'm not sure that's wise."

"Hey, don't worry, Doc. I'm not going to get any sicker." He grabbed Derek's arm and hauled himself slowly to his feet. Derek held onto him until Bert waved him away. He raised his hands and gazed at them. There was no tremor, no shaking. He smiled again. "Thank you, Doc. That was good."

Derek took his elbow and guided him onto the gurney. The older man grabbed Derek's hand. "It's all good."

"Let me do something. A couple of units of blood, that's all. You'll be all right."

Bert squeezed his fingers. "No, I've done all I was meant to do. I'm ready for this."

"I'm not. What if you're wrong? What if you're still needed?" Derek's voice dropped to a whisper. "What if I still need you? You're my friend. The best, maybe the only one."

Bert's eyelids drifted shut. "No, there's another. He's a friend closer than a brother." A tremor washed over his body, and he let go of Derek and folded his hands over his chest. "Okay," he said. "Now it's time. It's time to go home."

* * *

Paschek didn't have to be at the station at this time of the morning. He could still be at home asleep or at least enjoying a decent breakfast. He grimaced at the murky liquid in his cup. Even the rookie made better coffee than Blackburn. He swiveled in his chair to survey his office—dull beige cabinets stuffed with files, a pin-cushioned cork board covered with notices and alerts, half of them outdated, a grimy window with a view of the parking lot... all in all, not much better than the cells.

He stood and sauntered over to the framed photos hung on the wall. There weren't many. A formal one of him wearing his dress blues. Another of his graduating class from the Colorado police academy. He lingered there for a moment, tracing the lines of fresh-faced men and women. Moved back east. Retired. Dead. Lost touch. Another one dead. In rehab. Not much of a legacy for any of them.

Paschek touched the last frame. Its glass covered not a photograph but two newspaper clippings. Yellowed and dry, some of the lines were starting to fade. It didn't matter. He knew them all by heart. Especially the headline. *Police officer, son wounded in drug bust. Two dead.* He stalked to his desk and wrenched open the bottom drawer. The jar was mostly empty, with only a scattering of green candies. The deputies thought he hated the green ones. It was more that someone else loved them. The head wound had left the boy functioning at the level of a toddler, but he was still his son. He punched his intercom, his voice a low growl. "Blackburn, go get me some M&M's."

* * *

The temperature in his car rose as Derek sat and watched vehicles come and go from the hospital parking lot. A small car pulled up at the entrance, and a young man raced into the building. Hurrying back with a wheelchair, he helped a young woman into it. Her stomach protruded in the final stages of pregnancy, and as her husband wheeled her into the hospital, they were both panting through pursed lips.

Derek blinked and looked away. Death and life. *What's the point? It's all futile. You live and you die. So what?* He stared out the front window. The sky was clear and cloudless, the type of day where a person could see for miles. If there was anything to see. If there was anything to look at.

A shadow passed over him. Someone stood by his car. It was that cop. The one from the diner. What was his name, Joseph? He lowered the window.

"You all right, my friend?" Standingready asked.

"You don't want to be my friend. All my friends are dead or in jail."

The deputy bent down and rested his arms on the door frame. "I heard about Bert. He was a good man. He'd bring donuts by the station sometimes. We talked a bit."

"Oh."

"It was amazing how he kept going in spite of that disease."

Derek shrugged. "Yeah."

"He stayed real active, didn't he? I guess you'd call it a miracle, eh?"

"Miracle?"

"Well, yeah. He had a real bad disease, but he was always so happy. Joyful, even."

"He's still dead."

The deputy clasped his shoulder. "It hurts. I understand that."

"Do you?" Derek shook the hand off and stared ahead. "Bert's dead, and you've got Tyler in jail. What a great day."

The deputy straightened. "Hey, I don't have anybody in jail. But, yeah, Tyler Sampson is back in custody. All I did was help find some of the evidence. It was the DA who decided to charge him and the judge who set the bail conditions."

Derek fixed his gaze on Standingready's face. His voice was clipped when he spoke. "What evidence?"

The policeman hesitated. He scanned the lot before lowering his voice. "It's not a big thing. I found the witness who saw Sampson's truck leaving the yard on the day of the murder."

"Was the witness sure it was Tyler's?"

The deputy shrugged. "He only said it was a black pickup."

The sun bore down on the two men. Heat waves rippled up from the asphalt. A squirrel scurried across the fringe of lawn and up a tree. Derek screwed his eyes shut and clenched his teeth. He knew what he had to do. He reached for the key.

"I have to go."

THIRTY-THREE

"For murder, though it have no tongue,
will speak with most miraculous organ."
Hamlet, Act II, Scene II

"I'm in over my head." Rebecca paced the outer office. Paulina sorted papers and kept her head down while her employer spoke. "Who am I fooling? I'm not a criminal attorney. It's a murder trial, for heaven's sake. If I mess up, Tyler Sampson will go to jail for a long time."

She stopped and pressed her palms to Paulina's desk. "And the District Attorney. I can't stand the man. He's so smug, as if his evidence is completely air-tight. Ha." Rebecca shoved away from the desk. Grabbing a paper from the table, she waved it about. "Judge Hollister practically came out and said she'd never allow Jennifer's letter into court. Maybe as evidence of state of mind, but nothing else." She dropped the paper and Paulina returned it to a the pile.

"No way it could be accepted," Rebecca said. "The Supreme Court ruled on something like this already." She stopped and contemplated an odd waterstain on the ceiling. *Looks as messed up as I am.* "At least, I think it did. There was a case. What was it?" She collapsed onto a chair and wove her fingers through her hair. "I can't do it. I'm not good enough. Hollister won't be the trial judge. What if the letter is deemed admissible? What do I do then?"

Paulina rose and carried a clipboard over to Rebecca. Holding it out, she smiled. "These letters need to go out. Sign here, here, and here." She tapped the blank lines with a pen before handing it to Rebecca.

"I know what you're thinking," Rebecca said as she complied. "But who could I turn to?"

Paulina carried the letters to her desk and started making copies for the files. Rebecca scanned the pictures and diplomas on the wall. The letters were in their envelopes, stamped and ready to go when she turned to Paulina and shoved her hands into her hips.

"Don't say it. I'm not asking him. I am not asking my father for help."

* * *

He didn't want to go into the yard. He had driven by, twice in fact, and the same gray car was still parked in front of the house. McKenny might be home, and Derek did not want to tip him off. He pulled to the side of the road, well out of sight of the house, and glared at the farmyard. Deputy Standingready had told him someone had seen a black pickup leaving the Sampson place the morning Jennifer was killed. He was certain that he had seen a black truck hidden in the trees at the back of the McKenny place. That had to mean something.

Tyler was innocent, Derek was becoming more and more certain of it. That meant someone else was guilty. His money was on Samuel McKenny. The old man was so full of hate and anger that he was surely capable of anything, including murdering his own daughter to save her from a life of sin. He tapped his fingers on the steering wheel. How to prove it? What did he know about such things? He groaned and rested his head on the back of the seat. *I'm an ER doc, not a detective.* He massaged his forehead as a great weariness enveloped him. *I just don't know anymore.*

Do something. The urge seemed to grow, pushing away the fatigue. He hopped out of the Jeep and yanked open the tailgate. After rummaging through a box in the rear of the vehicle, he pulled out an old pair of binoculars. Holding them to his eyes with both hands, Derek scanned the back of the McKenny property. The trees were thick with foliage and he couldn't see anything. A small cloud had covered the sun, but it drifted past at that moment and his eyes caught a flash of light. *There. A reflection. From a tail light?* Derek focused in on the spot. It was there. The black truck was there.

The ragged chime of his cell phone startled him, and he almost dropped the binoculars. Ripping the phone from his pocket, he darted back inside the vehicle and uttered a breathless, "Hello?"

"Hey, it's Rebecca. Did I catch you at a bad time?"

"No, it's fine."

"Are you sure? You don't sound fine."

Derek took a deep breath. "I'm okay. It's been a rough day, that's all."

"Well, my news likely isn't going to help. My application to get Tyler's bail reinstated was dismissed. We're not through, although I do need to come up with a different approach. It might help to talk things over. Maybe we could get together for an early supper if you're not too tired?"

"I guess we could."

"Are you sure? It would help to get your input on things."

"Then let's do it. I have a few things to tell you as well." He shot a look in the direction of the truck before closing the tailgate of his Jeep and heading for the driver's seat.

"Great. It's a beautiful day out. Let's meet at the pizza place. They have a patio and actually make a good panini."

The thought made his stomach rumble. "Perfect. See you there."

* * *

The prairie sky was an endless, clear blue. A scattering of feathered clouds touched the broad expanse like the remnants of a daydream. Derek played with the food on his plate without eating any. Rebecca watched him quietly and waited, her sandwich sitting untouched. At last, she reached out and touched his hand.

"It will really help the case knowing about the McKennys' truck. Anything that points away from Tyler is good. Seems like something else is on your mind, though. What's happening?"

Derek blew out a long breath. "Do you know Bert Cavanaugh?"

"I've heard of him. Doesn't he have some disease?"

"He did. Huntington's. He died today. He was my friend."

She flinched and grasped his fingers. "I'm sorry."

He stared at her hand. It was soft in his. Smooth and pale against his skin. So much like Cassie's.

"Do you want to talk about it?"

Derek continued to study her hand. "Not much to say." Her nails were a glossy soft pink. "Bert kept going despite the Huntington's. He was always upbeat." Her fingers were long and slender. "One of those guys who'd always make you smile." It was becoming harder to concentrate. "He had a heart attack. Now, he's dead." Harder to breathe too.

Rebecca lifted his chin with her other hand. Her eyes were moist. The breeze caressed her hair. "I'm so sorry. He must have meant a lot to you. Let me help. I'm done working for the day. Why don't you come to my place. You could stay." She leaned across the table, her face close to his. Their lips touched.

Derek breathed in sharply, as if he'd been punched in the stomach. A sheen of sweat glistened on his forehead and his face blanched. He gave his head a small shake, as if waking from a dream. "I'm sorry," he said, his voice hoarse. "I can't do that. It would be… wrong."

Rebecca recoiled as though he'd struck her. A red blush touched her cheeks. Her eyes darted from side to side, like a wild thing searching for somewhere to hide. "Wrong?" Her voice quivered and then grew stronger. "Wrong?" The red in her cheeks deepened, and her eyes flashed. "Who do you think you are to judge me?" She shoved her chair away from the table and grabbed her purse. "I've been a fool. I thought we might have something. I even gave up a weekend in the mountains for you. With someone who wanted to be with me." She pulled some cash out of her bag and threw it on the table. "That's for dinner, Doctor. Go to hell."

"Rebecca, I…"

She spun and stalked away from the patio. Derek remained in his seat, frozen in shock. A waiter inched up beside him.

"Uh, would you like these to go?"

* * *

Derek couldn't run fast enough. He tried. After he had left the restaurant, he'd driven straight home and changed. The late afternoon was hot and airless, but still he ran. His legs and lungs were burning, but he only ran harder. His vision began to blur, flashes of red and black piercing the periphery until at last he had to stop.

He stood panting by the side of the road, sweat dripping from his forehead to evaporate on the hot asphalt. Gradually, his pulse slowed to a dull roar in his ears. When he could draw in a breath without his lungs hurting, he looked up. The town was a distant smudge on the horizon. Derek shook his head. *That's the problem with trying to run away from your problems. Eventually, you have to go back.* One foot in front of the other, he trudged back the way he had come.

* * *

Rebecca left tire marks at each stop sign as she roared back to the office. She half-hoped Paschek would show up with his stupid red and blue lights at one of them. It would feel good to strangle someone. She exploded into her office and snarled at Paulina to send a client in before collapsing onto her executive chair. Slow, deep breaths brought her pulse and blood pressure down to a simmer as she stared out the window. A tapping sound caused her to swivel back around.

Paulina stood at the desk, her arms crossed and her foot beating out a staccato rhythm.

"Did you get me some work?"

"No, I did not, Ms. Andrychuk."

"Why not? And what's with this Ms. Andrychuk stuff? I've told you…"

"Will you shut up for a moment?" Paulina's foot stilled. "Look, honey, I'm not sure what's got you so worked up, but now's not the time to be seeing clients. I like working in this town, and anybody you talked to right now wouldn't be a client much longer."

Rebecca stabbed the power button on her laptop. "I need to get stuff done. I've been spending all my time on this stupid murder case, and I'm behind on everything else. Get me something to do."

"No." Paulina rounded the desk and spun Rebecca around to face her. Gripping the armrests, she looked Rebecca in the eye. "You need to go home. You have to cool off and figure out whatever it is that's going on with you."

"But…"

"No buts. Go home. You can fire me in the morning. But make sure you're here on time. You have a busy day with all that work you're so concerned about."

Rebecca watched her secretary leave. Only after the door had clicked shut did she think to close her mouth. She blinked and looked around the office. Then she laughed out loud.

* * *

After stepping out of the shower, Derek grabbed a towel and walked to the kitchen. He pulled one of the paninis from the Styrofoam container and took a bite. Although he hadn't been sure his stomach could handle food, it actually went down nicely. The first sandwich disappeared quickly, and he reached for the second. His gaze strayed continually to the phone on the end table. *Should I call her?* He set the sandwich down and strode over, picking up the device then setting it down again.

She should make the first move. He grabbed a set of clean clothes and hurried to get dressed.

* * *

Rebecca didn't head straight home. A couple of quick stops, though, and she was ready to. She glanced at the passenger seat of her Mustang. Two new Blu-rays, a pizza, and quart of rocky road ice cream. She was ready for anything now.

* * *

Grabbing his car keys, Derek headed to the door. As he touched the handle, his eye was drawn back to the night stand. Resting beside his Bible was a small picture of Cassie and Sarah, smiling up at him. He had taken the photo a week before they died. As he stared at the picture, his shoulders slumped as if a great weight had settled onto them. He blinked hard and yawned. *So tired.* He stumbled to the bed and fell onto it with a moan.

Had he meant to go somewhere? His eyelids fluttered and closed.

* * *

The pizza had grown cold. The ice cream had received every bit of her attention. The movie droned on, unwatched, as Rebecca sat and chewed on her knuckles. For the twelfth time, she picked up her phone. This time she got to the seventh digit before she slapped the device back down. *Forget it. He was the one who was wrong. Let him apologize.*

She sat and stared at the phone. It didn't ring. With a hiss of frustration, Rebecca snatched the remote and punched a button. The movie continued to flicker at her from the television screen, only now in silence. The quiet washed over her. When her angst had settled, somewhat, Rebecca moved. The pizza went in the fridge and the empty ice cream carton in the garbage. She had finished tidying the room and was wiping down the counter when her doorbell rang. A smile crossed her face as she hurried to the door and flung it open.

"I knew you'd change your—" She stopped, confused. "Oh. I wasn't expecting… I mean, come in. Would you like something? Tea, maybe?"

Her visitor nodded and entered the condo.

THIRTY-FOUR

*"For curses never pass the lips of those
that breathe them in the air."*
Richard III, Act 1, Scene III

The light was harsh and bright and shone directly in his eyes. He covered them with one hand, trying to force the last vestiges of sleep from his brain. He stretched and shambled to the kitchen. The coffee maker had started to gurgle cheerfully when his phone rang.

"Derek, it's Chandra. You're needed at the hospital right away."

"Why? What's going on?"

"It's Rebecca Andrychuk. You need to get here STAT."

* * *

The quickest way into the ER was through the ambulance bay. Leaving his Jeep double-parked, Derek tore inside. Chandra caught him at the door and waved him toward the casualty room. Even as he yanked aside the curtain, he heard the distinctive huff of a respirator. Rebecca lay on the gurney, a host of tubes running into her body. Two IVs dripped fluids into her and a trach tube had been placed into her throat. Derek watched her cheat rise and fall to the rhythm of the respirator. At least the heart monitor showed a steady, regular beat. He felt a hand on his sleeve and turned to Chandra. "What happened?"

"They found her like this. When her secretary couldn't reach her early this morning, she called Rebecca's neighbor, Judge Farr. He didn't get a response at the door, so he called 911. They had to break in to get to her."

"I don't understand."

"She was barely breathing when the ambulance got there. When the paramedic tried to intubate her, he found two fentanyl patches in her mouth."

Fentanyl. The word struck him like a fist. "Oh no."

"I found two more on her body. I've given her Narcan, and she's out of danger for now. But she may be unconscious for awhile."

"She could have died."

"I know. If her secretary hadn't called…"

"But how? How could this have happened?"

"That's a good question, Doctors." Derek and Chandra both turned. Sheriff Paschek and Deputy Standingready stood in the opening of the cubicle. The sheriff rested a hand on his weapon. "When did you see her last?"

"Yesterday. About five."

"When you had your big fight? Lover's spat, was it?"

He cocked his head. "You heard about that?"

"It's a small town, Doc. You didn't see her later?"

"No."

"So she was pretty upset the last time you saw her."

"Yeah, I guess she was."

"Upset enough to do something stupid?"

His mouth went dry. Was the sheriff suggesting their argument had driven Rebecca to try and take her own life? "No way. I mean, I don't think so." But how well did he know her, really?

"And you didn't see her later?"

Really? Trying to trip him up by repeating his questions? "I told you I didn't."

"Where were you for the rest of the day?"

"I was at my apartment."

"Any witnesses?"

No living ones. The photo of Cassie and Sarah flashed through his mind. "No. I live alone."

Chandra moved closer to Derek and glared at Paschek. "What are you suggesting? Derek had nothing to do with this."

Paschek offered her a mock bow. "Thank you for clearing that up, Doctor. Good to know. So tell me, who would have access to a drug like this? Don't see many of these patches on the street."

"I don't know," Chandra said. "Patients who got them with a prescription, I guess. A pharmacist."

"How about doctors? You keep these things in the hospital, don't you?"

"Yeah, we do," Derek said. "But not in the ER. Only in the hospital pharmacy or on the wards, and only under lock and key. No one is allowed to remove them without a witness present."

"Okay, we'll check that out. Thank you for your cooperation." Paschek whirled around and headed toward the exit. Standingready shrugged and gave Derek an apologetic half-smile before following his boss.

"What was that about?" Chandra asked after the doors had hissed shut behind the two officers.

"I don't think he likes me very much."

"You think? It's more than that."

"Could be." The sound of Rebecca's steady breathing calmed him. A little. "I think it's because of the murder case."

"You mean the Sampson thing?"

"Yeah, Rebecca's defending Tyler, and I've been helping her a bit."

"I thought I'd heard something. What's wrong with that?"

He lifted his shoulders. "Paschek seems so sure that Tyler's guilty. I guess he doesn't want us getting in the way."

"Well, I'm afraid Rebecca will be out of the way for a while."

Derek walked to the bedside and pressed his palm to Rebecca's forehead. "She'll be okay. Give it a day or two, and she'll be back on her feet."

"Derek," Chandra reached for Rebecca's chart on the tray table, "what happened yesterday at the pizza place?"

"You heard about that too?"

"Like the sheriff said, it's a small town."

He sighed. "Rebecca seemed to be pushing for the two of us to get together, and I panicked. Everything's happening a little too quickly. I'm not ready." He took the chart from her and scanned it. "When will you move her to ICU?"

Before she could answer, a middle-aged man in a dark suit strode into the tiny space. "You won't be moving her anywhere," he said. "She's coming with me."

* * *

Paschek stopped as soon as they'd cleared the doors to the ER and jerked his head toward the hospital. "Check things out here, Deputy. Talk to admin and the hospital pharmacy. Tell them I expect their full attention and assistance. Check out Kessler's story that no one's allowed to remove narcotics without a witness. See if anyone on staff has been in the pharmacy alone recently. Don't take any crap. Got it?"

"Yes, Sheriff."

"Good." Paschek squinted as he peered through the glass doors. "And find out who the suit is."

* * *

"Excuse me?" Derek moved to block the man's way. Two paramedics had followed him into the room with a stretcher. The stitching on their sleeves read *Seattle Air Ambulance*.

"I said Rebecca is coming with me," the stranger said. "I'm Maxwell Andrychuk. Rebecca is my daughter."

Derek exchanged a look with Chandra before facing the man. "I'm sorry," Derek said. "What did you mean she's going with you? She's in no condition to be moved."

The smile tightened on Max's face. "And you are?"

"Kessler. Dr. Derek Kessler."

"Well, Doctor, I got a call a short time ago from my friend Judge Farr. He told me what happened. I hired a plane and a medical team and flew down to take Rebecca back to Seattle. All the papers are in order." He tugged an envelope from the inside pocket of his jacket and held it up. "I am her next of kin."

"But she's stable now."

"No offense, Doctor." The man walked over to stand beside Rebecca. "But she's my only child. I need to make sure she's okay."

Derek took the envelope from him and slid a thin sheet of paper out of it. He scanned it and his shoulders sagged. It definitely looked legitimate. Chandra pushed back the curtain and left the cubicle. Derek folded the letter and returned it to the envelope before thrusting it at Rebecca's father. "I want it on the record that I opposed moving her."

The man's lips twitched as if he was amused. "So noted."

Chandra returned with the hospital's respirator tech, who set to work disconnecting her from the respirator. He used an ambu-bag to pump air into her lungs while the paramedics slid her onto the stretcher they'd brought.

"We're ready to go, sir."

Max nodded to Derek and Chandra and followed the stretcher out of the ER to the waiting ambulance. Derek watched them go before speaking. "Will she be all right?" He wasn't looking at Chandra or the respiratory tech. His gaze was turned upward. Neither of them responded.

As the ambulance disappeared from view, Derek remained standing at entryway doors. He barely felt the hand on his arm.

"You okay?" Chandra asked.

"I don't know."

"Do you want to talk?"

"No, thanks. I need to think."

"She'll be fine. God will take care of her."

Derek knew she and John were church goers. They prayed over every meal and their faith had seemed stronger than his own. Was it enough? "Do you really believe that?"

Chandra's voice was strong. "Yes, I do."

He stared at the doors where Rebecca had disappeared. *I'm not so sure. I'm just not sure.*

* * *

The ER was never quiet for long. Derek wandered around the department and into the staff room. He drank two cups of bad coffee before heading for the exit and a couple more hours of sleep. A voice called him back. He turned slowly and grimaced. Julia Antosh strode toward him through the ER, Maggie and a young woman in a white coat following close behind.

"Dr. Kessler, we need to talk."

"We already talked. I got the message. No more praying."

"It's not that."

Derek ran a hand over his face. "Well, whatever it is, can it wait? It's been a bad day."

"That's what I need to speak to you about. Would you come up to my office?"

His legs felt suddenly leaden. "Not sure I can walk that far."

"All right, let's step into the staff room."

Would he never be allowed to sleep? Repressing a groan of frustration, he followed the women into the small room, After closing the door, Antosh motioned to the stranger. "This is Noelle Richardson. She's covering the hospital pharmacy while Charlie Watson is away on holidays. Noelle, please tell Dr. Kessler what you found today."

The young pharmacist blushed and ducked her head. "I'm really sorry. A policeman came in and wanted me to check the narcotics records, particularly to see if anyone had gotten access to the drugs on their own. Charlie's logs were a mess. He hadn't finished them before he left for his holidays. I couldn't reach him. I tried. The thing is, I did find an irregularity. You were there on your own on the 26th. I didn't want to cause any trouble, but I had to report it."

Derek's chest tightened. "What does that mean?"

Antosh's voice was cold and professional. "You signed out a fentanyl patch from the pharmacy two nights ago."

Derek's eyes narrowed. "So?"

"No one countersigned and confirmed it. And with the logs not up to date, there's no way to prove that you didn't take more than that. Four of them, even."

Red flags popped up in his mind. Four fentanyl patches? Like the ones Chandra had found on ... "Maggie was there." Derek spun toward the head nurse, but she shook her head.

"I'm sorry, Doctor," she said. "I wasn't there the whole time. I got called away, remember?" She held up both hands in a helpless gesture. "I can't confirm that you only took one patch, because I left before you did."

They think I did this to Rebecca. Heart pounding, Derek shifted his gaze back to the administrator. "Okay, so I was briefly in the pharmacy alone. What are you suggesting?"

"I'm not suggesting anything, only stating facts. The facts are that a woman you had an argument with came in this morning. In a coma. With four fentanyl patches on her. And you're the only one in the hospital who could have taken them from the pharmacy without anyone knowing."

It had become as hard for him to breathe as it had been after his long run in the heat the day before. "Do you actually believe I had anything to do with that?"

"Dr. Kessler, I'm sorry, but consider how it looks. You have a heated and public argument with Rebecca Andrychuk, and then she turns up in the ER after OD'ing on fentanyl patches. Which you had access to, and at least one of which you signed out of the pharmacy without anyone countersigning."

Maggie stepped forward. "I explained how that came about."

"I know, I know." Antosh patted Maggie's arm. "It's not your fault. These things happen."

"They shouldn't. I was responsible for making sure it didn't."

"No one's blaming you, Maggie. And no one is blaming Dr. Kessler." Antosh turned back to Derek. "However, we need to be certain. We have to protect the hospital... and you."

"What are you saying?"

"I'm sorry." Antosh straightened and took a deep breath. "But until we finish an investigation to clear this up… I have to suspend you."

This is not happening. "Are you serious?"

"I'm sure it will only be for a couple of days."

Maggie pressed her lips together as though trying to keep them from trembling. "I'm so sorry, Doctor."

Maybe they'll give me the cell next to Tyler. That will make Sheriff Paschek happy. Shoving back the cynical thought, Derek spun around and headed for the door. "Forget it," he said. "I'm out of here."

He was almost to his Jeep when Chandra caught up to him.

"Derek, I don't get it. What's going on?"

"I'm suspended. As you know, someone tried to kill Rebecca with fentanyl patches, and it looks like I'm the only one on staff who could have gotten them out of the pharmacy. Which makes everyone think that I might be the murderer."

"That's crazy."

"Yeah." Derek didn't look at her as he reached for his vehicle door handle.

"Are you okay? Is there anything I can do to help?"

"I need to be alone."

"Derek, please, let me help. You're hurting right now. I understand that."

He let go of the handle and whirled toward her. "How? How can you understand it? You've got the perfect life. How can you understand anything?"

"Derek…"

"You've got it all. Great practice. Fantastic marriage. Everybody loves you." He ignored the tears that sprang to her eyes and started to open the door to the Jeep, but Chandra thrust out an arm and pushed it shut. Tears flowed down her cheeks as she poked him in the chest.

"No, it's you that doesn't understand. You think you're the only one to lose someone? The only one to be hurt? You lost a child. Well, so did I. A stillbirth hurts just as much. You lost your family. Well, mine disowned me when I married a Christian. I'm dead as far as my father is concerned. So don't accuse me of not understanding pain. Don't."

She turned away sharply and strode back into the ER. Derek started to follow her but stopped. Letting his hands fall to his sides, he stood and watched her go.

It was quiet. Even the birds in the trees had ceased to sing. Derek climbed into the Jeep. As he drove away, he looked up at the prairie sky. It was stark and empty.

THIRTY-FIVE

"They do not love that do not show their love."
The Two Gentlemen of Verona, Act I, Scene II

Derek drove mindlessly, not watching for landmarks, turning when he felt the urge to turn, not stopping at all. Only when the gas gauge pinged a warning did he pause to look around. He barely resisted the urge to bang his head against the steering wheel. *Can't even run away properly.* There on his left, only a couple of miles away, was Stockton.

Like the rest of life. Going in circles.

The gas station attendant tried to make small talk, but when Derek only grunted in reply, he took the hint. Wandering through the aisles, Derek pulled magazines out but replaced them without even a glance. He picked up a bag of chips and stood staring at it. Glancing over at the counter, he caught the attendant watching him. He put the chips back.

"Anything else?"

"No. Just the gas."

Back at his apartment, Derek slammed the door so hard a mirror rattled against the wall. It was all wrong. Who would hurt Rebecca? How could they think it might possibly be him? Grabbing a notepad, he dropped onto a chair at the kitchen table and began to write. His own name went on the top left and Rebecca's on the right. He connected the two names with a line then drew a circle in the middle. Tyler's name went in the circle. Arrows shot downward from Tyler, pointing at other names. Jennifer. Paschek. Samuel McKenny. Marsh.

He tore the page from the notepad and began to write on the clean page. Julia Antosh. Simon Cudworth. Maggie? Chandra? He grimaced and scratched the last two names out. They were his friends. He tapped his pencil against the paper before scrawling another word across the bottom. *Why?*

Derek stared at those three little letters and then snatched the page and crumpled it into a ball. He took the first page and stared at the names. *This is it. The pattern has to be here.* He circled Jennifer's name and wrote below it. *Who did it?*

At a noise from his kitchen, he lifted his head. The timer on his coffee maker had kicked in and it was beginning to perk. He trudged to the kitchen and contemplated the machine. His work calendar lay on the counter beside it. He'd been scheduled to work last night. Twelve hours on, sleep until the afternoon, then wake up to a pot of fresh coffee. It seemed pointless now.

Even as his thoughts wandered, the scent of the coffee rolled up his nostrils to wrap around the primeval parts of his brain and exhume another thought from his subconscious. He was hungry.

Derek pulled open the cupboard doors and rolled his eyes. Two packages of instant oatmeal and half a bag of sugar. Walking over to the refrigerator, he yanked open the door and stuck his head in. He recoiled just as quickly. Trying not to breathe, he lifted the take out containers out of the fridge and carried them to the garbage. He was about to drop them in when he paused. Cautiously, he sniffed each one. The first he tossed into the can. The second he carefully opened. It had once been beef stew. Now, it was a putrid mess. Which made him think of something else. Dying flesh smelt the same. A tumor bursting through to the surface. More thoughts came to him. *Weight loss. Weakness. Jaundice.*

Pain meds when the cancer was advanced. When it was terminal.

He released the container into the can and let the lid drop into place with a clatter. Stalking back into the living room, he grabbed the notepad and wrote another name on the paper. Tabitha McKenny.

* * *

Paschek hovered over his deputy's shoulder as Standingready finished typing the report and scowled. He reached for the delete button, but the sheriff stopped him.

"Looks okay. Print it up."

"You don't really think Dr. Kessler had anything to do with this, do you?"

"What does the report say? Who had a nasty fight with the Andrychuk woman? Kessler. The girl's poisoned with those patch things, and who's got access to them? Kessler. And who goes into the hospital pharmacy while nobody's watching? Kessler."

"I don't think he'd do something like that."

"So you're an expert now?" Paschek cocked his head. "Are you friends with the guy or something, Deputy?"

"I've only met him once or twice."

"Listen to me. Kessler is a suspect in a police investigation. He's not anybody's friend. Not anymore."

"Yes, sir."

Paschek straightened. "We may need to keep an eye on him, now that the hospital has suspended him. Don't want him taking off or anything. At the moment, I've got bigger fish to fry. Bring me Tyler Sampson's file."

Paschek grabbed the report from the printer. *Good.* One less amateur to worry about. One less do-gooder to mess up the investigation. He tapped the back of Standingready's chair. "Buck up, Deputy. You can always get another friend. Tell you what. Go get me two bags of M&M's." As he sauntered into his office, the sheriff called back over his shoulder, "You can keep one for yourself."

* * *

The list of names had shrunk. Samuel McKenny's had a red circle around it. Derek ran his finger down the page and added a question mark below the names. Dropping the paper on the counter, he pulled out his cell phone

"Stockton County Police Station. How may I help you?"

The two minutes it took for the receptionist to get Deputy Standingready on the line felt like thirty. Finally the familiar voice came over the line. "Standingready."

"Deputy, it's Derek. Can you talk?" After a few seconds of silence, Derek could hear footsteps, as though the deputy was moving. *Somewhere private?*

When he spoke, Standingready's voice was low, hushed. "Yeah. Okay."

"I need your help."

"With what?"

"Someone tried to kill Rebecca. It wasn't me, but I have an idea who it might have been."

"Maybe you should talk to the sheriff."

"Do you really think he'd listen to me?"

Standingready huffed out a breath. "No, I guess not," he said. "What do you want me to do?"

"I believe Mrs. McKenny has a serious illness, probably cancer. If I'm right, she could be on fentanyl patches. Her husband would have access to them. I think he's the one who attacked Rebecca."

"I guess it's possible. But why?"

"To stop her from defending Tyler. He hates him."

"Yeah, I can see that. What do you need from me?"

"Check it out. See if I'm right."

"I don't know. I'm not really part of the investigation."

"Deputy, I need some help here."

"What you're asking is really tough. I can't promise anything."

Derek forced himself to keep his voice calm and steady. "Will you try?"

"I'll think about it." The line crackled with static. "I'll call you back when—I mean if—I figure out if there's anything I can do."

"Please."

Derek stared at the cracked photo of Cassie on the end table, waiting in grim silence until Standingready spoke again. "I'm really sorry. I wish I could do more."

"Yeah," Derek said. "Me too."

* * *

Paschek had been a cop for a long time. Sometimes he got this feeling that something was going on. Today he sensed it almost as soon as he closed his office door. He had turned back in time to look through the window and see Standingready take a phone call and move off to the side of the room. *Odd.* Paschek slipped out of his office and crept closer to the deputy, close enough to hear his half of the conversation.

He watched with interest as Standingready clicked off the cordless phone and turned to return it to its cradle. The deputy froze at the sight of Paschek standing grim-faced behind him.

Paschek jerked his thumb over his shoulder. "My office. Now."

* * *

Derek tossed his cell phone onto the counter and smacked his hands down so hard they stung. There had to be a way. The information was out there. How could he get his hands on it? He tipped back his head and shouted at the ceiling. "What am I supposed to do? I need to know if she's using a fentanyl patch."

He stalked toward his laptop on the table. Yanking it open, he contemplated the screen, chewing his bottom lip. His hospital access would have been shut down with his suspension. Even if he could get into the system, the ethics of it gnawed at his gut. Patient privacy and confidentiality had been drilled into him since med school. *But didn't Tyler's and Rebecca's needs supersede the rules? He could ask someone else to check. Yeah, and put his or her job at risk. Ends and means, right? What would Cassie do?* Throwing his hands in the air, he shouted, "Stop it, okay? Just stop it."

Exhaustion overwhelmed him. Stretching out on the couch, he covered his eyes with his forearm and tried to think about nothing. His mind drifted back to the ER, to the woman with fatigue. *Guillain-Barré.* The words echoed like a voice in his head. Different, somehow, than the first time. No matter. He knew what it meant. He wasn't alone. All the guilt, frustration, and anger were just background noise. All the pain a shadow trying to hide the truth. God had not left him.

His joints creaked like an old man's when Derek threw his legs over the side of the couch and stood. After a brief stretch to loosen them up, he walked over to the counter. He closed the laptop and nodded. "All right, then. I don't need to check. I already know." He squared his shoulders. "I can do this myself. That's how it should be."

Clutching his car keys, he started for the door but stopped. A red circle on the calendar by the door caught his eye. Three weeks ago, Chandra and John had invited him over for supper. Part of the family, they'd said. He set the keys on the counter and checked his watch. It wasn't too late. She'd still be at work. John, too. He reached for his phone but pulled back. Talking to her wouldn't work. She might try to stop him. He would leave a message on their home phone. The ringtone sounded in his ear three times before their answering machine kicked in.

"Hi, you've reached John and Chandra's, but we're not in right now. Here comes the beep. You know what to do."

"Chandra, it's Derek. I wanted to say I'm sorry. I didn't realize you had lost a child too. I'm really sorry you had to experience that. I've got to go now. There's something I have to do."

* * *

Paschek was happy with himself. He had managed not to break anything and had kept the volume below jet engine level. The rookie got the message, though. The sheriff held the office door open and waved Standingready out. With more backbone than Paschek had given him credit for, the deputy lifted his chin as he passed.

"He could be right about some of this, Sheriff."

"And I told you that Dr. Kessler was under investigation. You should not have been talking to him about anything."

"I know, but…"

"No buts. If I have to keep you in my sight to teach you to follow orders, I will. Now bring a patrol car around to the front. We've got work to do, but I need to make a phone call first." Only after the deputy left the office did he stalk over to his phone.

"Melansen, it's Paschek. You said to call if I needed anything. We have a new lead I think we should explore. Can you do some checking on the McKennys? Here's what I need…"

* * *

Derek forced himself to slow down. It would seriously hamper his plans if he got stopped by the cops now. If they weren't going to help, they should keep out of the way. Derek squealed off the highway onto a gravel road. *Who cares, anyway?* He pushed hard on the accelerator, causing his tires to spin and the rear end of the Jeep to fishtail. He regained control and raised a cloud of dust as he sped down the road. Only a couple more miles.

He slowed as he approached the yard, checking his mirrors and out the side windows repeatedly. No other vehicles were on the road. The Jeep crawled ahead as he peered around the trees lining the driveway. The McKennys' car was gone. He heaved a sigh of relief and turned in the driveway. Pulling up to the grove of trees behind the old farmhouse, he rolled down the window and turned off the ignition. Derek sat and listened. The only sounds were the pings of contracting metal from the cooling engine and the sputtering sizzle of water dripping from the air conditioner. The yard was quiet.

Easing the door open, he climbed out and crept over to where he had seen the black pickup truck. He kept glancing back at the house, studying the windows for any movement. There was none. When he reached the shed, Derek sidled along the outside wall until he reached the back corner. He peered around it. The truck was still there.

Wiping damp palms on his pants, he bent forward and ran towards the vehicle. Carefully opening the driver's door, he scanned the interior. It was empty. He ran his hand along the dash and reached across to the other door. Nothing in the glove compartment, either. Derek backed out of the cab and rounded the truck to check out the box. A burlap sack had been tossed into one corner. Was it empty? Maybe… maybe not.

* * *

Something was beeping that didn't sound like her alarm. Rebecca reached for her nightstand, but something blocked her arm. Was that a pole? Her hand hurt, and her throat felt like sandpaper. She tried to roll over but stopped when a searing pain ripped through her head. Something large, dark, and hazy stood beside her bed. She blinked, trying to bring the object into focus. It wasn't something. It was someone.

Rebecca struggled to sit up. The pounding was starting to lessen, but a wave of nausea hit her. With one hand, she clutched at the sheets while with the other she covered her mouth. A soft groan escaped from her lips. A face shrouded in white appeared on the opposite side of the bed.

"Careful, Miss, you've had a rough time of it. Best lay back down."

Her vision was starting to clear. She could make out the face of a woman leaning over her. Her voice cracked. "Where…?"

"You're in a hospital. In Seattle."

"I don't understand. How…?"

"I brought you here." The voice came from the large, dark shape. She turned to look but had to wait until the waves of light stopped dancing before her eyes. The shape swam and coalesced into a face. Rebecca blinked twice. It was her father.

She tried to speak but coughed harshly. Max Andrychuk leaned forward and held a chip of ice to her lips.

"Here. Take this," he said. The ice was soothing. As it melted it ran along her tongue to her throat, easing her parched discomfort with its passage. She nodded and accepted a second piece. Rebecca studied her father's face closely. His hair, normally perfectly coiffed, was disheveled. He had loosened his tie, and his suit was creased and wrinkled. She raised her eyebrows when she noted that he was unshaven. "You look awful."

"You're not looking so great yourself. How are you feeling?"

"Like I've been hit by a truck. Everything's a blur. Why did you bring me here?"

He gripped the bed rail with both hands. "I needed to make sure you were okay."

Rebecca's gaze lifted over his shoulder to the window. The sun was high above the horizon, its harsh brightness making her eyes water. "What happened to me?"

The nurse stepped forward with a cup. "You managed the ice, so let's try some water." She held the straw to Rebecca's lips. "You were drugged. They found four strong narcotic patches on you. You could have died. It's been almost eight hours since they found you, but no one knows how long you were out before that." Rebecca drank deeply from the cup and lay back on her pillow. The nurse set the cup on the table beside the bed. "The police wanted to talk to you when you woke up. Are you feeling up to it?"

Rebecca struggled to sit up. "The police. That's it. I have to get back to Stockton."

The nurse took her shoulders and tried to ease Rebecca back onto the bed. "That wouldn't be wise, Miss. You had a lot of drugs in your system. You need to rest."

"I can't rest." Rebecca shook off the nurse's hands. "I need to leave. Someone tried to kill me, and they're not going to get away with it. Please bring me my clothes and whatever papers I need to sign, because I am out of here."

The nurse continued to protest, but Rebecca's father held up a hand. "There's no point in fighting it," he said. "She's always been stubborn. If she wants to go back to that little town, I'll take her."

Rebecca's eyes widened. "You will?"

"Yes, I will. I have a plane available. We can be in Stockton in a couple hours. On one condition. Well, two really."

"What are they?"

"One, I'm coming with you. And two, we're going to talk."

* * *

Derek lowered the tailgate and pulled the burlap sack toward him. Something clinked inside when he moved it. The neck of the sack had been tied with a length of cord, and he struggled to loosen the knot. He was finally able to pull the sack open and peer inside. A brick. *For weight, maybe?* Some sort of glass container. A fancy-looking tumbler. He frowned. He'd heard there was a broken tumbler on the floor when they found Jennifer. Could this be from the same set? Did McKenny remove it so they wouldn't find his fingerprints at the scene?

There was something else in the bag. A small black plastic bottle. Why hadn't be brought a pair of surgical gloves with him? Not wanting to touch the bottle, he leaned over to look at it more closely. The lid was off and it was empty, but he could see the label. Gas line antifreeze.

As he straightened, a shadow passed over him. A white-hot splash of light stabbed through his head, and then everything went black.

THIRTY-SIX

"The world is grown so bad that wrens make prey
where eagles dare not perch."
Richard III, Act I, Scene III

The nurse insisted on a wheelchair. Rebecca gritted her teeth and fumed as her father pushed her to the curb. She was on her feet before he had a chance to open the car door.

"I've got it," she said as she wrenched the door open and collapsed onto the passenger seat. Crowds of people were entering and leaving the hospital, and it seemed that half of them were walking by their car. Rebecca hunched low and covered her eyes with her hand in a futile attempt to hide. As Max pulled out into traffic, she lowered the sun visor to peer at her reflection in the mirror. Wincing, she tried to straighten her hair with her hands. "I look awful."

"There's a bag in the backseat. I picked you up a few things."

"You did?" Rebecca stared at him. He looked like her father, but he wasn't acting like him. "Uh, thanks. Can I use your cell first?"

Without asking any questions, he reached into the pocket of his suit coat, extracted the sleek silver device, and handed it to her. Rebecca punched in Derek's number. Her frown deepened with each unanswered ringtone. Finally, she disconnected the call and dialed a second number.

"Stockton Police Department. Deputy Blackburn speaking."

"This is Rebecca Andrychuk. Is Sheriff Paschek there?"

"No, the sheriff's out on a call. Can I help you?"

"What about that other deputy? Standingready. Is he there?"

"No, he's with Sheriff Paschek. What's this about?"

"It's about the Sampson case. And about the person who tried to kill me."

"Ah. Right. I heard about that. Why don't you come in, and we'll take a statement?"

"A statement? Are you crazy? I'm hundreds of miles away at the moment. You need to do something now."

"Miss Andrychuk, I assure you we're already working on your case. As soon as we confirm that Kessler was involved, we'll pick him up."

Rebecca almost dropped the phone. "Derek? You're not only crazy, you're an idiot. Derek had absolutely nothing to do with what happened to me."

"But he had access to those fentanyl patches."

"So did every doctor in the hospital. And a lot of the patients." She tightened her grip on the phone. This was getting them nowhere. "When will Paschek be back?"

"He should return in an hour or two, but I…"

"Tell him I'm on my way." She snapped the phone off and smacked it against her palm. "Idiots."

* * *

He still drove like her father. They were at the airstrip only minutes after leaving the hospital. As he pulled up to the tarmac, a corporate jet was being taxied into position. Rebecca gawked. "Is that yours?"

"Well, mine and my partner's. Wait." Max hopped out, rounded the front of the car, and pulled open her door. "We use it for business mainly. It's a Cessna Citation I/SP. Not as big or as new as the one I hired to get you here—that one was fitted as an air ambulance. This one will do the job today." He held out a hand to help her out then grabbed her bag from the back seat and took her elbow as they crossed the tarmac.

The interior of the jet was not nearly as posh as she had expected. All but the front two passenger seats had been removed, and the rear of the plane was bare except for cargo hooks and straps. She was fastening her seat belt when her father settled in beside her and tapped the pilot on the shoulder. "You know the flight plan, Chuck?"

"Yes, sir, Mr. Andrychuk. Sorry the plane's a mess. We hadn't had time to reconfigure from the Haiti flight. But don't worry, we'll be there in no time."

Rebecca squinted at her father. "Haiti?"

He shrugged. "No big deal. We had a chance to fly in some medical supplies."

"Oh, new commercial venture?"

The pilot lined up the plane on the runway. "Hardly, Miss. Mr. Andrychuk and his partners have been sending me on mercy flights for over a year."

Rebecca stared down the tarmac stretching out ahead of them. "Are you kidding me?" she whispered.

The roar of engines sent new spasms of pain through her head, and she fought a wave of nausea.

The jet was soon airborne. As the noise lessened, so did her pain. Rebecca pulled out her father's cell phone and was about to dial a number when the pilot turned around.

"Please don't do that, Miss."

"Why? I thought it was only a problem during takeoffs and landings."

"On a commercial flight it's safe anytime, but here you're dealing with older avionics, and you're seated right behind the pilot."

"Better do as he asks," Max said, holding out his hand. Rebecca placed it on his palm. Her father pocketed it and reached into his bag to pull out a couple of cans of diet cola. "You want a drink?"

Rebecca glanced at the soda can and shook her head. "Have you got a hairbrush in there?"

Her father smiled and produced a comb, hairbrush, breath mints, and a sealed package of towelettes. "I've got a toothbrush as well, but there's no place for you to use it."

As Rebecca worked on her hair, he sipped on his cola. Once she had wiped her face clean and popped a mint, she nodded at the can. "That's not your usual drink. Is it because of your new girlfriend?"

His forehead wrinkled. "What are you talking about?"

"I saw her picture. Your pro bono immigration case. She's very pretty."

"Nalini?" He tipped his head back and laughed. "Yes, she is pretty. She looked especially nice a couple of months ago when she got married. To a legal clerk from our office. They just moved to Portland."

Warmth crept into Rebecca's cheeks. She stuck out her chin and tapped a fingernail against his soda can. "What is this about, then?"

"I'll tell you. We did have a deal, after all. To talk, that is."

Rebecca folded her arms. "So talk."

"Okay." He lifted the can as if giving a toast. "I haven't had any alcohol in over eighteen months. I guess I had hit rock bottom. Did rehab and then AA. The whole twelve-step thing. I've been working on number nine for a while."

"Number nine?"

"Make amends to everyone I've harmed whenever possible."

"That's what this is about? Making amends?"

"Yes."

"Try making amends to Mom."

Her father deflated in front of her eyes. "I wish I could. Every day, I wish that I could." A tear slid down his cheek and he wiped it off with his palm. "I let her down so many times. I couldn't see it. I didn't really know how much I hurt her until she took all those pills, and by then it was too late."

"So you ran away."

"Yeah, I did."

"Why?" Rebecca's voice was tight. She blinked rapidly and gripped both armrests until her knuckles turned white. "Why weren't you there? She needed you. I needed you."

"I know. I'm sorry." He covered her hand with his. She didn't pull away. "I am so sorry."

Slowly, Rebecca allowed her hand to unclench. A shiver moved through her body as she turned her hand until it was cupped in her father's. She sat staring at their hands. After a long moment, she looked over at her father. "So, do you want to hear about this case of mine or not?"

* * *

He was being transported somewhere. Each jolt sent a spasm of pain coursing through his head. Derek tried to open his eyes, but a wave of nausea washed over him. He groaned softly and closed his eyes. Darkness edged in on him again.

* * *

A car was waiting for them, as her father had promised. They climbed into the back seat. As soon as they started driving, her father reached into his pocket and silently handed her his phone. Rebecca grabbed it. There was still no answer at Derek's apartment or on his cell phone. The hospital was no help, so she called Chandra.

"I don't know how you managed to get out of the hospital so fast," Chandra said. "But I sure am glad you did. Things are all wrong. They're accusing Derek of poisoning you."

"He didn't do it."

"I knew it. I just knew it. But, I… I didn't help things. I blew up at him. He was being so stupid, so full of self-pity that I got mad."

"Yeah." Rebecca wrinkled her nose. "I did that, too."

"I tried to call him. No answer. I got home right before you called, and there was a message on my machine from him."

"What did it say?"

"He said he was sorry, and that he had something he needed to do. Rebecca, I'm worried. Where could he be?"

The car slowed. They had arrived at the police station. Rebecca reached for the door handle. "I think I know where he went."

* * *

He tried to open his eyes again. The nausea was easing, thankfully. Derek wanted to wipe his eyes, touch the aching sting on the back of his skull, but he couldn't move his hands. He groaned again.

"You're awake?" a woman's voice said. "Good. I was worried I hit you too hard."

Derek turned his head slightly in the direction of the sound. He clenched his eyes shut as another wave of nausea threatened him. When it abated, he opened his eyes. His vision gradually cleared and he squinted at the woman. "Tabitha?"

"You remembered my name." The woman smiled. "How sweet. I always thought you seemed like such a nice young man. I'm sorry I have to do this, Doctor."

Derek tried moving his hands again, to no avail. He was in the driver's seat of his Jeep. His wrists were wrapped in strips of cloth that looped under the seat, and the seatbelt was cinched tight around his waist. When Tabitha McKenny appeared at the open door, he stopped struggling. "What's going on? How did I get here?"

"It wasn't easy. If you hadn't fallen into the back of the truck, I don't know how I'd have managed."

"What do you mean?"

"I simply backed the truck up to your car and dragged you across into it. It took me so long. I'm not as strong as I used to be. I was worried you might wake up on the way here, but you didn't."

The Jeep was surrounded by a dense bluff of trees. "Where are we?"

"It's a nice place," she said and smiled again. "It won't hurt, you know."

"What do you mean? What won't hurt?"

"Your death. You're about to commit suicide."

* * *

Sheriff Paschek was standing beside his police cruiser when Rebecca and Max pulled up and jumped out of their car. He crossed his arms as they approached. "Looks like you've recovered pretty quickly from your little ordeal."

"Nice to see you too, Paschek." Rebecca's voice was sharp. "We need to talk."

"First things first." Paschek inclined his head toward Max. "Who's this?"

"I'm Maxwell Andrychuk. I'm Rebecca's father and an attorney. And we need your help."

Paschek uncrossed his arms. "What can I do?"

"You can start by arresting the person who drugged me," Rebecca said. "At least I think she did."

Paschek raised an eyebrow. "She?"

"Yes. Tabitha McKenny came over to my place. I thought she wanted to talk. I made her a cup of tea, and the next thing I knew I was waking up in a Seattle hospital."

"So you have no proof she did anything?"

"No, but who else could it have been?"

"Maybe your boyfriend, Derek? He had access to the drugs. Not many people around here can get those patch things."

"I said it wasn't him. It was Tabitha." Rebecca glanced at her father and then back at Paschek. "That's not all. I think Derek went out to the McKenny place. And if he did, he's in a lot of danger."

* * *

"You're crazy," Derek tugged harder on the cord around his wrists. His heart thudded erratically in his chest. "No one will believe that."

"Oh, but they will, Doctor." She held up his cell phone in her gloved hands. "You're about to send a suicide note. It's so sad, really. You lost your wife and family. Had a big fight with that Jezebel. And then got suspended from the hospital. It was all more than you could take."

"How do you know all that?"

"Oh, well, I know that gossip is a sin… but I listen anyway. And I'm real good at doing research on the computer."

"Look, you don't have to do this. Not to protect Samuel. He doesn't deserve it."

"Don't you talk about Daddy like that. He didn't do anything."

"Daddy? How can you call him that? He killed your daughter."

Tabitha laughed. "Daddy didn't kill her. I did."

* * *

Paschek held up both hands. "Okay, I'll bite. Why would Kessler go out to the McKenny place?"

"Because he knows that the McKennys are behind the murder. I'm sure he went out to their place to get proof." Rebecca was about to say more when a movement caught her eye.

Deputy Standingready climbed out of the passenger side of the police car and came around to join them. "She could be right, Sheriff. I told you what Dr. Kessler said when he called."

"And I told you to stay with the prisoner," Paschek said.

"Prisoner?" Rebecca peered into the rear of the cruiser and then spun toward Paschek. "What's my client doing there? Just because I'm not around, you think you can do whatever you want with him?"

"Whoa, hold on there, Counselor. We were about to move Sampson to the county jail in Cut Bank."

"He was supposed to stay here in Stockton."

"Yeah, well, that was before the plumbing in this old building exploded and left us with only one holding cell. The judge sanctioned the move, okay?"

Rebecca gritted her teeth. Making sure Derek was safe took priority at the moment. "So, are you going to help us or not?"

Paschek's reply was cut off when Deputy Blackburn stepped from the building. "Sheriff, phone call for you. It's Detective Melansen."

* * *

Derek screwed up his face, trying to claw through the pain enough to grasp what was happening. "I don't understand. Why would you kill your own daughter?"

"I couldn't let her come home. Daddy loves me. There's only room for one of us. She would take him away. She tried before. I had to do it."

"That's crazy."

Tabitha stiffened. "You don't understand. My Daddy has always loved me. He does things to… no, with me. He loves me. He told me." Her voice had gone higher, like a little girl's. "He told me lots of things. Never tell. Never tell anyone. Jennifer knew. She knew too much. She wanted to hurt me. Take Daddy away. She had to be stopped."

"So you poisoned her?"

"It wasn't hard. I used Tyler's computer to find out how. Jennifer liked to go out lots. So, I would babysit, and everything was there that I needed. I didn't even have to buy the antifreeze. Tyler had some in his garage, and I simply took one. Then I put it in her lemonade. She always liked it sweet, so she didn't notice it at all."

"Then you framed him."

"That worked out well, didn't it? He's a bad man. He drinks and uses bad words sometimes. Not like you. You seem nice."

"Then why this? You could let me go."

"Oh, no. You and that woman lawyer would accuse Daddy. You would try to take him away from me."

"Samuel will see you. He'll stop you."

"No, he won't. I convinced him to take that child to town. 'Go for ice cream,' I said. 'Go to the park.' Daddy listens to me. He'll listen later, too, when I tell him the child can't stay. That she has to go live somewhere else. Then it will just be the two of us again."

She walked to the rear of the Jeep. Derek was able to shift his body enough to peer into the side mirror. She was crouched near the back of the vehicle. When she straightened, his chest tightened until it hurt to take a breath. She'd attached a hose to the exhaust pipe.

* * *

"Let's go, Deputy!" Paschek shouted as he ran from the station. "Leave Shooter in the car. We need to hurry."

Rebecca stepped in front of the sheriff. "Where are you going?"

"Out to the McKennys' place." Paschek batted a hand through the air. "Look, I don't give a crap about your opinion, but I happen to be a good cop. I check everything. Melansen confirmed that Tabitha McKenny is on a narcotic patch for cancer treatment. That makes the McKennys suspects."

"I'm coming with you."

"No, you're not." Paschek brushed by her. "This is police business." Before he could get to the driver's door, his way was blocked by Max Andrychuk.

"Tell me, Sergeant," Max said with a smile. "Was that Detective Oliver Melansen? I'll be seeing him next week at the National Police Fund meeting. You know, for widows and orphans. We're on the steering committee together, and I'll be sure to tell him how helpful you were."

Paschek frowned and then jerked his head at the car. "Get in the back. You two can ride with Sampson."

* * *

She stumbled as she shuffled to the passenger door and leaned heavily against the side of the Jeep. Derek watched her as she breathed slowly in and out. Her knuckles were white where she clutched the hose. She was weak. Somehow he had to take advantage of that. He tugged again on the cord but only managed to tighten it further. He gave up with a grunt of frustration. Maybe if he kept her talking long enough, McKenny would come back.

After a minute, she pushed away from the vehicle and opened the door.

"You're ill," Derek said. "Is it cancer?"

Tabitha nodded sharply. "It started in my breast. They cut me but it came back. And then it spread. There's some in my brain. It makes it hard to remember, to think sometimes. Maybe we should have done something different, but it grew so fast. It hurts. It hurts a lot."

"Do the patches help?"

"Yes, they do. But I'm a few short right now."

"You did drug Rebecca. Why?"

"Are you trying to keep me talking, Doctor? No matter." She held up his cell phone so he could see the screen and then pushed the send button. "There goes your suicide note." She pursed her lips. "She's not a nice person, you know. She spends too much time with men. Some of them married men. But that's not why I had to do it." She dropped the cell phone on the passenger seat and started to roll up the car window. "She was trying to get Tyler released. To prove him innocent. If she succeeded, the police might suspect Daddy. They might try to hurt him. I couldn't let that happen. So I visited her. A little sleeping pill in her tea and then the patches. I thought it was clever to do it different from Jennifer."

She slipped the end of the hose through the crack in the passenger window and made sure it was secure. Then she reached across the seat and turned the ignition key. The Jeep's engine roared to life.

* * *

Tabitha came around to his side of the Jeep and started to close the driver's door. Derek swung his head from side to side and pulled on his restraints. "They'll know it wasn't suicide when they find me tied up."

"Oh, don't worry. As soon as you're unconscious, I'll untie you."

"But… but they'll see my head. They'll know."

"Why, thank you for mentioning that." She reached in and swiped a finger through the wound on the back of his head. Blood coated the finger of her latex glove. "I believe you slipped and hit your head when you were attaching the hose. There'll even be a little blood on a rock by the back of the car. No one will suspect a thing."

She pushed the door shut and stepped back. Derek stared at the hose in the passenger window. He could already smell the fumes filling the Jeep. His breathing was becoming ragged. He coughed and tilted back his head. *Is this how it ends? God? Are You there? Is anyone there?*

THIRTY-SEVEN

"It seems to be most strange that men should fear, seeing that
death, a necessary end, will come when it will come."
Julius Caesar, Act II, Scene II

The car skidded to a stop in the McKennys front yard.

"Stay put!" Paschek shouted as he and Standingready leapt from
the cruiser. The sheriff waved at the black pickup truck parked by the
house.

"Check out the house," he called. "I'll get the truck."

Paschek ran to the pickup. The cab was empty, but the tailgate was
down. A few drops of blood were splattered across the box beside a
burlap sack. He glanced inside and then lifted his head. An engine was
running. It was coming from behind the house.

* * *

Derek smiled slightly. She was right. It didn't hurt at all. He was only
feeling a bit sleepy.

* * *

Paschek raced around the house and over to the riding lawnmower. Grabbing Kyle Hendry by the collar of his T-shirt, he yanked him off the mower. The machine sputtered to a stop while the boy stared wide-eyed at the sheriff.

"I didn't do nothing," he said. "I swear. I stayed in the ditch the whole way."

"How long have you been here?"

"I don't know. Half an hour, maybe more."

"Did you see anything? Anyone?"

"I don't know. Something, maybe. Am I in trouble?"

"No, just tell me what you saw."

"A blue Jeep left when I was getting close."

"Where did it go?"

"North, I think."

Paschek sprinted to the front of the house as Standingready barreled outside.

"No one in the house, sir," the deputy said. "Anything out here?"

"The kid saw Kessler's Jeep headed north. Let's go."

As Paschek threw himself back in the car, Rebecca grabbed his shoulder. "What's happening? Where's Derek?'

"Not here." Paschek spun the car in a tight circle and was accelerating to the driveway when another vehicle turned into the lane. He slammed on his brakes. Samuel McKenny pulled his gray car up and screeched to a stop. He was scowling when he stepped from his vehicle.

"What's happening here? Why are you people in my yard? And what is she doing here?" He pointed at Rebecca as she pounded on the side window.

"Let her out, Deputy," Paschek said as he stalked toward McKenny. "Where have you been the past few hours?"

"In town. At that ice cream place and the library with my granddaughter."

"Witnesses?"

"What are you talking about? You had better explain yourself, Sheriff."

"Where's your wife, Mr. McKenny?"

"Resting in the house. You still haven't…"

"She's not there. No one is there."

"She has to be. Where else could she be?"

"Mr. McKenny," Paschek said, "I believe there could be a problem with your wife. I think she may have been involved in the murder of your daughter."

"You're insane. How dare you suggest such a thing?"

"Mr. McKenny," Standingready pointed at the pickup. "Is that your truck?"

"Yes."

"In the back of your truck there's a glass tumbler just like the one missing from Jennifer's house and an empty bottle of gas line antifreeze. That's what killed her. The evidence is there."

"That can't be right." McKenny strode over to the truck and glanced inside. When he came back, his face was white. "There's blood," he said.

"We think it might be Derek Kessler's," Paschek said. "We know he was here, and we think Tabitha left with him. She might be taking him somewhere."

"Where?"

"The boy cutting the grass saw them go north."

McKenny shuddered and lowered his head. When he looked up again, his eyes were wide. "I think I know where they went. Tabitha has a favorite place. A clearing in a bluff of trees a few miles from here. She used to go there before she got sick. It has to be the place."

Paschek jerked his head toward the back seat of McKenny's vehicle. "Is your granddaughter in the car?"

The old man shook his head. "No, I took her to the Vermettes' so Tabitha could rest."

"Then take us to your wife." Paschek yanked open his car door. "Now."

* * *

He was getting so tired. He couldn't open his eyes anymore. Derek coughed weakly. His head lolled to the sidet, and he was silent.

* * *

Rebecca clasped her fingers together to keep from hitting something. Or someone. *Too slow. We're going to be too late.* Her father's hand covered hers. She turned and looked into his face. There was a strange calmness in his eyes that she didn't understand. It made no sense at all.

* * *

He was falling. Maybe he was flying. His face felt strange, and his lips were tingling. Like a kiss.

* * *

"Wake up, you fool. Wake up." Rebecca lowered her face to Derek's once more and blew into his mouth. His chest rose and fell. Paschek took a step forward, but she threw up a hand. "I said I'd do it!" She tried again.

* * *

Samuel McKenny knelt on the grass, holding his wife tightly in his arms. She kept trying to break away. They were both crying. Paschek shook his head as Standingready walked over to him. "The ambulance is on the way. They'll be here in a few minutes."

The sheriff glanced back and forth between the two couples. "What a mess," he said. "What a complete screw-up." He snatched the handcuff keys off his belt and handed them to his deputy. "Let Shooter—I mean, Tyler—out of the car, and take the cuffs off him."

* * *

Why was his head hurting? There wasn't supposed to be any pain. Where was the light? There was supposed to be a light. Something wet was dripping on his face. Derek opened his eyes and coughed.

* * *

Rebecca froze. The tears continued to fall from her cheeks onto Derek's. He smiled weakly. "Hi."

Max knelt beside Rebecca, and together they helped Derek sit up. She turned when Tabitha cried out and held her thin arms toward them. "No, Daddy," she said. "They're ruining everything. Make them stop."

"Hush, Tabitha," he replied, stroking her hair. "It'll be all right."

* * *

Paschek crouched beside Samuel McKenny. "Why did she do it? Why all this?"

The old man looked at him, his eyes red and puffy. "It's my fault. I should have known." He took a deep breath. "Tabitha was abused as a little girl. Her own father. It affected her, affected her relationships. I didn't know about it until after we were married. It took over a year of prayer and counseling before we could be together—as husband and wife. Things improved for a while.

"Then Jennifer was born. Tabitha always resented her. It was as if she didn't want to share me. It didn't help that Jennifer was so rebellious. No matter how I tried to control her, she fought us all the time. It was almost a relief when she ran off. It seemed that Tabitha was coping better. That we had dealt with it. But then the cancer came. It was everywhere, her chest, her skin, her brain. The pain became so bad that she needed more and more drugs, and things got worse and worse." He paused to kiss her forehead.

"I couldn't admit that we needed help. I thought if Jennifer came home, we could take care of things together. I kept pushing her to leave Tyler. I didn't see what it was doing to Tabitha. I was a fool."

Tabitha touched his cheek. "I never told, Daddy. I never told anyone. Just like you said. Never tell. Never."

"I'm sorry, dear." McKenny brushed her hair back from her eyes. "I'm so sorry." He kissed her once more. "She didn't mean to do it. She needs help, that's all."

"I'll do what I can." Paschek glanced over his shoulder. Tyler Sampson stood behind them, looming over the McKennys. He slowly clenched and unclenched his fists. His face was flushed scarlet. Paschek stiffened and shifted his hand to the butt of his pistol.

McKenny looked up and opened his mouth as if to speak. No sound came. He lifted a trembling hand toward Tyler, and then dropped it. Paschek could barely hear his words. "I'm terribly ashamed. I was wrong. I've been so wrong."

Tyler's eyelids fluttered, and the color washed out of his face. In a slow jerking motion, the young man knelt beside Samuel McKenny and gripped his shoulder.

Paschek let go of his weapon and stepped back. "Don't that beat all."

* * *

Derek couldn't take his eyes from Rebecca. Was she really there or was he hallucinating? He started to speak but was stopped by another cough. Standingready knelt beside him and offered him a bottle of water. After taking a few careful sips, Derek asked, "How did you find me?"

"God must have heard you call," the deputy said.

"How did you know I'd called out to him?"

"I just knew. I was praying myself, and I knew God would help us get to you in time."

"How could you be so sure?"

"Because God's got plans for you. He's not through with you yet."

Derek offered the deputy a slow smile. "Maybe you're right." He shot a glance over to where the McKennys and Tyler sat huddled on the ground. "I guess He still loves us, no matter how damaged we are. No matter how far we try to run away from Him."

* * *

Paschek tapped his deputy on the shoulder. "Help them out over there," the sheriff said, jerking his head toward the McKennys. "Give them a bit more time before getting her in the car." He squatted and fixed his eye on Derek. "You gonna be okay?"

"Yeah, my head is throbbing, but I'll live."

Paschek straightened with a groan. He stared at the horizon for a moment. "I guess you were right. This time. But do me a favor?"

"Sure. What is it?"

"Stick to medicine from now on, and leave the police work to the professionals."

"I'll try." Derek said, forcing a half-smile.

* * *

When Paschek sauntered away, Derek touched the back of Rebecca's hand. "Hey, I'm sorry about what happened. About everything."

"Me too," she said. He started to say something more, but she stopped him with a finger on his lips. "You don't need to say anything. It's okay. I think I understand." She glanced over at her father. "In fact, there are a lot of things I understand a bit better now."

"Then we're friends again?"

She smiled and hugged him close. "Friends. That's enough," she whispered in his ear. "For now."

THIRTY-EIGHT

"I am for the house with the narrow gate, which I take to be
too little for pomp to enter: some that humble themselves
may; but the many will be too chill and tender,
and they'll be for the flowery way that leads to
the broad gate and the great fire."
All's Well That Ends Well, Act IV, Scene V

Rebecca was awake. Her beeper was silent and her alarm clock mute, but she was still awake. It was Sunday, too.

She sat up and looked at the clock. It was only nine. She flopped back on the bed and pulled the covers over her head, but it was no use. With a disgusted grunt, she sat up and swung her feet out of the bed. Her toes crinkled the weekend paper where she had dropped in on the floor the night before. She looked down at it.

It was open to the church page. Rows of friendly invitations listed times and places. Which one was it that Derek went to? She spotted the ad and glanced at the clock again.

Plenty of time. So many new things were going on in her life—what was one more?

Maybe it was worth a try.

ABOUT THE AUTHOR

Dr. Kevin Dautremont is a graduate of the University of Saskatchewan College of Medicine. He is a Clinical Associate Professor of Medicine with the U of S Department of Family Medicine and a family physician in Moose Jaw, Saskatchewan.

In 2008, The Word Guild of Canada awarded him The Word Award for Best New Canadian Christian Author for his historical novel *The Golden Conquest.*

His short stories include "Dazed", *A Second Cup of Hot Apple Cider* (That`s Life Communications, 2011), and "Affliction", *Christmas with Hot Apple Cider* (That`s Life Communications, 2017).

Dr. Dautremont has a blog at http://thestethoscopeandpen.com/